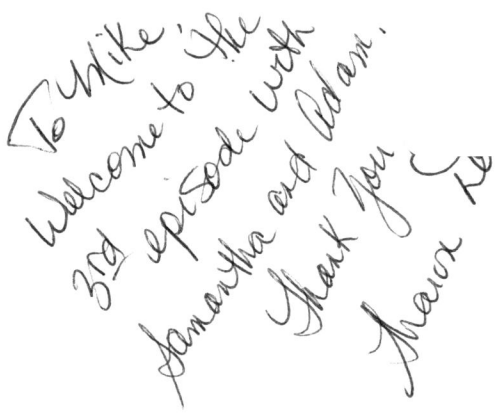

Middle Plantation

Sharon Dobson

Copyright © 2017 Sharon Dobson

All rights reserved.

ISBN: 1537445014
ISBN-13: 978-1537445014

DEDICATION

I would like to dedicate this book to Trish Dobson for her help and suggestions. To Matt Roman and Bill Dobson for putting up with me while I wrote this book.

CONTENTS

	Acknowledgments	i
1	Day One	3
2	Day Two	42
3	Day Three	54
4	Day Four	76
5	Day Five	96
6	Day Six	103
7	Day Seven	136
8	Day Eight	180
9	Day Nine	197
10	Day Ten	228

ACKNOWLEDGMENTS

A big thank you to Bernie Moll, Stephen Koehler, Billy Gill and Tracy Davis for volunteering to be characters in the book. While the story is fiction many of the characters are the people in my life.

Day One
Williamsburg, Virginia

I live in a world that is connected. My life revolves around and is controlled by my cell phone. This morning is no different. It is ringing before the sun comes up. My first thought is to roll over and go back to sleep. I am on vacation and last night was not a good night. My wife and I got home early but I tossed and turned until after three in the morning revisiting an argument I had at dinner with one of my oldest friends. I walked out before the meal was finished and now I have to find a way to mend the friendship. Most of the night I thought about what I can say to him. I don't want something stupid to destroy the friendship.

The ringing is not stopping and I answer more out of curiosity than duty. Something has to be pretty important for the office to call me at five forty-seven in the morning during my vacation. I look at the number calling before touching the screen to answer. The call is coming from Margaret Cho's cell phone.

This makes me sit up in bed. Margaret is a good employee and a friend. She has always gone above and beyond her duties to get the job done and has dropped everything she was doing to come to my house and help protect my family on two occasions. If she is calling me this early something big must be happening. I hear her just above a whisper on the other end. "Adam, I am sorry I woke you. I don't know any other way to tell you this but Scott Llewellyn is dead. His body was found at around four thirty this morning lying on the Palace Green. The police are on their way to your house. No one saw him after he followed you out of the restaurant last night. Please tell me you have some sort of eye witness and that you went straight home? You are a person of interest!

It takes a few seconds for my mind to process what she has just said. My wife, Samantha, and I had gone to dinner with Scott and his wife, Karen, last night. Scott has been lecturing at the college this week and is my reason for a vacation. I have been attending his lecture series every day on the early settlers of the Middle Plantation area of Virginia. Last night we met at a tavern in the historic area for dinner. The girls were bored with us but he and I were talking about the legends of the lost treasures of the Knights Templar. Scott believes that Nathaniel Bacon brought the treasure to America and it is buried in a vault under Bruton Parish Church. His wild ideas and insane notions of digging up the side of the grave yard led to last night's argument. He feels finding the treasure is for the greater good. Bruton Parish is one of the oldest churches in American and a historic treasure. For that matter Williamsburg is a national treasure and should be preserved. Digging around and under the church could cause structural damage and is not worth the risk.

The church is located on the corner of the Palace Green and is the center piece of the mile long living history museum. Even the cover of darkness gives very little cover for a murder. Yet, it has happened.

This phone call explains the loud knocking on the front door. I get out of bed and put on a pair of jeans before heading into the hallway. Our nanny, Christina, is already at the door looking out the window asking for identification. The person on the other side shows something that seems to satisfy her request. She looks up the stairs at me and I nod my head to let them in.

Doughnut is beside me barking and growling. I grab his collar just before he bolts down the steps to greet the cops who are walking in the door. I try to get him to quiet down before he wakes up the kids. He's one hundred and twelve pounds of labradoodle. We joke about getting him a lion cut because he is tall and long like a lion with a solid frame. In the back of my mind I know one day I will come home and be greeted by a lion at the door. The girls will give in and do it one day. I think I would like to have a lion by my side this morning.

Two men dressed in Virginia State Police uniforms walk in and look up the steps at me. "We are looking for Special Agent Adam Clay. Would you mind coming downstairs to talk to us sir?"

I don't see much choice at the moment. The cops don't appear to be leaving without talking to me. I'm also not sure what to say. The food was good and the atmosphere was excellent. All was going well until Scott started again on his tirade about digging up the cemetery and palace green. I understand the lure of looking for the Arc of the Covenant, but to dig up historic ground on a snipe hunt is insane. There is no actual proof, only legend, that anything is buried there. Yet, his need to explore this area and prove whether there is anything to the legend overpowered his ability to listen to reason. In the end, it might have ended our friendship and his life.

I hear Alina stirring in her room. She is a light sleeper. Luckily our baby, AJ, can sleep through a bomb blast. Samantha joins me at the top of the stairs looking worried. I walk down the stairs and invite them to follow me to the kitchen. Doughnut is whimpering next to me and I am trying to walk him to the back door to put him outside. He is a strong dog and very protective. He is well behaved but I think he can sense my tension. I make it to the back door and shove him out telling him to go pee.

With only two and a half hours sleep, I am going to need some coffee. I tell Samantha and Christina to go back to bed, I can handle this. They of course don't listen to me and busy themselves around the kitchen getting coffee cups and making breakfast.

I look at the two cops. They look uncomfortable standing in my kitchen. I wonder how they got to draw the short straw and wake the FBI agent up to ask him some questions. I decide to see what they have to say before I tell them my office has already called me. "So may I ask why are you here? Did you just decide to pay a social call or are you here on business? It's not even six o'clock."

The taller cop shuffles his feet and won't even look me in the eyes. I look at the shorter cop. He's slightly overweight. Not bad but not in top shape. They both look young. I try to decide if they are an unlucky duo who grabbed a call at the end of their shift or early car and they will have all day to stand there. Finally, the shorter of the two pulls out a chair. "Do you mind if we sit down?"

I nod and tell them to go ahead. I also take a seat at the table. "Since I assume this is not a social call would you like to at least tell me why you are here?"

The taller one begins to timidly speak, "We don't know how to tell you this, Sir--."

They look back and forth at each other. I get the feeling these guys are rookies so I give them a break. "My office has already called me and told me Scott was found dead. Since we had dinner with him and Karen last night, I assume you want to know what I have to say about the argument he and I had. We ate dinner, he and I argued over an insane idea of his, then my wife and I left. He was still sitting at the table with Karen when we walked out. What else do you want to know?"

Samantha puts coffee cups on the table and brings the pot over to pour. The tall cop shakes his head. The other seems grateful to have something to hold in his hands. "Agent Clay, we have already spoken to Karen Llewellyn and she told us that you and Dr. Llewellyn did argue and you walked out of the restaurant. Did you see Dr. Llewellyn after that? Did you speak with him outside of the restaurant? Can you tell us your whereabouts between midnight and four this morning?"

I take a sip of coffee. So, I am being questioned about Scott's murder. "Both my wife and nanny can verify that I came home and went upstairs to bed. I assume since the word murder has been used his death is obviously not an accident. Can you tell me what happened?"

The two cops look at each other again. I wonder why they don't want to have a straight conversation with me and appear to be communicating with telepathy. The taller of the two finally looks me in the eye. "Dr. Llewellyn was shot in the head. Some may call his injury an execution style assassination."

I pause to absorb this. "Someone shot him in the head on the Palace Green of Williamsburg in the middle of the night? Did anyone hear gunshots? Was this a primary scene? Did anyone see anything?"

The shorter cop puts his coffee cup down. "Agent Clay, we are the ones asking the questions. We can either do it here or go to the station."

I can feel annoyance building. I need to maintain control. I'm normally the person asking questions and not accustomed to being interviewed. "When my office called me before you arrived, they also told me that I am a person of interest. I didn't kill Scott. I want to find out who killed him as much as you do, so why don't we work together?"

They look uncomfortable and glance at each other again. The tall one shuffles his feet under the table, then looks me in the eye again. "Agent Clay, according to Karen Llewellyn you argued with her husband and stormed out of the restaurant. He followed after you and was not seen again. When he was found it was pretty obvious someone roughed him up before shooting him in the head. Right now we have to follow the leads we have. You and your wife are the only people we know he encountered last night. Can you see your hands please?"

I thrust my hands out in front of me and then turn them over. "No bruising, no cuts. I haven't hit anyone. I haven't roughed anyone up and I certainly haven't shot anyone. Do you want to swab me for gunshot residue? Would you like my clothing from last night? What do you want from me? Why are you here when you should be looking for his killer? The street is lined with houses full of families who work in Williamsburg. Did you do a door to door canvas to see if anyone heard anything? Or is this a rush to judgement because Scott and I got into a heated discussion about history in a restaurant?"

I am making them uncomfortable. I guess I shouldn't but I need them to understand they are wasting time focusing on me. Scott must have been a few minutes behind us. I try to think if we passed anyone on our walk up Duke of Gloucester Street.

Samantha and I had walked holding hands. The cressets were burning and a couple of the taverns and the bake shop had bonfires burning along the sidewalk. Small groups of people were gathered around the fires for warmth. Behind us I heard the clip clop of one of the carriages being pulled by a team of horses. Williamsburg at night in the fall can take you back to the seventeen hundreds. The street is dark and quiet. The smell of wood smoke fills the air. It is calm and peaceful. It defused my anger with Scott quickly. I was happy to just spend a few minutes walking up the street with Samantha. We stopped at the corner of the Palace Green and got cups of hot apple cider and ginger cakes. If Scott was behind us he would have easily caught up.

By then, it was about nine forty-five. There were a few people walking on the street. I saw two people taking their dogs for a walk. A man was riding his bike up the middle of the street. There was the carriage with its driver and passengers. I doubt the people standing around the fires noticed us. They were lost in their own conversations. The woman working at the hot cider stand might remember Samantha. She was about to pack up for the night and we spoke for a moment. Samantha was nervous about leaving AJ home, she hadn't had too many nights out without him yet. She and the cider women bonded over missing their young children. The holiday decorations are almost complete in town. This is the quiet before the storm. Soon the streets will be packed with tourists coming to town for the Grand Illumination. We bought her last two ginger cakes and cider. Since we didn't stay through dessert, this was a good ending to our evening. It took my mind off of Scott.

We walked past the Palace Green. The tall iron poles with fire baskets, the cressets, were burning down along both sides of the Palace Green and in front of the gates of the Palace. One of the last few ghost tours of the night passed by us stopping at the corner of the graveyard of Bruton Parish. We stopped for a moment as well at the corner of the church. I can't believe Scott wanted to dig up part of the grave yard and the tower of the church. He isn't the first person to try, a group was caught once before and they had dug up along a grave and to the wall of the church one night. Luckily, graves were not disturbed and they didn't make it to the tower. They did uncover a foundation which may have been part of the original church, but it was meaningless to them. Scott just has crazy ideas searching for a treasure that doesn't exist. Once again, if he was behind us, he could have caught up.

I know Scott and Karen drove separately. Scott was staying in a hotel on route sixty. Karen had driven down from their house in Fredericksburg and was going to spend the night. Scott would have walked Karen to her car. She had mentioned she was lucky to find a close space in the lot on Francis Street. He had either moved his car from the west end of town at the college or it was still parked there. It is possible he walked west on Francis Street to the parking lot between Nassau and Henry Streets, where we had parked. If so, he would not have been seen on Duke of Gloucester Street.

I realize my mind has drifted off and the two cops are looking at me. "I'm sorry. I was going over last night in my head. Samantha and I walked up Duke of Gloucester Street. You can check with the woman who was selling hot cider along the Palace Green. Samantha suggested we stop and get some cider and a cookie before we drove home. It was her way of cooling me off. The woman selling the cider may remember us. You need to talk to Karen again. Find out where she parked her car and if Scott walked with her to her car. He may have walked up Francis Street and avoided Duke of Gloucester. Or if he was trying to catch up with us, he may have thought we left the restaurant and walked up Francis. Instead, we walked back to the main road through town. Francis Street is not well lit."

The tall cop is shaking his head. "Scott left a minute after you to try to catch up with you. Karen waited in front of the restaurant for nearly a half hour before she drove to the hotel. She thought he might be meeting her at the hotel. She also tried to call his cell phone and he didn't answer. His phone was not on his body when he was found."

"She fell asleep waiting for him. She assumed he had met up with you and you were talking. His body had found by the time she called us to report him missing."

Samantha has been standing in the kitchen leaning against the counter and has been quiet until now. "He didn't catch up with us. After we left the restaurant, we didn't see him. I understand you have to do your job but you are wasting your time. I was with Adam from the time we left the restaurant until you just knocked on the door."

Christina slams a plate of pancakes and bacon on the table a little harder than she should have. "I saw them walk in the door. I was watching TV in the living room. My bedroom is on the first floor. I would have heard him walking around downstairs or open the door. I have a monitor to the baby's room and to Alina's room. I hear anything moving in the house from the rabbits to the dog. No one came back down the stairs and the alarm was set. Until Adams phone rang and you rang the doorbell, no one moved around this house."

The tall cop stands up and looks at the other cop. He also stands up. "I guess we don't have any other questions right now, but keep yourself available in case we need to speak with you again." They turn and walk out of the kitchen. Samantha follows them to the door. Christina and I walk to the living room and we watch Samantha close the door behind them.

She locks the door. "Well, I'm not going to be able to go back to sleep right now. Breakfast is ready, we might as well eat." We turn and head back into the kitchen.

I'm not hungry but I put a pancake on my plate and take two pieces of bacon. I don't understand why Karen would think I had anything to do with Scott's death. She knows this was just a trivial disagreement. Scott and I have known each other since college. I was studying criminal law and he was a history major. We met freshman year when we were assigned to a four person dorm room. Our other two roommates were the party type. Scott and I were nerds who spent more time at the library than at a bar. We became close when one of the roommates over dosed just before Christmas. We found him in the living room one afternoon after class. The other roommate didn't come back after Christmas. That left Scott and I to deal with the death and spring semester.

We got an apartment the next year and kept it through graduation. It gave us a chance to pay attention to school, work our part time jobs on campus, and stay sane. We were the best man in each other's weddings and he was by my side through Elizabeth's funeral. My instinct now is to go to Karen's side but, I don't know if she will slam the door in my face. Scott was like a brother to me. I can't believe he's dead.

Samantha is pushing her food around her plate. I guess she is not hungry either. Christina is concentrating on stirring her coffee. It was well stirred a minute ago. Now it is mindless activity. She looks up at me. "Why would they think you killed him? It makes no sense. You are an FBI agent. You investigate murders, not cause them. Do you think you should call Karen? I'm sure she isn't sleeping."

I don't know who is with Karen right now. I hope she is not alone and she called her mother or sister. I don't think I should call her. I think after the sun comes up I will drive up to Fredericksburg and talk to her. Then again, maybe she has stayed in the hotel. Before I drive to Fredericksburg, I should find out where she is staying.

We force ourselves to eat. The kids will be up in less than an hour. I promised Alina I would drive her to school this morning. I was planning on driving to Williamsburg and attending the last day of the conference. Now, I guess it will be cancelled. Scott was the keynote speaker. He was scheduled to lecture at two sessions today and was on the panel for the closing program.

After breakfast, Samantha and I go back upstairs to get dressed. She pulls up her schedule for the day and sends a couple emails. "I have canceled my appointments for the day. If you are going to see Karen, I am going with you. And do not argue with me Adam Clay! You are a hard headed man but you just lost a good friend. While you pretend to be a rock, you are human somewhere deep inside."

She knows me too well. Right now I am focused on finding out who killed him. I can mourn his loss later. At the moment, this is a victim who needs a voice. I go into the bathroom and shave. The man looking at me in the mirror appears to be a stranger. I know I should feel loss but right now I can't. Murder victims don't scare me. They are bodies on a table. The man in the mirror is telling me to get to work and bring a murderer to justice. The man looking into the mirror knows I just lost one of my oldest friends. I don't let myself dwell on that fact and finish shaving.

I come out of the bathroom and look at my phone. It's after seven and I call John. He answers on the first ring. "Hey, I didn't know how long the cops would be at your house. What the hell is going on? I'm at the office. The rumor mill says you are being investigated for murder. The agent in charge wants to see me in his office at nine. What do you need me to do? Damn, Adam. This is messed up!"

I have to laugh. John and his partner, Chris, are close friends. They are like uncles to my kids and Samantha calls them her gay husbands. If I was at work, I would know John has my back. I am somewhat hesitant to get him involved with this because I do not want to have him accused of anything. "John, when I know more I will tell you. All I know at this point is that after Samantha and I walked out of the tavern Scott followed us. We never saw him and drove home. From what I gathered, he took a bullet execution style. Karen was waiting for him at the hotel and fell asleep. His body had been found by the time she called in a missing person report. She told them about the argument Scott and I had and that Scott had followed us out the door. That brought them to our house."

The other end of the phone is silent for a moment. "So you are telling me you are a person of interest because you walked out of the tavern before he did and went home before you got into a further altercation? You have Samantha as an alibi. What about Karen? Has she been fighting with Scott? Why has she been home all week and just come down to join him now? Is she also a person of interest?"

John is asking a very interesting question and one I have not allowed myself to think about. How was Scott's relationship with Karen? He hasn't talked about her lately. All week long his only mention was that she had stayed home this week but was coming down Thursday night for dinner. Karen had been a friend of Elizabeth in college. Scott and I double dated the girls and proposed at about the same time. After Elizabeth's murder, Karen had talked to me about taking my time to begin dating again. She welcomed Samantha into their lives but was cold at first. She warmed up to her eventually, but she has not been as close to Samantha as Elizabeth. This put a strain on my friendship with Scott. The couples weekends and weekends at each other's houses stopped when Samantha came into my life. Of course, Samantha and I had a child in our lives. When Elizabeth was alive, she made it clear she did not want to have children. Karen and Scott don't have any children either. Alina made the over nights and trips more difficult. We could leave her home with her nanny, but we tend to do things as a family with Christina and the kids. I guess things just changed.

Now more than ever I feel as if I should be by Karen's side. I know what it is like to get the news that your spouse has been murdered. Dying suddenly from a natural death is hard but murder is different. There is no right time to be murdered. There is no acceptance of murder.

Someone took someone you loved from your life too early. It is a deep dark chasm with no answers and no solace. No one can tell you the person is in a better place. They were fine before their murder. This isn't like a release from a painful disease or a valiant fight for life. It is not something you will ever understand, it just becomes something you accept. I tell John I will let him and Chris know when I need something. For right now keep his eyes and ears open.

I finish getting dressed and go back downstairs. Alina is up and eating her breakfast. AJ is in the highchair currently wearing more than he has eaten. Christina is trying to catch his mouth long enough to get a spoon full of cereal in. I hear the shower running upstairs and know Samantha is finishing and getting dressed. We will take Alina to school and then drive to Fredericksburg.

Samantha comes down the stairs as Alina is getting her coat on. We head out to the car leaving Christina and AJ to settle in for the day at home. Christina is taking college courses at night and in her free time during the day works on homework. AJ is learning to walk so his day is spent trying to defy gravity and stand firmly on his own two feet. Our biggest challenge right now is keeping him out of the rabbit and dog food bowls. He still likes to put everything in his mouth. The pediatrician assures us a few rabbit pellets and dog nuggets won't hurt him but we shouldn't let him get in the habit of eating them as a meal.

The carpool line at school isn't complete mayhem as we drop Alina off. We pull into the circle in front of school. She unbuckles, grabs her backpack and jumps out. She waves goodbye at the door before running inside. The cars in front of us are about to move and the crossing guard signals for us to leave the circle so that the next group of cars can enter and drop off. From there I head to I-95 to head north through Richmond to Fredericksburg.

Traffic through Richmond is heavy but we are going the opposite direction of most commuters. We make the seventy-six mile trip in about ninety minutes. Scott and Karen own a house just off the

Rappahannock River in a cul-de-sac. It is normally a quiet neighborhood but today we have a hard time finding a parking space. The news crews have parked outside the house. I find a place to park and look at Samantha, "Well, are you ready to face the vultures?"

She looks at me and grabs my hand, "I am, but are you? They know who we are and they will be trying to find out why the FBI is involved in the murder. We can still turn around and go somewhere to call her. You don't have to do this."

I think I owe it to Scott to be here. He would not want her going through this without us. I open my door and step out. We keep our heads down and walk toward the house. In moments, I see a microphone poking in front of my face. "Agent Clay, would you like to comment on the report that you are a person of interest in Doctor Llewellyn's murder? What are you doing at the house? What is your connection to Doctor Llewellyn?" I push the microphone out of my face and mumble "No comment."

How do they know I am a person of interest? Why are the police releasing information on this case so quickly? My head is spinning but I know better than to stop and talk to them. We push forward and make it to the front door. I can feel the crowd of reporters closing in around us. Karen's sister, Linda, opens the door and hugs me. "Adam! I'm so glad you have come. Karen is a mess. Samantha, maybe you can talk to her. We are trying to get her to go to the doctors and get a prescription. She needs something to help her through this." She looks out at the sea of reporters with cameras rolling. "Oh my God! Hurry and come inside. This is insane!"

Samantha pushes the door closed behind her and locks it. Karen is sitting on the sofa. Her mother, Anita, is sitting by her side with a box of tissues. Don, Karen's brother is sitting on the other side of her. Joyce and Kurt, old college friends are also nearby. Karen looks up at us with red eyes and tear stained cheeks. She starts to stand up and wobbles, reaching quickly for the arm of the sofa. Don jumps up and helps her to her feet.

Her eyes are nearly swollen shut. She looks frail and seems to have aged about fifty years since last night. She melts into my arms when I hug her. I can feel my shirt getting damp from her tears. "Adam, I'm sorry they are trying to pin this on you. I know you had nothing to do with this. I don't know who killed him. Why would anyone want to kill him? He was a history professor for God's sake. Who murders a history professor?"

She breaks down into uncontrollable sobbing. Don is standing behind her and urges her to sit back down. She allows him to help her back on the sofa and she slumps against Anita. I get down on my knees and put my arms around her. Her tears are bringing on my tears. There was so much history between him, Karen, Elizabeth and me. The four of us were tied together until Elizabeth's murder. Now Scott is dead. At least with Elizabeth there was someone to hate immediately. It was assumed her murder was part of the trial she was working on and it proved to be true. I don't know who would hate Scott enough to kill him and a street robber rarely shoots the victim between the eyes. That is a personal crime.

I hear Samantha on her phone behind me. "This is Dr. Samantha Callahan-Clay. I need to call in a prescription for a patient. Linda…Anita…do you know if Karen has any drug allergies?" They both shake their head. "Has she ever taken Diazepam?" They both respond that they aren't sure. Karen shakes her head no. "Karen, are you taking any other drugs?" Again she shakes her head no. "Let me call this in for you. Hi, I'm sorry. I was talking with the patient and the family. I think Diazepam five milligrams PO." She is listening to the pharmacist and pauses. "I would say standard. Thirty tablets for right now. My DEA number is Bravo Charlie four-two-one-three–five-nine-eight. This is for Karen Rebecca Llewellyn." Samantha pauses and looks over at Don. "Don, do you think it would be better for you to pick it up or for them to try to deliver?" He tells her it would be better for him to pick it up. That way the press won't see a pharmacy delivery pulling up to the house.

Samantha thanks the pharmacist and tells Don it will be ready for pick up in about fifteen minutes. When Don stands up Samantha sits down next to Karen and puts her hand on her shoulder. "Sweetie, in a few minutes Don can get the prescription back to you and it will make you feel a little better. It will take the edge off. Now have you eaten? Would you like a cup of tea or anything?"

Karen looks at Samantha, "Thank you. Tea would be fine. Thank you for calling something in for me. I don't know what I am going to do. Scotts gone. I don't know how to live without him. What am I going to do? How am I going to survive? I am alone now! I don't know what to do."

Joyce stands up and goes to the kitchen to make the tea while Samantha takes Karen in her arms. "You are going to find a way to survive this. You have friends and family who love you and will help you get through this. Life will go on and you will find happiness again. It just takes time. For today, tomorrow and for the next few weeks, look at the people in this room. Lean on us and we will get you through this."

Samantha, Karen and I have our arms around each other crying together. Karen looks up at Anita and Linda as Don gets ready to leave to pick up the prescription. "Mom...Linda...Kurt...do you mind? Can you give Adam and me a few minutes? Samantha, you can stay. I need to talk to you both in private."

Kurt, Anita and Linda nod their heads and leave the room as Karen tries to compose herself. "I'm glad you both came. I think I need your help. I know the police think you had something to do with Scott's murder and I have told them this is ridiculous. I have tried to think all morning why someone would want to kill him. I think I know but I don't understand why. Adam, you might. A few weeks ago Scott was very excited. He told me he had found a copper tube. It may be one of the scrolls you were talking about last night. He didn't bring the tube home. He thought it might put us in danger. Would someone kill for that treasure? Is a copper tube that might hold a scroll worth someone's life?"

I guess it all depends on the copper scroll. The Masonic Scrolls are thought to hold the information on the location of what was taken by the Knights Templar from Solomon's Temple. The legend covers everything from the Holy Grail to the Arc of the Covenant. "Karen, did he say anything about the copper cylinder? Did he say where he found it or what the scroll said? Did he tell anyone else?"

She reaches over and takes a tissue from the box and blows her nose. "He just told me he found a copper tube and inside it he thinks he would find a scroll. He was doing some archeology work somewhere near James Island. I don't know if it was sanctioned. He was very secretive about it. He didn't bring it here and I don't know who he may have spoken to about this. I do know that he went to Baltimore for a few days."

I'm not sure why going to Baltimore is significant. "Did Scott go to Baltimore to talk to someone?"

She shakes her head and leans in toward me. "No." She looks around to check that no one else is in the room. Just above a whisper she says, "He had a small office up there. He occasionally taught at a few of the colleges and he rented an office in the downtown area. I'm not sure where. There was some work that Scott did and kept to himself. I think it was his Masonic Treasure stuff. It was not work he wanted to do at his home office. He would drive to Baltimore at least once a week to work. Occasionally, he would sleep in his office."

Karen stops talking as Joyce walks into the room with a cup of tea. She takes it and gives Joyce a smile. "Thank you. We will be finished talking in a moment. Adam or Samantha will let you know when we are done." Joyce smiles back at her and puts her hand on Karen's shoulder, then walks out of the room.

Karen sips her tea for a moment. "Samantha, you were right. I needed this tea. It's hard to think of anything but Scott's body lying on the Palace Green. I didn't see him, they wouldn't let me. Now I guess he's somewhere in the morgue." She whimpers and takes another drink to compose herself. . "I guess you are curious about why Scott had the office in Baltimore. I wondered also. Our relationship has been strained. I thought he might have a mistress. I'm still not entirely sure there wasn't another woman. I hate to ask but if you go to Baltimore could you see if you can find out? He told me the second office was for when he taught and for him to work on his treasure hunting. I don't understand why but he thought it was better to not have that information at the house. As for Scott and I, after I had fertility problems things went downhill."

She is sitting there looking out into the room. I have seen this look before in a victim's family member. They are looking back at what was, and wondering what if... I just sit back and let her go. This is the beginning of the process of recovery. I went through this myself. I possibly suppressed much of this and didn't deal with it until I met Samantha. I ran from it rather than face it. "We went to a fertility doctor. We had been trying for nearly a year and it just wasn't happening. Physically we were both fine, so the doctor thought it was a matter of timing. I started tracking my life on a chart and taking my temperature a couple times a day. When it was the zero hour and an ovum was being released it became time for sex. I can tell you trying to make a baby is not as much fun as practicing and accidentally making one."

Samantha looks at me. I can almost read the look in her eyes. Because of our ages, we went to a fertility doctor. We were recommended to have sex on a schedule and given a list of positions to try. It was not romantic or exciting. After walking out of the doctor's office she looked at me and suggested we leave having a baby up to fate, if it happened it happened. If it didn't happen it was not meant to be. Allowing fate to make the decision seemed better than what the doctor described. Samantha moves to sit next to Karen and takes her hand.

Karen smiles at Samantha, "if you ever get to that place in your life where the mind wants a child but the body does not. I advise adopting over doctor prescribed sex. When the calendar and the thermometer said it was time it was pretty horrible. I would lie on my back and Scott would do the deed. There was nothing erotic or exciting about it. It was procreation sex. Scott felt like he was being forced to perform. This eventually led to Scott having difficulty. He first had problems getting an erection. If he could get one the sex was so horrible he couldn't keep one. There was also the image. I went from sexy erotic wife who fulfilled fantasies to the sperm receptacle. We were told for me to lie on my back during sex and to stay in that position for 30-45 minutes afterward. It was preferable after sex to elevate my vagina so that the sperm could basically run downhill. It would allow the sperm to travel into my uterus better and be in a position to meet up with the embryo for fertilization. This would give the whole fertilization thing a better chance. Trying to have a baby ruined our sex life. I became familiar with the ceiling and he lost the ability to have sex entirely. So we quit trying. I think we also quit being a couple about the same time. We were two people living in the same house. Of course now I regret all of this. We weren't happy. Scott died existing rather than living."

She dabs her eyes again. "If I can be honest with you, if you go to Baltimore and find another woman I will almost be relieved. I feel I failed him. My body failed both of us. Trying to have a baby ruined our marriage and made us strangers. That is why I don't want mom and Linda to know what I am telling you. They would try to blame this on Scott but it was both of us. We just fell out of love. It made Scott focus and try to follow a dream of treasure. That at least had some excitement. Now, someone has murdered him. I think the answer to both our questions might be in Baltimore."

I ask her if she told the police about this office. She shakes her head. "No. Adam, this is why I am telling you. If someone killed Scott because of what he found I don't want it in the hands of the police. If Scott found something historically important I want him to get credit for it. The police will just release the information. I don't know if he will get proper credit for all of his research. I also didn't tell them that I suspect he had a lover. If they find someone in his history I will accept that, but I don't want them digging through the mud in his life and going to the media with speculation."

I tell Karen that I will look into what I can but I can't promise I will go to Baltimore to find and go through Scott's office. This is probably something she and the family should do, not me. Having dinner with Scott last night and walking out over a conversation about what he might have found brought the police to my door to interview me as a person of interest. My finger prints on a secret office could make matters worse if they find out about it and do any investigation.

Don walks back in the front door. For a moment we are able to see the crowd of reporters camped on the front yard. I also see a couple police cars. I hope this new addition does not create a problem for me. Samantha gets up and goes to the kitchen to get a glass of water for Karen and sticks her head into the office where the others have been waiting. She comes back and hands Karen the glass and one of the pills. "I suggest you take this and go lie down. It might make you sleepy, but it will help get you through the next few days. I will leave my cell phone number with your mom in case she has any questions or you need someone to talk to outside the family. You may have the urge to skip a dosage and see if you can tough it out. I don't advise doing that. Let the medicine work. Take one every six hours at least through the funeral. After that we can talk and see if you need them anymore. I would also like to set up grief counseling for you when the time comes." Karen nods her head and takes the medicine.

There is no way for us to leave other than walk out the front door. We put our heads down and walk out not looking at anyone in our path. Samantha walks behind me and I use my body to cut a path through the reporters. I hear them asking how she is doing? What did we talk about?

And a jumble of other questions. The police are sitting in their cars watching the scene. I wonder what they are doing here. I would have thought they were dispatched to keep the reporters away from the widow. Instead, they are observers to media harassment.

Once inside the Jeep, we are surrounded by reporters and cameras. One outside my window is reporting that I am a person of interest in the murder and had just visited with the victim's wife. He is speculating that I might be trying to influence her to draw the police away from me. His camera person is taping over his shoulder. Samantha and I just look forward and inch our way out of the cul-de-sac. The officers in the police cars watch the scene without opening their car doors.

As soon as we break clear of the reporters and get on open road, I try to relax. I had planned on going to Scott's funeral but now I am not sure. I am torn between paying respect to a friend and fueling more speculation on his murder. I hear Samantha sigh and glance at her. "Okay, it's just us. Let's talk. You give me your educated impression and I will listen and drive."

She shakes her head. "First, I think she told the police you and Scott argued, but I believe her that she did not suggest in any way that you are guilty. I don't think her family does either. I don't know about Scott's family but you are not close to them. I am concerned and confused about the reporters knowing you are a person of interest. I feel there has been a rush to judgement and the information has been released to the press for some reason."

Karen seemed happy to see us. Scott's family has always been distant. While we were in college his parents were more interested in their trips to Europe and somehow managed to miss most major holidays. He spent holidays either at school or at my parent's house with me. I will never forget our graduation. He got a message the morning we were scheduled to walk across the stage to tell him their flight had been delayed but they were on their way and would get there in time. Our graduation took over four hours. When it was over we stayed with him to meet up with his parents. They never came. Eventually we left and went out to dinner. This cemented Scott's decision to look for a job and move to Virginia. I'm not sure how much contact he had with his parents since then.

I take the exit to get back on I-95 south. Once we are on the interstate she continues. "I am worried about what I saw going on with the police and the press. I feel like there are too many leaks. The press knows the police talked to you and too many details. Releasing that you are a person of interest so early in the investigation will turn the court of public opinion against you. They will convict you on the five o'clock news without any evidence. Scott's murder is being treated as a high profile case. Karen is right, Scott was a history professor. Why is his murder being elevated by the press to a red ball case?"

I have wondered this myself. It may be a result of his body being found in the historic district of Williamsburg. "Besides his murder being in Williamsburg, can you see any other reason they are red balling this?"

I glance over and see a scowl on her face. "Adam, I have no idea. I am still trying to figure out how the two of us walking out of the restaurant transitioned to you being a person of interest in his murder. It doesn't make any sense. It is a rush to judgment. His body was found an hour before the police were at our door. They had to find his body, identify him and talk to Karen. When does a murder investigation move that quickly?"

She has a very good point. I became a person of interest in an execution style murder in sixty minutes. From the surface this seems someone has an agenda. For the moment all I can do is watch my back. Luckily, I have both Samantha and Christina to vouch for me throughout the night. I also have the vendor at the apple cider stand who should remember both Samantha and I together walking up the street.

I drive on in silence for the rest of the drive. I think we are both lost in thoughts. Christina comes out of the house when we pull into the driveway. "I'm sorry. I have been watching for you to get home. I didn't want to call you with this. I had to call the police while you were gone. The kids are fine but I'm concerned."

We walk in the door together and she turns and locks the door and sets the alarm. "Come with me. I need to show you something." She walks into my office and pulls up the video from the security system. "I sent a copy of this to the police who responded. I was in the kitchen making AJ a bowl of fruit. You hadn't been gone long. I glanced out the window and I saw a man in the yard near the tree line. I know I set the alarm when you left. Anyway, he was walking from tree to tree heading to the house. I thought he was a reporter or something. I ran to the front door and set off the panic alarm. The dispatcher was speaking to me in seconds and sent the police. I glanced back out and the audible alarm made the guy run back down the path to the boat house."

She types a code into the keyboard and brings up the video and security log. "This is where it gets weird. Watch this and watch the perimeter alarms." As the man walks up from the boat house, I see individual perimeter detectors turning off and once he passes turning back on. Once the log shows the panic alarm was pressed and the man running I see the perimeter alarms indicating they have been set off. "Guys, I think this guy hacked our security system. I am not going to lie to you. I am scared!"

I sit down at the computer and watch the video and the log on split screen a few more times. Christina is correct. As the man begins to walk into the perimeter of the next detector it turns off. Once he clears the area it turns back on. He is somehow controlling my security system. If Christina had not seen him in the yard, this man could have gotten into my house. For the second time in my life I do not feel that my family is safe in my own home. Samantha has been sitting by my side as I have been looking at this. "I think we need to pack the kids and Christina up and get them out of here." I look into her eyes and see the same fear I am beginning to feel.

I hear a noise behind me and jump. It is Christina standing in the doorway. She has her hands folded across her chest. I can't tell if this is fear or determination on her face. "The kids are already packed and I have thrown a few things in a bag for myself. You both know I won't let anything happen to these kids. I will take them where ever you think they need to go."

I smile for possibly the first time all day. Christina is like a female tigress. She will protect the young at all cost. She proved that when Alina was a toddler and she ran from Tyler Braden. I trust her with my children's life. "I'm going to call John and see if you can stay with him and Chris for a couple days. Samantha, I'd like you to go also. Take the dog and rabbits. I want my family safe. I don't know what's going on right now but something is happening." One person has already died and I don't want my family to be next.

I look over at Samantha. As I expected she is now glaring at me with her arms crossed. I can ask her to go to safety but I can't make her go to a safe place. "Look, I don't know who this guy might have been. He could have been someone from the press with some sophisticated device that blanks out security systems. He could have been the guy who killed Scott. Until I know who he is, I don't want to put anyone at risk. Nor do I want my kids plastered over the news by some photographer. Either way I want the kids out of here until I figure out what is going on."

Christina nods and walks out of the room. I hear her walk up the steps toward the kids rooms. Samantha has not moved. I wait to see what she has on her mind. Rather than speak she walks across the room and opens the gun safe. She takes out her box and pulls out her 9mm. I hear the clip pop and see her reach into the bottom and pull out a box of ammunition. She walks back across the room and puts the box on my desk before she speaks. "I guess you know I am not leaving your side. As this day has progressed, I have seen some things I can't explain. I'm getting scared but I am not going to let whoever is behind Scotts murder get to anyone in my family, including you Adam. Let's get the kids and animals packed up and moved off site. Then we will discuss what we are going to do tonight."

She is interrupted by the doorbell. She tucks the gun in the back of her jeans and pulls her sweater over it before heading to the door. I follow her. Outside are two cops with their hands on their guns. I signal to Samantha to back away and open the door. "May I help you officers?"

The first thing I see is a search warrant in the hands of one officer. "Agent Clay?" I nod my head. "I am Officer Neal Rogers and this is Officer Howard Macks. We have been sent here with a search warrant for your premises. The warrant is specifically for your Glock 22 service weapon. May we come in and search your premise for that weapon?"

I am confused but swing the door open for them to come in. "You would come in whether you have my permission or not with that warrant, but I have no problem taking you to my office and getting it out for you. Come with me."

I notice Samantha has fallen in behind us. I walk across the office to the gun safe and unlock it, taking out my box and handing it to the officer. "Anything else while I have this open?" He shakes his head and takes the box from me. "Can I ask what this is about?"

Officer Macks holds the box in his hand and looks me in the eye. "The autopsy on Scott Llewellyn has been completed and ballistics has matched the bullet to this weapon. Has anyone else had access to this weapon other than yourself?"

I can't believe this is happening. I haven't touched my service weapon in a week. While I have been on vacation it has been locked in my gun safe. "My wife has access to the safe but has no need to handle my service weapon."

He opens the box and looks inside. "Would you mind telling me where your weapon is at this moment?" I'm confused until he turns the box around showing an empty case. The last time I saw my weapon was when I put it in its box and locked the safe. There is no way anyone could have gotten into the safe and taken it. "Agent Clay, I think you need to stick close to your home. We just have a warrant for your weapon at this time. We are going to take this back to the station. I'm sure someone will want to speak to you in the very near future. You also might want to think about getting a lawyer."

They turn to walk out of the room and pause at Samantha. "Mrs. Clay, I'm sorry we had to disturb your afternoon. As I recommended to your husband, it might be very important for you to contact a lawyer as well. You both might need a representative in the next day or so." They continue walking through the house and out the door, taking my FBI issued gun case minus my now missing service weapon to their vehicle.

She stands at the door and watches them back out of the driveway and drive away before she shuts it and locks the door. "Adam, what the hell is happening?" She turns and looks at Christina. "Get my kids out of here!"

Christina walks back upstairs to finish packing the kids toys as my phone rings. I see it is from the office and I don't want to answer it. The voice on the other end is the last thing I need right now. "Adam, this is Special Agent in Charge Roger Sacks." Roger Sacks is the agent in charge of the entire field office. In the pecking order, this guy is the top of the pyramid. My boss reports to him. I know what is coming before the words leave his mouth. "I wanted to call you and talk to you. I don't know if you would like to come into the office and talk or if you would like to do this over the phone?"

I know what he is going to tell me. I run my fingers through my hair and lean against the wall. "You are putting me on administrative leave aren't you?"

There is a pause on the other end before he answers. "Yes. I see no other way around this. We can't risk any cases you touch right now. If you are indicted, anything you have worked on will be in question. It is too much of a risk. I believe you. Hell, we all believe you are innocent, but until this plays out I can't let you work. You are still being paid for right now. Look, take a couple days for a vacation. Spend time with your kids and your wife. Get outdoors and enjoy yourself for a few days. I'm sure this will all work out and everything will be fine."

I feel like I can't breathe. He is telling me to spend time with my family. I know he means before I end up in jail. I tell him I understand. My mind is screaming help me, don't put me out to pasture, but of course I can't say that. Instead, I tell him I will keep him up to date on the investigation. He starts to say good bye and stops. "Adam, if you need anything— call us. We are your family. I don't know what is going on and I'm sure neither do you but if you need anything from us— anything—call us." I thank him and hang up the phone.

The doorbell rings and Samantha spins around. There is a small red car in the driveway. On the porch is a pizza delivery guy from the local pizza shop. We have seen him before when he has delivered. Samantha opens the door for him. "Hey, Charlie. What are you doing here?"

Charlie is standing in our doorway looking confused. "I'm delivering your pizza." He holds out the pizza and Samantha takes it. She turns and looks at me.

Doughnut has come running out and has his nose pressed to the bottom of the box. She holds it higher and hands it to me. "Do I owe you anything Charlie? I hate to sound crazy but we didn't order a pizza. Are you sure you have the right place?"

He pulls a slip from his pocket. "Yup. Someone from the house ordered a pizza about twenty minutes ago from your online account. They added the tip. It is the same as usual. Do you want me to take it back?"

He is as confused as we are but Samantha tells him it is fine. He turns and goes back to his car. I walk into the kitchen with the pizza and put it on the table. Samantha and Christina join me. If the day had not been so strange, this might have been comical. We are all standing around the table looking at a pizza box.

I look at the box for wires and feel its weight. It doesn't feel or look unusual. I decide to be the one who opens it. Inside is a pizza. I assume it is safe to eat but I hesitate. It smells like a normal pizza and looks like a normal pizza but I have no idea how it was ordered or why. Christina and Samantha seem to be having the same thoughts. "Well if we are going to vote on this, I vote we send this to the trash can. Anyone have any other idea or do you want to trust eating it?" Both women shake their head no. Christina takes a step back from the table.

Samantha leans in over the pizza. "Well someone ordered it for a reason. It could have been to be nice. The cops could have felt bad but I doubt they would hack our pizza account and bill us to order it. It could be poisoned. I don't think I want to try my luck with it." Christina shakes her head no also.

I pick up the box. I don't want to put a potentially poisoned pizza in the trash and have Doughnut knock down the can and eat it. I open the back door and walk to the trash cans. I sit it on top of one can to unlock the lid of the other. Samantha is standing on the back porch watching me. As I start to dump it in the can, the pizza slides from the box and she yells at me to stop.

Inside the box, under the pizza is an envelope. It has been stained orange with oil from the pepperoni. I know I am getting paranoid and I look around to see if anyone is near us and can either see inside the box or hear Samantha. No one is around but the three of us. I pull the envelope off of the box and walk back inside.

The note tells me to follow the Colonial Parkway and to the pull off at Indian Field Creek. In the fourth post on the bridge, I am instructed to reach in and locate the magnetic box of the geo cache. From there I should read the tenth name on the geo cache list. Once located, I am instructed to look up the user name, specifically the profile comments attached to this geo cache user. There I will receive further instructions.

I'm not sure if I should follow the instructions or not. Someone has gone to great lengths to send a message to me. My gut tells me to check this out. I walk back into my office and pull my personal gun from the safe. Indian Field Creek is near James Island and according to Karen this is the area Scott was doing a dig. If I am going to get to the bottom of this, I think I have to take the risk.

I tell Samantha that I am going to drive there and check it out. It will take me about an hour in drive time and hopefully no more than an hour to see what this person wants. I will check in with her by phone throughout my journey. I walk to my office and make a copy of the note and hand the original to her. "If anything happens, here is the evidence. I have to do this."

She looks me in the eye and then nods her head. "Be careful. I don't like it, but I understand. Are you sure you don't want me to come along?"

I tell her no and grab my jacket as I walk out the door. I hear the lock click behind me as I walk toward the Jeep. I hear her yell "I love you" from behind the locked door.

The road is wide open with very little traffic and I make good time. I call Samantha when I get there and park the car to let her know where I am. This all feels a little cloak and dagger to me but I walk toward the bridge. There in the fourth post I find a small metal box with a magnet glued to the back. I slide the lid open and pull out a small scroll. It is a four inch strip of notebook paper. Line ten says Moonshiner.

I open my browser to the geo cache website and type in Moonshiner. This takes me to a very elaborate web page. I'm not sure what to do or go from there until I see a Masonic symbol with the letters A and C on them. I have seen Easter Eggs in games before and this looks like a classic Easter Egg. I tap the screen and it immediately asks for a password. I see four boxes followed by a space and four boxes. Taking the hint I type in Adam Clay.

The screen blinks for a second before the message appears. "Welcome Adam. I gambled on you being smart enough to discover the link and to guess the password. You have not let me down. Now, I will not let you down. Continue to cross the bridge. Once past the guardrail walk to the tree line. Look for a red string tied to a tree branch. Enter the woods there. Look for a drink can under a pine tree twenty paces away. Inside the drink can is the next step of your journey."

I am already getting tired of the games. I take out my gun and click the safety off. I'm not sure if I am walking into a trap, dealing with someone who is mentally disturbed or someone who needs to be careful. I am gambling on someone who needs to be careful.

I see the can and pick it up. In the opening I see a scroll of paper and remove it. "You have trusted me. I am going to trust you. At this point both our lives depend on it. Walk to the left twenty paces. You will see three trees growing together. Walk behind these trees. From a distance this will look like a dense stand of trees. Find the door knob. Knock twice so that I know it is you."

I walk over and see the stand of trees. He is correct. This appears to be a stand of trees until I run my hand over it and find a door knob molded to look like a knot in the tree. I knock twice on the tree and turn the knob. Nothing happens. The door appears to be locked. I can hear noise behind it and a man's voice asks, "Is that you Clay?" I respond that it is and the door opens.

The door opens to a foyer with a staircase leading down into a cement chamber. The room is much larger than I thought it would be. It appears to be a ten by twelve foot room. In the center sits a still. He was not kidding about being a moonshiner. Inside the building, the smell of corn mash is strong. I look up expecting to see the sky, but instead see a roof with an elaborate air purification system.

The man notices me looking up. "Can't be too careful these days. I have been making shine here for forty-five years and I have never been caught. Of course back then the smell of wood smoke and corn mash would not have drawn the cops on me either. Now a-days I have to be more careful."

He wipes his hands on the back of his pants and then holds it out to me. "I'm sorry. I guess I should introduce myself. I know who you are but you have no idea who I am. Oh and to be honest, guns make me a little uncomfortable. I can understand my instructions and ordering that pizza put you on edge and it is understandable that you have your gun out. I just ask we shake hands, have a seat at the table and have a conversation. Oh, and I will pay you back for the pizza. It was the only way I could slip a message to you. By the way, it is not as easy as I thought to get a job making pizza at that store. I found out I suck at making pizza. I don't think they want me to come back again. As a matter of fact, I was fired soon after making your pizza. I'm slow. I can't keep up with some twenty-something spinning dough and getting a pizza into the oven quickly. They want you to make a pizza in under three minutes. For me it was more like six."

I push the safety back on my gun and slide it into my shoulder holster. He smiles at me and holds out his hand to shake mine. "My name is Roddie Clark. Please, come and sit down. We have a lot to talk about."

I walk over to the wooden table and pull out a chair. He sits across from me. I am still amazed at the construction of this building. The woods are narrow and this sits only a few feet from the Colonial Parkway. Yet, this is completely invisible from the road.

Roddie Clark is an older man. My guess is somewhere in his late sixties. He has a trimmed snow white beard and mustache. His skin is well tanned. He is wearing a blue and white pin stripe shirt with the top three buttons undone and a pair of denim jeans. I can see the telltale scar from open heart surgery running down his chest and beyond the first button. His body looks tired and old but his eyes tell another story.

They are wrinkled and he has a perpetual squint from drooping eyelids but his eyes sparkle with life.

"I guess you want me to get down to business and tell you why I asked you to come here today? I know about your friend Scott Llewellyn. I know about a lot of things around here. What would you like me to start with? The serial killer? The things the military hides? Or things that go bump in the night from the place known as The Farm?"

There are some things I don't think I want to know. I look him in the eye and see a man who is in control of his environment. "Tell me what I need to know about Scott Llewellyn's death. If it's connected I need to know. If not, some things are better left unsaid."

He takes a drink from a glass. If the swirls in the liquid are any indication, this man is drinking moonshine in the middle of the afternoon. Then again, I don't know what the appropriate hour to drink from a still might be.

He smacks his lips and sits the glass down. "Can I offer you a drink?"

I shake my head no and he nods his head. "It is a little early for some. I work during the night when it is cooler and less people are around. I know it looks bad drinking in the early afternoon, but this is after my midnight."

He takes another drink. "I will ask again after I tell you what I know. You might be ready for that drink by then."

He stands up and flips on a computer screen. "Sorry, I want to keep an eye on things. They have cameras in the woods and so do I. I stay out of their field of vision and I expect them to stay out of my area. I don't want anyone to hear some of the things I want to tell you."

I have no idea who this guy is or what he is doing in this woods. He is more than a moonshiner. If anything the still is a cover for whatever he is actually doing.

He sits back down and takes another drink. "I know you are wondering who I am. I was a farmer and insurance agent for over thirty years. I made moonshine here during that time and I've been making it here ever since."

I feel as if he is playing with me. He has drawn me to his hiding place in the woods as part of a game. I'm not entertained and I want to stand up and leave. "Why was your profession important? What are you hinting at? Tell me or I'm walking out of here."

He holds up his hands with his palms facing me. "I will come clean with you. There are things I am not allowed to say outright, but I think you can follow along." He takes another drink and looks me in the eyes. "I was a special agent for the Company of Independent Agents. Do you know the company?"

I nod my head. He is telling me he is or was a CIA agent. Looking around his building hidden in plain sight I can understand where the technology originated. "And you were a farmer. I assume you worked as an instructor at the Farm?"

He looks down as if he is ashamed. When he looks back at me there is sadness in his eyes. "Back in the days of the Cold War, things were different. We knew where the enemy was located and what they were trying to accomplish. The world is different now. It's hard to look at someone and be able to determine friend from foe."

He gets up and starts to pace around the room. "I retired from the company but I found it is not something you can leave. Now I sit in the woods and watch the people that once employed me. I built this bunker back in the early eighties. Little did I know that I would be an eyewitness to a couple murders. Things were tested on this road. Tourists can disappear and no one knows they were even here. It was a testing ground for a hit man. When I realized who was doing this, I realized there was no one I could turn to. So I spread rumors and tried to warn people to stay away. It worked for a while."

He sits down again and reaches across the table and grabs my arm. "Listen, you can't repeat any of this, but I want you to understand just who you are dealing with. Scott Llewellyn didn't want to listen to me and he ended up dead this morning!"

My head is swirling. If I had drank any of his moonshine I might have thought I had been poisoned. This guy knew Scott and he claims to have warned him about something. He also seems to have been able to get through the fire wall on my computer and order a pizza, which he claims to have made and got it delivered to my house. I try to clear my head and agree to listen to him.

"I will assume you have some idea of the training that goes on at The Farm. It isn't your run of the mill education. We train or I should say I did train agents to stay alive. Sometimes you can talk your way out of a situation. There are other times you have to kill your way out. Back in the 1980s I had a young recruit. He was good. He trained and followed directions well. At the time I thought he could be one of the top covert agents I have ever seen. One night, I was in this woods cooking down some mash and I heard something out on the road. It was a scream followed by someone pleading for their life. I went to the tree line to see what was happening and if I could be of assistance. To my surprise I saw my student. The next day the murder of the couple I saw pleading for their lives was reported in the newspaper. I couldn't prove it and it was dark, but I was pretty sure the recruit practiced his lessons on live humans and left his homework along the Colonial Parkway. I tried to keep an eye on him after that, but it was hard. He was good at slipping out and making his kill before anyone knew he was even missing. The police suspected a serial killer. Then one day the killings stopped. I had finally gotten through to my superiors and we transferred him into the field in a foreign country where his need to practice his craft was easier to go undetected."

He stops and takes a drink of moonshine. "You ready for that drink yet, because it just gets worse from here?" I tap the table and nod. He pushes a glass to the center of the table and pours about an inch of liquid in the bottom of the glass. Then he refills his own. I pick it up and smell it and smile at him. Then, in one motion drink it down. If he is trying to prove who is "the man", I will raise my glass and match him.

He smiles at my action. "He has returned to this country, and returned to The Farm. I can't tell you his name, but he is no longer a red faced recruit. He proved himself over and over in the Middle East. He has been one of our top assets there and now he has come home to raise the next generation of agents in the company. Scott was digging around in the wrong place at the wrong time and I think he came onto this individual's radar."

I push the glass toward him and he pours more into my glass. If what this man is saying is true, Scott was killed by the CIA. "What could a history professor do that would cause a CIA agent to kill him? I have heard he was on an archeology dig somewhere in this area. Did he stray onto CIA grounds? Or did he see something he shouldn't have? And what would warrant him being executed?"

Roddie pushes his glass around the table. He is watching the glass slide on the table leaving a damp trail. "I don't know. I saw Scott poking around in the woods. An associate of mine engaged him in a conversation. This associate knows more about the item that was removed from under a fallen tree than I do. You should probably talk to him. I can set up a conversation between the two of you if you want to know more about that?"

At least now I have confirmation that Scott found something in the woods around James Island. I guess my next step will be to talk to this associate but first I need to know specifically why Roddie Clark went to the trouble to have me come out here. "I assume you did not ask me here to tell me the CIA has an agent who has a questionable history and that Scott found something under a fallen tree. Getting a job making pizza just so that you can send a message to me seems a little drastic. You could have called or come to my house. Can we get down to business? I am scheduled to check in with my back up in ten minutes."

He stops moving his glass around and looks me in the eyes. I have seen eyes like this before they are stern and serious. This is a man you want on your side. "I want to scare you. The hit on your friend came from The Farm. I believe they are setting you up to take the fall. I also think you and your family are in danger. I don't know who did it or what was in the copper tube but I do know this is a hit being pinned on you."

This man is either part of the plan or telling me the truth. I decide to trust him. "Okay, today my wife and I went to Fredericksburg. While we were gone my nanny watched someone turn off areas of my perimeter alarm as they walked through my yard toward my house. This would take some fairly sophisticated equipment. What do you know about that?"

He has not blinked the entire time I was talking. His hands are flat on the table. "When I saw what was happening and I saw this being pinned on you I hacked your computer. I have seen the video. That was one of the reasons I paid an employee in the parking lot of the pizza joint you regularly order from and walked in saying I was the uncle of the regular guy and I was going to take his place for the day. They were pretty desperate at the moment and told me to make pizzas. It was a good lie until I actually tried to make a pizza. They are more complicated than I had imagined."

He offers to pour another drink for me but I decline. "The man in your yard was a CIA agent. He had a device that controlled your alarm system and gave him invisibility to your system. What you might not know is that while you were at the conference and your wife, nanny and son were in the house yesterday, the same man entered your house, was there for just under ten minutes and left through your kitchen door. He waited for your dog to be outside in his run. Your wife probably thought your dog was barking at squirrels. He had a boat hidden near your boat house and left via the James River. My associate has been watching your house from the water since this morning."

This explains how my gun disappeared. "My service weapon is missing. The gun box was in my safe but it was empty when the police came. I have been informed that it was used to kill Scott. I agree that I am being framed. I just don't know why."

Roddie nods his head and sips from his glass. "Is it possible over the last week that Scott told you something about what he found? Or for someone to believe he told you?" I know he is trying to figure this out as well. I didn't know anything about Scott finding a scroll until Karen told me today and I tell him this. Last night we did talk about his desire to do a dig at Bruton Parrish. Someone may have overheard us.

I am watching his reaction to what I am saying. He looks puzzled about something. "Scott Llewellyn was here to lecture at the conference on the early settlers of Virginia was he not? I have not taken time to look at the outlines for each of his sessions. It could have been something in one of his sessions. I have found over the years if there is history to be covered up our government puts a fence around it and makes it an installation. Call it a red herring, but I have walked onto a facility grounds and seen dinosaur bones sticking out. Talk about an elephant in the room. In order to keep scientists from disclosing a large extinction event site near Washington, DC, they put up a fence and built some military buildings. I've also seen this happen in Alaska. I took a picture of a tyrannosaurs head as I hiked a trail in a federal park. If we are willing to hide something as big as a dinosaur imagine how easy it is to hide the little stuff. I don't think it was something he said last night or the day before. It had to be something earlier in the week. This was planned before yesterday."

There was a time in my life that I was naive and believed our government didn't hide anything from us. Then I encountered the life and motive of Lilly Ward, one of the country's first female serial killers. Now I believe John Wilkes Booth was allowed to ride out of Washington, DC and lived until he committed suicide in 1903. What if this is about the Masonic treasure legends of Williamsburg? What if the treasure was brought over on one of the early resupply ships and hidden on James Island? The legend has the treasure moved from Jamestown to Williamsburg when the settlers relocated to higher, less mosquito infested ground. Could Scott have uncovered something left behind or a clue to the location of the treasure? And what if that clue was located on CIA land? Could other secrets have been housed nearby that could change the course of history and make Scott a target?

My thoughts are interrupted by Roddie. "I think he or an associate of his may have seen something while he was digging around. Or at least friends and associates of this agent think he saw or found something. Whatever the case, Scott Llewellyn was murdered and you are going to go to jail for his murder unless you can perform a miracle and clear your name. I believe in the next few days you will be arrested and charged. The argument gave them motive and the autopsy finding a bullet that matches to your now missing weapon gives them enough circumstantial evidence to convince a grand jury. I wouldn't wait too long to disappear, but I think you need to go underground and get off the CIA and police radar."

Normally, I would have thought running and hiding was a sign of guilt. I have seen this happen in the past and it convinces me that the person is guilty. Innocent people know there is a real criminal out there and once they are found everything will be okay. "Adam, I know it will look bad if you run, but with the chips being stacked against you by the professionals, I don't think anyone else will be able to clear your name. You need to get your family to safety and step off the face of the earth. Don't come back until you have rock solid proof that you are innocent."

I am afraid he is right. I have already made arrangements for Christina, the kids and the animals to go to John's house. He and Chris will keep them safe. I had envisioned myself protecting my house. Now I see that my best option might be to go away for a couple days and see if I can find an answer.

I stand up and shake his hand. "Adam, I want to wish you good luck. You have the entire deck stacked against you and I am sorry. I wish I could give you more information or anything to steer you in a direction. All I can tell you is that you are up against a powerful force that is using you as a sponge to clean up their mess."

I walk back to the Jeep and call Samantha. Christina has left with AJ and the animals to pick Alina up at school. They are going straight to their safe house. Alina is just being told I am on a case.

I am not sure what is safe anymore. I want to get home and look at my alarm system to verify someone walked into my house while I was in Williamsburg. If that is the case, I cannot trust my own walls. For all I know, there are cameras and listening devices throughout my house. Every move I made over the last two days may have been recorded somehow to use against me.

I leave the Jeep in the driveway. I intend to be out of the house by nightfall. I smell dinner cooking in the kitchen and Samantha sticks her head into my office as I am pulling up the security program. The food will be ready in about thirty-five minutes and she is going to take a shower before dinner. I reset the time on the security program to nine in the morning and start to fast forward through the video. I stop when I see a figure dressed in black walking through my yard. The split screen shows my perimeter alarms being turned off and then coming back on as he passes. He walks to the kitchen door and in seconds has picked the lock and entered my house. Twelve minutes later he exits the same door and disappears into the woods along the river.

I hear the shower come on upstairs. This may be my only opportunity inside my house to talk with my wife without being heard. I head to the bathroom and strip off my clothing. She is surprised to see me but turns and puts her arms around me.

Naked in the shower with my wife is always a pleasure. This time is different. I have no way of knowing if there is a camera somewhere recording our movements. We kiss and I allow my hands to run down her body. She is smooth and slippery. I take the body soap and pour some in my hands and begin to wash her. The water is hot and steam billows around us. I hope it is clouding the lens and allowing us some privacy. "Samantha, don't freak out and continue to play along."

She looks at me through the stream of water. I can tell she is confused. I lean down and begin to kiss her neck. As I do I whisper in her ear, "Baby, I think the house may be bugged. I don't know if there are cameras. Our every move and every sound may be recorded. From what the guy in the woods told me, Scott was murdered by the CIA and he and his colleagues think I am being framed by them for the murder. I have to leave and go into hiding. It might be the only way to prove who killed Scott and not end up charged with his murder."

She leans in toward me and rubs her body against me. I wondered whether the threat of being watched would make her uncomfortable. It doesn't seem to affect her that way. She raises her leg up and hooks her foot behind my knee and pulls her body closer. Her soapy hands reach between my legs and I slump back against the wall and groan. "It's fine, Adam, but I am going with you. This is a partnership and I love you. I will do what I have to do to keep you in my life. Now rinse off. If the CIA is watching us, I intend to give them a show which will make them blush."

The timer is beeping on the oven when we walk back downstairs. I pull dinner out of the oven as Samantha grabs a bottle of wine out of the refrigerator. She leans over and kisses my neck. "Just remember, we are a pair. Where you go, I go. Now eat your dinner so we can go upstairs for round two."

This is incentive for me to concentrate on eating dinner and getting ready to go to bed. I feel bad for the CIA guys who might be watching this. My wife is an absolute knock out. When she walks down the street men turn and look at her. I just smile because at the end of the day this incredibly smart, beautiful woman curls up against me when we go to bed at night.

We are both having a hard time falling asleep. I feel like someone is watching me and I worry about someone walking in my front door. Samantha is restless also. We need to get some sleep. I have no idea what tomorrow might bring, but my thoughts of tomorrow help keep me awake.

I get up and walk into the bathroom. When I come out Samantha is sitting on the bottom of the bed with a stack of pillows in her arms. "Grab the quilt and the blankets. Our first night in this house was one of the most romantic nights of my life. The power was out and the house was cold with no heat. I loved sleeping in front of the fireplace with you. We haven't had the house to ourselves since then. Tonight is our opportunity to do something crazy. Let's sleep in the living room in front of the fire."

Sleeping downstairs would allow me to hear anyone coming inside. I don't know how well I will sleep but I'm not sleeping in our bed. I grab the quilt and the blankets and follow her down the stairs. Samantha gets a bottle of wine while I start a fire and pull the sofa a little closer to the fireplace. She comes back with glasses and a couple candles. There is enough room on the floor for us to sleep and until we do we can sit on the sofa and have a glass of wine.

It has been a while since I made love to my wife three times in the same night but the wine, fire and candlelight set the mood. Afterward, we wrap up in the blankets and snuggle together watching the flames flicker in the fireplace. I forget everything else in the world and drift off to sleep.

Day Two
Dutch Gap, Virginia

The house is quiet. Samantha is curled next to me. Being the only ones in the house seems strange. The fire has burned down to coals. I can see sunlight coming in the windows in the living room. It is warm and cozy in the blankets but I know I need to leave her and get moving.

I work my way out of her arms and walk into the bathroom. I put on a pair of jeans and a sweat shirt. According to Roddie Clark, his associate has been watching my house from the water since yesterday morning. I decide to walk down to the dock and see what I can see from there. I strap on my gun and put my cell phone in my pocket. I no longer feel safe in my own home or in my own yard. As I walk out the door I lock it and set the alarm on the house.

My boat house is still locked up tight. I walk out on my dock and look over the river at Henricus. I see a man fishing out in the middle of the river. It is a peaceful early Saturday morning. I hear a boat motor and look up to see the fisherman heading back up the river. He drives up to my dock and yells to over the roar of the engine. "Adam, I've been waiting for you. You are late. Hop in so we can get some fishing in."

I have never met this man in my life but he knows my name. I look at him in the boat. He has a southern accent and a strong muscular build. He's wearing a pair of camo pants and a black tee shirt with a faded fire department baseball hat. As he pulls tight against the dock he yells, "I didn't know if Roddie was coming out with us today or not. When I talked to him yesterday he told me he might get up early enough to join us." He angles the boat across the river and stops to let the boat drift.

He is laughing. "I brought you out in the water where we can talk for a reason. Fish don't have ears and the river is wide enough if we talk low a parabolic microphone won't pick us up. I guess I should start with formal introductions. I am Tracy Davis, fisherman and hunter by day, fireman by night." He tips his baseball cap at me. "As for the recently deceased professor, I believe your boy got in over his head. He was poking around James Island with an antique book. He believed he had found clues to a Masonic treasure and it led him to Roddie's woods. Roddie called me to come engage whomever was creeping around his little piece of paradise and find out why they were poking around. Like a true explorer, he was snooping around and under things until he came across a fallen tree. There in the roots he pulled out what looked like a copper telescope. It was inside a tree that was about 350 years old. He told me he was looking for a tree that was planted by the Colonists and this fit the bill."

He stops and is watching the end of his rod. "Hey get the net ready. I have a bite. I hate to interrupt this very important conversation, but I am about to shake fins with tonight's dinner." Whatever is on his line is starting to fight him. He turns a few turns on the reel, and then pulls up the rod to pull the fish forward. He turns the reel a few more turns and I see a bass break the surface. It's a nice size fish and I put the net in the water and let him pull the fish closer to the boat. I don't want the fish to see the net going into the water and make it run in the opposite direction. Tracy pulls the rod up again and the fish comes alongside the boat. In one motion, I slip the net under it and raise it from the water.

After getting the net inside the boat, Tracy puts his rod down on the floor and pulls his fish from the net. It's a nice sized fish. He has hooked the mouth in the corner and pulls it out. "Hey Adam, open that cooler." He bends down and slides the fish into a box on the sidewall of the boat. "Thank you. Now get the lid on that before he decides to jump out." Inside the cooler I see at least two tablets and cell phone boxes. I follow his direction to put the lid back on the cooler as he kicks the lid down on the side box.

To anyone watching from shore we just put a bass into the cooler. He nods toward the cooler. "When I drop you off back at the dock, carry that off the boat with you. There are burner phones and tablets that are completely off the grid for you to use. Don't use them to check personal emails or link back to family. Create neutral identities and go dark." Tracy puts more bait on his hook and casts it out across the water. He sits down and turns to look at me. "Don't look but we have company in the woods. Carefully take a look about twenty feet west of your boat house. You want to know about John Wake. I would like to introduce you to Joseph Callan. He is a current employee of John Wake. They both work for the company of independent agents, specifically in the command and control of the farm bureau. John Wake is the chief agent at the farm bureau."

This is interesting information. So the head of the CIA covert agent training program is somehow behind Scott's murder. This is not going to be easy to prove. "Do you have any proof that he is behind this?"

Tracy reaches down into a cooler near his feet and pulls out a beer. He hands one to me and opens another for himself. I glance at my phone and it is just after eight in the morning. I think what the hell, I might as well. I am being framed for a murder by the head of the Central Intelligence Agency covert training facility. There is very little chance that I will be able to find my way out of this. I am one man trying to fight city hall. Maybe one of the biggest and most powerful city halls in the world. "So besides getting out of Dodge and going on the run, what do you suggest I do? How do I prove a hit was called on Scott by John Wake?"

He downs the can of beer and crushes the can between his thumb and fingers. "The first thing you need to do is find that copper tube and figure out why the contents have pissed off a very powerful man."

He makes it sound so easy. Karen does not think the tube is at her house. Of course she has probably not gone through his office. I doubt I can get into her house right now. I know he has an office in Fairfax at the college. I'm sure the police have been there and are watching it. This leaves finding his office in Baltimore. I am looking for a needle in a haystack.

I glance over at the woods and Joseph Callan is gone. "Tracy, where did our spook in the woods go?"

He looks over to where we last saw him and scans the area. "Aw shit. Is your wife still sleeping?" He has to be kidding! I set the alarm before I left but this guy has the ability to walk through my alarms like a ghost. He has started the boat motor and is heading directly to my dock. He cuts the power and hands me the cooler. "Put this in your Jeep first. He isn't going to hurt your wife. He is probably there to plant more evidence in your house or return your gun. Do Roddie and me a favor and get the hell on the road as quickly as you can. They are going to try to set you up no matter what you do, so put road between you and your house."

I jump out of the boat and thank him for the fishing trip. As he pulls away he yells back at me, "Give Roddie or me a call if you want to do some more fishing. Don't lose our numbers in your phone, ya hear? I don't mind sharing a beer and drowning some worms with you."

I take the hint. He has put phone numbers in the phones to contact them in the event of an emergency. It is tempting to go into my house first but I want to protect the contents of the cooler. I throw it in the back of the Jeep and push the lock button. The house seems quiet. I run into the living room and Samantha is still wrapped in blankets on the floor in front of the fire. She wakes up when I walk in the door. "Hey baby, I just met Tracy and got some fishing in. I'm going to get a shower and why don't we get breakfast and take the fish to Chris. He said he wanted to make dinner for all of us. I have a nice bass I caught this morning and if we get it to him this morning I bet we can talk him into making fresh fish for dinner."

She is confused but nods her head. I go upstairs and get undressed and turn the water on. As I step in I hear her entering the bathroom. In a few seconds she has joined me in the shower. She pours body wash on her hands and starts to run her hands down my body. I'm not sure if this is driven by being alone in the house, the possibility of us being on camera, or her playing along to be able to talk without being heard. "I take it we are leaving the house. Should I grab some clothing? Where are we going?"

I have no idea where we are going and I have not thought of what we should take with us or how we will get it out of the house without being seen. I guess it doesn't matter if they know we are leaving. "We should grab some clothing and the weapons maybe some outdoor gear? I'm not sure where we are going. I just know we need to get out of here and soon. While I was out on the water fishing, there was a guy along the water's edge watching us. For all I know he is in the house right now. While I would love to take this from here to the bed, I think we need to get the hell out of here as soon as possible. If this guy was here to plant the gun back in the house, the cops may have been tipped off and they are about to knock on the door. I could end up in jail before lunch if I am not careful."

She rinses off and kisses me. "Okay then, let's get dressed, get a few things and get out of here. I don't want you to end up in jail, so if we have to bug out, let's go now." She beats me to the closet and is already putting things into each of our backpacks. "Hey, Adam, if we are going to take the ferry should I grab pillows and blankets? Last time I got cold as hell and standing or sitting on deck is brutal. Between waiting for them to load all the cars for the crossing and then unloading everyone ahead of us I could have taken a nap. We might as well be warm and sit in the car."

I like her cover and play along. "I had forgotten about that. Yeah, also could you grab my winter coat; it can get cold on the island." While Samantha packs some clothing, I go downstairs and grab guns and ammunition out of the safe. I check and my service revolver has not returned. I wonder if it is gone forever. I have visions of it being thrown into the James and me having to fill out the pile of paperwork for a missing/lost weapon. When this is over I will have to do the paperwork and go through all the interviews to determine if I will be given a new one or charged for it. That is, of course, unless I am doing twenty-five years to life for a murder I didn't commit.

We start to put our things in the back of the Jeep. Samantha runs back into the house to grab a couple snacks for the road while I disable to GPS and turn off my cars onboard navigation system. I guess I can live without my Jeep emailing me that it needs air in a tire or its time for its oil change for a couple days.

We pull into John's house about twenty minutes later. Chris is pulling into the driveway as we pull along the curb. Christina, Alina and AJ are inside. I hand our cell phones and tablets to John along with one of the cell phones from the cooler. This way he can contact us or either Tracy or Roddie. I will pick up a throw away phone on the road for Samantha and get the information on that phone back to them. John had the electronics team sweep his house and it is clean. Once Samantha and I are clear, he will get my house swept and cleaned of whatever bugging devices have been planted.

Samantha is trying not to cry. I know it is hard on her to say goodbye to the kids and not know how long we might need to be away. I feel emotionally drained. I am running on adrenaline right now. I need to survive and prove my innocence. My life is being taken away from me and I don't know why, but, before I can come home I need to find some answers.

We say goodbye and drive away. Samantha is sitting on the passenger side wiping tears from her eyes. "Where are we going?"

I glance over at her and take her hand in mine. "I don't know, baby. Right now I'm driving north. After Richmond, we are going to have to stay off of I-95. We can be tracked by the traffic cameras mounted on the over heads. I guess we will head west on some back roads. We need to get away from Washington, DC. After that I don't know. I want to find the office in Baltimore. To do that, I need to come up with a plan, so one step at a time, for now we drive north."

Samantha is chewing on her upper lip. I know she is trying to think. I want to avoid larger cities and major roads. Doing that becomes tough without a GPS but I can't risk connecting to a satellite and giving our position away. The CIA can tap into anything electronic that they can identify. I'm sure they have my GPS and onboard communications identified. Which are why they are turned off and the GPS is still sitting on the shelf in my garage. "Adam, let's find a library. We can either look up a route or get something from a printed map."

I think that's a great idea and drive to Chester and park at the library. Samantha goes over to a computer and pulls up a street map. "What if we take 60 to 522? In Culpepper, we can take 29." I grab a piece of paper out of a box near the computer and a golf pencil to write down the route. Samantha is moving the screen up. "Okay, after Warrenton, we need to take 15. If not we will drive into Washington, DC." She zooms in to the area around Leesburg. "We have to pay attention here. There is a business 15 and a bi-pass. I think we should stay on the bi-pass. This route will take us right through Harpers Ferry. If we are going to drive to Baltimore maybe we should find somewhere to spend the night in that area."

I finish copying down the route and we both make a trip to the rest rooms before getting back in the Jeep. We need to stop for gas before beginning our trip to disappear. According to the computer, the trip will take about four hours. There was also a warning about restricted routes. From what I could find on the maps there are some height restrictions and possibly truck restrictions.

As we are leaving town, I stop at a gas station with a mini-mart. Samantha runs inside with two twenty dollar bills and hands them to the cashier for the pump. She also gets two bottles of ice tea from the cooler and watches for me to motion to her that I have finished filling up. She walks out with the tea and our change. "I will have to become accustomed to paying cash for things. I haven't paid cash for a long time. I swipe a card and go. It's funny but money has lost much of its meaning to me. Now that we have a limited pile of cash, it seems such a precious commodity."

Going off the grid has made me think. I am a connected person. My car communicates with a satellite to tell me everything from where I am and how to get where I need to go to the tire pressure and miles to go before my oil needs to be changed. I have ATM cards and credit cards that I swipe and pay. My paycheck goes into a bank account. I never even see a dollar of my money unless I go to the ATM and get cash. Normally, I get twenty dollars to last the week. Not that I only spend twenty dollars a week but it's the just money to carry around. I swipe my card for everything from gas to groceries to fast food. If I walk into a store, I pull out my card. Shopping online, I pull out my card. It gets deeper than that. I have store cards to get discounts. I find that most people use the individual store cards for discounts on products. The stores track our purchase information. They even reward us with discounts designed specifically for us. We hand so much of our life over to complete strangers all the time and never realize it.

I have also thought about cameras. They are in stores to make sure we don't shoplift. They are at banks and ATMs to watch us access our money. Over highways there are cameras to monitor traffic and report back ups to the traffic system. At every toll booth there are cameras. We have speed pass lanes that scan our cars as they drive at highway speeds. Even on street corners to watch us walk around cities. I wonder how many businesses that we pass have cameras focused on their parking lots or houses on their front yards.

I know I use people's unconscious scanning to track their lives when I am investigating them. I can tell the route they take to work by the places they stop to buy gas and coffee. Their Social Security number will give me their company and normally the address where they work. I know where they go to lunch and where they eat dinner. Where they shop for groceries and what they buy. I can even pull up someone's register receipt and see the individual items they purchase and what time there were in the store. Being connected is easy, disconnecting will be hard but I realize if I am being framed by the CIA they have the same ability to track me the same way I have used the information to track others.

As I drive, we talk about everything we must avoid and try to keep our eyes out for anything designed to protect us or track us. Samantha and I have to step off the face of the earth today and not come back until we have the answers to clear my name. The drive is primarily rural broken by small towns. I try to stick to the bi-passes and side roads as we drive through Warrenton and Leesburg. Toll roads are also not safe for us to take right now. If you do not have an electronic device in your car to be scanned, there are cameras that focus and take pictures of your license plate and a person that takes your money in a booth. Every street corner and highway has become my enemy.

At about four o'clock, I start to think about getting something to eat. Tracy had suggested we find someplace crowded and hide in a crowd. That works for big towns but strangers stick out in a small town. Our route is taking us through all small towns.

I see a sign that says Harpers Ferry twenty-three miles. This might work. While it is a small town, it is a tourism town. Strangers walking around or entering a restaurant will not be remembered.

I make the left and drive down into the old town of Harpers Ferry. I park in the park and ride lot and we lock the Jeep as we get out. The town is busy and we wait for a few minutes to cross the road. I can see people out on ladders putting up the finishing touches on store front Christmas decorations. The thought makes me sad. I hope I can solve this and we are able to be home for Christmas. As it is now, Samantha and I will miss AJ's second Christmas. This will be the Christmas that he will begin to understand Santa Clause. Alina is looking forward to being the big sister and teaching him the ropes of giving Santa his list and opening all his gifts. Thanksgiving is this Thursday and I doubt we will be home by then. John and Chris will make sure Christina and the kids have a good Thanksgiving but Samantha and I will probably be hiding out for the day. The thought is very depressing and I try to not focus on it.

We have walked to a small corner restaurant. I can see evidence of a recent fire on the street. One building is completely gutted. Two others show charring and soot on the exterior. We walk inside the restaurant and order hamburgers. The place is not very crowded. There is a group over in a corner looking over a map. A middle aged couple sit near the window holding hands across the table. Besides the woman at the counter, there is a cook in the back. The only other noise comes from a game show on the television mounted on the wall. The young woman behind the counter keeps looking at us and I wonder why. She brings our burgers to the table and stand there staring, "I swear I know you from somewhere. Do you live around here?"

Samantha looks up at her and smiles. "Yes we do. We are local authors. You may have seen us on television being interviewed recently. Our book is rising on the best seller list."

The waitress smiles and mumbles, "That must be it. Well enjoy your meal." as she walks away. We eat our hamburgers quickly. I want to be out of here before the evening news comes on. I am afraid our pictures may have been on the noon news in connection to the case.

The burger is dry and tasteless but it is food. I hope we can find something better for dinner but there are no promises. I want to concentrate on eating and getting out of here before someone recognizes us. I don't want any surprises and my fear is to see my picture appearing on the screen.

We finish and I leave a tip on the table. I drive in the direction of one of the only places I know that is quiet with a good vantage point, the Correspondents Monument on South Mountain. Being a trail head for the Appalachian Trail, there is a rest room with showers available. There are grills and fire rings but no restaurants nearby. I hope we can have the camp area to ourselves and no one will think it's odd for a couple to camp along the trail right now.

I stop in Frederick at a grocery store. The evening crowd is still grabbing dinner and tomorrow's breakfast. A few kids are trying to talk their mother into some sugary breakfast cereal. I see Samantha smiling at that. She has been in that mothers shoes before and knows how to win the war of junk for breakfast. We find beef chopped into cubes and walk around the produce section getting mushrooms, a pepper, an onion, a zucchini, cherry tomatoes and olive oil. Searching for bamboo kabob holders is harder. I'm not sure where to find them in the store and we don't want to ask anyone. We finally find them in the isle with laundry detergent and candles. I'm not sure of the store logic but I am glad we have found them.

I would love to buy a nice bottle of wine but I think we need to have our wits about us. Instead, I find coffee in individual bags that we can just add water and steep. We get sugar in individual packets and travel mugs. At the last minute, Samantha remembers to get a case of water. Our only problem is how to heat the water. We don't have a pan or anything to put over the fire.

We begin to drive and look for a discount store or someplace to buy camping goods. I see the sign for a thrift shop and pull into the parking lot. I have paper towels and a small bottle of dish liquid in the back of the Jeep. Normally I use these to wash my Jeep or clean my windows. If we find some sort of pan or pot that will sit on a grill top I can wash it for us to use tonight and to make hot water for coffee in the morning.

I see a small cast iron dutch oven. It has some rust on it and the lid is cracked but it will work for us. The cashier points out the crack in the lid but we tell her that's okay. It isn't important for our intended use.

Once we make our purchases I drive west on I-70. The sun is down and this section of road does not have any overhead traffic cameras. I take the exit for Gathland and drive up the road to the top of South Mountain.

As I had hoped, the trail head is deserted. I don't want to park in the parking lot and sit there with the Jeep visible from the road. We park and walk around. There is room for us to drive off the service road to the parking lot and pull in behind the rest room. This will block the visibility from both roads. If I maneuver carefully, I can turn the Jeep around and be able to drive out quickly if anyone comes to investigate.

While I gather some sticks to start a fire in a fire ring, Samantha takes the dutch oven into the rest room to wash it. We get some light from the spot light in the front of the restroom. I pull my knife out of my backpack and wipe it on my pants. I laugh. I doubt Samantha would approve of my knife cleaning skills. I chop the vegetables into cubes and begin to put them on the bamboo sticks. We have to eat everything we purchased or throw the left overs away. It looks like a lot of food, but we have not eaten much today.

We sit back and watch the fire burn for a while. When the sticks burn down to a pile of coals I sit the dutch oven on them. I drizzle olive oil down the inside of the dutch oven and take a paper towel to spread it around. The warmth from the fire on the iron feels good. It is getting cold enough to see my breath. Once coated, I place the kabobs across the bottom. They pop and sizzle as soon as they hit the hot metal.

In a few minutes I turn them. They smell good cooking over the wood fire. We are standing over the fire for warmth. This is going to be a cold night. I'm glad we brought blankets with us. While the food cooks, I open up the back doors of the Jeep and put the seats down. Once we eat we can clean up and then wrap up in the Jeep. I'm tired but I know I will have an interrupted sleep. Every noise in the woods will wake me.

We finish the ice tea with dinner. When we are finished, I wash the dutch oven in the men's room and put it on the back floor under the seat. I don't want to leave anything outside. If we have to leave quickly, I don't want fingerprints left on the scene to identify us. We bank the fire and spread the blankets inside the back of the Jeep and get inside and try to go to sleep.

Day Three
South Mountain, Maryland

I must have been exhausted. I think I fell asleep immediately. When I wake up I am disoriented. I hear the sound of a helicopter overhead. I wake Samantha up and we get out of the Jeep. The helicopter is not directly overhead and I try to determine its location. I think it is hovering over I-70. It drops out of sight. There must be an accident on the interstate. I look at the time on the cell phone and it is just after midnight. It is cold and we get back in the Jeep under the blankets. It is hard to get back to sleep. So much has happened in the last forty- eight hours. I can't stop running the events over and over in my head.

Samantha knows me too well and leans over to kiss my forehead as she strokes the back of my hair. "Let it go for the night." She is whispering even though we are the only people for miles. We are alone on the top of the mountain. "Let it go for now. We can't solve anything until we get more answers and those answers can't be found here tonight,"

I know she is right. The downfall of being married to a psychiatrist. She can read me and know what I am thinking. I look at her in the dim glow from the light on the corner of the building, her blond hair catches the light. I take my hand and smooth it down and brush it away from her eyes. "I love you. No matter what happens in this crazy life of ours never forget that I love you."

She smiles and kisses me. "I knew the morning we woke up together in Austin, that I would follow you to the end of the world and back. I didn't get much sleep that night. I kept waking up and my head was screaming that we had unprotected sex. After having Kali, I had a no condom, no sex rule. John said it would be the first time, awkward and bad. I had known awkward, bad sex all my life. Sex had always been either rape or a business transaction. With you it felt different. I felt like more than a guy inside me getting off."

I interrupt her with a kiss. "Shhh— before I stop thinking about the case and have to make love to you again."

She giggles, "that's just what I'm talking about. I'd always laid there moaning and telling guys how good they were and I was faking it. If I moaned and made them think they were amazing, they would get done faster, I would get my money and get cleaned up for the next job. With you, my body responded in ways I never responded before. I didn't need to fake it. All I could think about was the next time. My only real concern was why you pulled the sheet over me when you rolled off. I still wasn't sure you and John weren't a couple. Why do you do that, every time we have sex you pull a sheet or blanket over me?"

Confessions in the dark. She has managed to take my mind off the case. I sigh and I see a look of concern on her face. "Adam, is it bad?"

I smile at her and tighten my arms around her. "No, it's not bad. We were both hot and sweaty but the air conditioning was blasting. I looked down at you and saw your eyes closed with a smile on your face. That's when it hit me that we had unprotected sex. It didn't scare me. I knew that I could have just made you pregnant. The miracle of life could be happening inside your body. I didn't want you to get a chill. I cover you up every time to protect you and our possible baby. Believe me, I don't think about this before or during sex, but afterward I have this primal drive to protect you and hold you in my arms. When Karen talked about having sex to make a baby, I thought of how badly I want to make a baby grow inside you."

She is smiling. "If it wasn't so cold I would take my clothes off and let you try again right now, but I don't think any amount of instinct could keep me warm afterwards. Consider this a raincheck. I love having reckless sex with you and letting nature decide the outcome. Now get some sleep and maybe it will be warm enough in the morning for you to take me over the back tailgate."

We wake up again and it is early morning. A thick layer of frost covers the outside of the windows. I get up and pull my sweat shirt on before crawling out the back hatch of the Jeep. The cold morning air hits me and I get out quickly to preserve some heat in the Jeep for Samantha.

I walk into the men's room and look at myself in the mirror. A morning growth of hair covers my face and I decide to leave it. Very few people have ever seen me with any facial hair. It will help hide my face. I hear the shower come on in the ladies room and assume Samantha has gotten up also. After my shower, I walk back to the Jeep and get the dutch oven and partially fill it with water from a bottle. The fire has gone out overnight. I put some sticks in the fire ring and start a fire. Samantha comes around the corner from the women's room and finds the box of doughnuts in the back of the Jeep. I think we are both a little stiff and sore from sleeping in the Jeep. As soon as the water is hot, we put a coffee bag in each mug and pour the water in. I take the rest of the water and pour it on the fire to put it out.

We sit at a picnic table eating the doughnuts and drinking coffee. Samantha has pulled the hood of her sweatshirt over her wet hair. We have to figure out our next move. I think we need to go to Baltimore and find Scott's office. That was one of the reasons I drove north. We need to find out what Scott uncovered on James Island. Since the copper tube is not at Scott's home it may be at his Baltimore office. I wish I had any clue where the office was located. "Finding Scott's office in downtown Baltimore will be like trying to find a needle in a haystack. We can't risk calling Karen to see if she has found any information on the office address." I hate flying blind but right now we have no information to go on. My hope is to find Officer Bernie Moll and hope he will help us.

The thermometer on the dash of the Jeep reads thirty-one degrees. That will explain why I feel so stiff and the frost I have to scrape off the windows. We are probably half frozen. I turn on the heat and drive toward Baltimore on I-70. The morning traffic is heavy driving into Frederick. We are able to keep moving but the pace is slow. I know there are traffic cameras the closer we get to Baltimore. At the first possible opportunity, I take the exit off of I-70 and work my way over to Frederick Road. I have driven this road before when I was investigating Lilly Ward's killing spree. This is at least familiar ground.

I am not sure if we should drive and park in Baltimore City and risk all the cameras or park the jeep and take the subway into the city. If we take the Jeep into the city we risk being seen, the tags being identified and being cut off from it. If we park the Jeep and walk to the metro we can find alternate ways to get back to it. There are buses and cabs that we can use as a back-up. I decide to park near the Owings Mills Metro station. Of course we will be seen on cameras in the metro. If our pictures have been on the television, we will be recognized and someone will call the cops. I'm not sure how we can find out if anything is on the news about us being fugitives. I try to listen to the radio for any information on out drive toward Baltimore.

I park at the movie theater on an abandoned mall parking lot. There is a path along the side of the theater to and demolition site from a former mall and metro parking lot. I look around and don't see any cameras in the parking lot. We both pull the hoods up on our sweatshirts and walk with our heads down. As we pass the side of the library, we keep our heads down and walk to the underground station.

I have some difficulty getting the ten dollar bill in my pocket to work in the ticket kiosk. I finally get the machine to take the bill and select two round trip tickets. I hand a ticket to Samantha and we walk to the turnstiles. Once through, we walk to the escalator and ride it to the platform on top. A train is about to pull away from the station and we get on quickly as the doors are closing.

The train is full of early morning football fans dressed in team jerseys. Owings Mills is the end station and we don't have a problem finding a seat. I try to look at the map of the metro. I'm not sure if we should get off at Charles Street or at the Shot Tower. I think Charles Street will drop us off closer to the Inner Harbor and Officer Moll's patrol area. Of course, I know we are taking a chance that he is working today. My hope is that he still has the same schedule as he had last summer.

My ears pop when the train goes underground. The sound of the train on the tracks has a deafening roar. I can tell we are moving fast. There are some people standing in front of me holding on to the railing attached to the ceiling. Their bodies are bumping together. Outside the window the lights in the tunnel flash by as we pass. The train slows down as we near a stop. A few get off, more get on. I glance up at the map on the wall near the door. We have three more stations until Charles Street. The engineer comes over the loud speaker and announces the next stop. It is hard to understand what he is saying over the noise of the train. I look up and read the connecting buses on a display board mounted on the ceiling in the front of the train car.

I am glad to see the sign for Lexington Market on the wall of the station. I nudge Samantha as the train begins to roll away from the station. Ours is the next stop. We stand and work our way to the door. Our bodies sway and jerk with the motion of the train. Bodies bumping and grinding into strangers bodies. It is uncomfortable knowing these are all strangers bouncing into us. I put my hand in my pocket and clutch the wad of bills I put inside it. They make me feel vulnerable. I can feel the train slowing down and jerk to a stop. We bounce off of the people standing around us. The door opens and we join the crowd flowing off the train.

We keep our heads down and follow the crowd to the turnstiles and around the corner to the escalator. At street level, the crowd flows out into a patio area between buildings. There are some tables and chairs belonging to a coffee shop to our left. I fall into the crowd heading up the slight incline to the street. I figure from there I can get my bearings. I need to find the Inner Harbor.

The sea of people leaving the metro fans out. In the distance I see a sign for the shot tower. For the moment I walk in that direction. Then down the street I see an Inner Harbor landmark I recognize. I grab Samantha's hand and we fall into the morning crowd walking down the sidewalk.

I am aware of the cameras on the corners. These were installed to fight crime, but now cause me concern. We make our way to Pratt Street. With the morning vehicle and pedestrian traffic, the police are on every corner. I don't see Bernie anywhere. All we can do is find a place to sit down and look for him. Up the street I see a coffee shop. We walk there and go inside. Samantha uses the ladies room while I order two coffees. When she comes out I hand her the coffees and use the men's room.

I notice the streets are starting to become packed with both vehicle and pedestrian traffic and while it is warm in the coffee shop we need to keep moving. I glance at the time on my phone and it is after ten in the morning. We walk out of the coffee shop and down to the corner where we can cross to a pedestrian island and then to McKeldin Park. Men are working to build the platforms for their holiday display. Another group are making the final preparation for the ice rink that opens in a few days.

We walk to the wall of the amphitheater and sit down to drink our coffee. Here we can blend in with the tourists. There is a slight wind blowing but the temperature has moderated. It is turning into a pleasant day. I walk over to the water taxi stop and pick up a map. Not that I need it but more to use it as a cover story. It gives us purpose to the average person walking along the promenade. On my way back to Samantha, I see the familiar face of Officer Bernie Moll walking toward me. He hasn't seen me and I walk back to Samantha. I wait for him to pass and we fall in behind him. "Officer, can I bother you for a moment?" He turns around and I see recognition in his face. "Can you help us? We are just here for a few days and I am trying to find the building that was used in the television police show. A friend told us it was right along the harbor and we have looked everywhere. I was a big fan and wanted my wife to take a picture of me in front of it."

Bernie looks confused but walks over to us. I open the map up and ask him to show me where we need to go. The crowd on the promenade parts to walk around us. He nods his head and points to the side of the World Trade Center, "There was construction in the area and most of the memorabilia from the show has been taken down for the moment. It still looks like the front of the police station so you can't miss it." He looks again at the people walking around us. "Why don't we get out of everyone's way so that I can give you directions?"

We walk past the dock for the Dragon Boats. They have been tied up for the winter and the area looks cold and empty. The dock is chained off with a sign indicating they will reopen in the spring. He leads us up the steps and around the lobby of the World Trade Center to the benches on the other side. We stop a few benches away from where Ronald Jones body was deposited by Lilly Ward after she murdered him. "Here, this will get us out of the wind and where we aren't blocking a walkway." He looks around. "Okay, you two, what is going on? You are giving me the distinct impression that something is wrong!"

The closest people are about twenty feet away. I lean in toward him pointing at the map as a cover. "I am wanted for murder in Virginia and we are on the run. I need your help."

He takes a step back from me. "What? You know I'm a cop, right? You can't walk up to me and say 'Hey, Bernie. I killed someone and I'm running away. Please hide me!' What the Hell? I have to take you in!"

I look around to see if anyone noticed his outburst. "I didn't kill anyone! I'm being framed by the CIA. You know me. I do things by the book. Please! I need your help. I wouldn't have come to you if I could do this any other way. Look, I don't even know if a warrant has been issued for my arrest yet. I just know it is probably coming and I need to solve this before I end up in jail for something I didn't do!"

He looks around for a few second. His hands are on his hips and I am having a hard time reading the expression on his face. "I can't help you right now. I'm wearing the uniform and I'm on duty. I'm sorry I just can't. Where is your vehicle parked?" I tell him Owings Mills Metro. He makes a face and bites his upper lip. "You are putting me in a very bad position. I want to believe you but I want to hear your entire story first. This is not the time and place to do that. I get off at three. You are going to have to lay low for a couple hours. I'm sorry about that but not much I can do right now. Meet me at the Shot Tower. Be along the road and I will pull up and pick you up. Be there at three fifteen. If you are not there, I am going to keep on driving."

We agree and he walks away from us. I look at the time on my phone and realize we have four and a half hours to kill before we meet him. Samantha looks at me from the bench and asks "What do we do now?"

I wish I knew. I point over at a bookstore on the other side of the pedestrian bridge. I need to get my bearing on the city. "Let's go to the bookstore and see if we can find anything with a current map of the city. If nothing else we can walk back to the Charles Street Metro Station and follow the signs from there. I saw a sign for the Shot Tower."

She stands up and we start to walk to the bookstore. "Hey Adam, what's a Shot Tower?" I shrug my shoulders. I have no idea but in the next four hours we will find out.

The store was built, in part, from the old power plant for the city. Some of the old brick work and piping remain in the store. I look around and find the local interest shelves in the back. There is a book on the Baltimore Shot Tower. I pull it out and look for some place to sit down and look at the book. Samantha taps my arm with her finger and points up. On the second floor is a seating area with tables and chairs. Behind us is an elevator and we ride it to the second floor.

It is another coffee shop. I get the feeling this is going to be a coffee shop kind of day. We order two coffees and take the book over to a table along the wall. I find a picture of the Shot Tower. It was built in 1828 and at the time was the tallest building in America and remained the tallest until 1846. It was designed to melt lead and pour it through a sieve then drop it over the side of the tower. By the time the pelts reached the bottom they were round droplets. It is much faster than melting and casting individual bullets. Of course, now it is not the tallest building in the city but it should stand out. According to the map, if we walk north from here, we can spend some this afternoon in Little Italy. We can get lunch there. The Shot Tower is one block over from here and three blocks up. We walk out of the bookstore and walk up the street.

In the distance, we see the side of a building painted with an Italian scene and Little Italy in big letters. The area is filled with stores and restaurants. We can smell bread baking and tangy garlic sauce as we walk. Down the street we hear a group cheering. We look in to see a group of older men on a Bocce court. A few other people are cheering on the players.

We stop for a few minutes on the sidewalk and watch the game. The Bocce court is sandwiched between two buildings. What may have once been the space for a kitchen garden has been cemented in and painted for tournament play. Wooden benches sit along each side against the brick walls of the building. It seems everyone in the court area knows each other by name. My guess this is where the locals come to play after church services on Sunday. The ages range from young children to old gray haired men. There are very few women watching. I guess they are home working on dinner while the men and children stay out of their way.

The street around us is lined with stores and restaurants. It looks like a wonderful place to explore. I wish this had been a different time in our lives. Today we can just walk and look around. We pick a spot and walk in for lunch. We can take our time and eat. It's a nice day and we look like any other couple having lunch.

I open the menu and see the history of the restaurant. It has been in the family for generations. The pasta is handmade daily and the sauces are made in the restaurant from old family recipes. We can smell fresh bread baking and mingling with the smell of garlic and basil.

The waitress brings us a basket of garlic bread sticks. They are hot from the oven and covered in a sheen of butter and spices. With that she puts a bowl of marinara for us to try their sauce while we wait for our order. We both order baked ziti with the house salad. The salads come out immediately along with our drink order. It has been hours since we ate a donut in Frederick and we are hungry.

The salad dressing is tangy and laced with fresh grated parmesan cheese. It's a small salad and I hope the portion of ziti isn't also small. I don't know when or where our next meal will be. The ziti comes out as we finish our salad. I see the staff moving food around the room. They are efficient. The pasta is delicious. The claims of the menu have not let us down. The sauce is fresh and spicy and a perfect complement to the pasta. When we are finished, we are full but not uncomfortable.

We decide to skip dessert even though the cannoli looks delicious. The waitress tells us they are handmade just down the street. If we change our minds they are worth walking into the shop and getting an expresso with a cannoli. We thank her for the advice and pay our bill.

Back out on the street, we walk off lunch for a while. We window shop and look at the offerings in a few stores. Christmas is coming and the street is decorated for the shopping season. We can hear holiday music playing in the stores when we walk by.

As we pass the bakery, we walk inside and split a cannoli. This is cup of coffee four for the day and I am feeling a little jittery but the expresso is a perfect complement to the sweet light cream inside the cannoli.

I look at the time on the cell phone and we have an hour left before we meet Bernie. I'm not sure where we are in Little Italy and which direction to walk in order to find the shot tower. We head for a street corner and read the signs. We follow one that points us back toward the inner harbor. This should take us to a location that we will be able to see the Shot Tower.

I hear bells ringing and the clip clop of a horses hoof. We turn and see a Baltimore icon walking toward us. They are called the Arabers. In the early days of Baltimore, a man would take his wagon into the city to sell his fruits and vegetables. Today the tradition continues. Many of the wagons have been in the family for years and it is passed from father to son. Samantha and I encountered the Arabers the last time we were in Baltimore and she was charmed by them. It is a good to see her relaxing and enjoying a few minutes.

The horse is wearing an elaborate harness decorated with bells. It is pulling a cart filled with fruits and root vegetables. Along the sides of the cart hang wreaths for sale and on the back are small Christmas trees available for sale.

The man walking beside the horse is old and bent. His face shows the lines of age and his hair is snow white. He talks to the horse as Samantha walks up and the horse grunts and comes to a stop. It lowers its head and closes its eyes. I wonder if it naps while people shop.

She walks back from the Araber cart with a bunch of grapes and a pomegranate. I look up and see ahead of us the tall brick tower building that is the Shot Tower. We find a bench and take a seat. She pops a couple grapes in her mouth and begins to take the skin off the pomegranate with her fingernail. Soon I can see a few of the individual gems inside. She pauses and looks at it. "I think like the platypus, a pomegranate proves God has a sense of humor. In designing things, why create something that is filled with hundreds of individual parts, each with a seed, and package it in a complicated structure? If you try to break one open with any force you crush the arils and your hands get stained with the juice. Plus you are crushing the best part." She holds the pomegranate out to me with about twenty arils exposed and I take a few. Eating this will at least help pass the time we have to wait for Bernie to get off work.

Traffic flies by us. People are in a rush to get out of town. I guess many of them are on their way home after being downtown for the day. No one pays any attention to us sitting on the bench. At three fifteen we stand up and stand along the sidewalk. I see a gray car pull up and the driver stops in front of us. I look in and see Bernie. I open the door and we get in.

I sit on the front seat and Samantha is in the back seat. Bernie looks ahead and drives. He makes the merge onto the Jones Falls and we are on our way out of town. "Okay, now it is just the three of us. You have until I get you to the Owings Mills Metro to explain why I should not take you to the nearest police station and turn you in."

I'm not sure where to begin. "Three days ago I had dinner with my friend Scott Llewellyn. He and I got into an argument in a tavern and I walked out. That was the last time I saw him. His body was found lying on the Palace Green in the early morning. The police were knocking on my door before six in the morning. After that things have gone to hell. I was contacted by a guy who has a still along the Colonial Parkway. He told me he was retired CIA."

Bernie interrupts me. "Wait. The guy told you he was retired CIA. Did you verify any of this? How do you know this man wasn't some nut case?"

I know he is going to think I'm crazy, but I have no answer. "I don't know. Our normal pizza guy delivered a pizza that we didn't order. Inside the box under the pizza was a note from this guy. All I can tell you is that this guy had hacked my computer and ordered the pizza. He talked his way into working for the day at the pizza shop. He slipped the note into the pizza box. I followed his instructions and arrived at a very unusual set up in the woods. It was hidden and looked like a stand of trees. Inside it had a sophisticated air filtration system so that the smell of the fire and the corn mash didn't exist outside. The guy told me he was retired CIA. That is all I have to go on. The story of what happened is a little crazy. The cops showed up with a search warrant for my service weapon. The box was in my safe, but the gun was gone. No one has access to my gun safe except Samantha. Samantha and I went to see Scott's widow and extend our condolences. While we were gone, Christina saw a man walking up our yard from the river. She watched our perimeter security system turn itself off and back on as he passed so she hit the panic alarm. The guy ran and the police couldn't find anything. When we looked back at the security system on the night Scott was murdered we saw the same thing on video except the person came into the house with Christina and the kids inside. We think that is how my gun was stolen originally and while we were gone he was trying to return it."

I don't know if he believes anything I am telling him. I don't even know if I would believe this story if a suspect was using it as an excuse. "Yesterday morning, I met a guy. He picked me up at my boat dock and we were on the river in his boat. He pointed out someone in the woods along the river just below my house watching us. I sent Christina and the kids to a safe house and Samantha and I hit the road. Last night we slept in the Jeep in Western Maryland. I don't know where we are sleeping tonight."

The afternoon traffic is beginning to build slowly. Traffic is heavy, but moving at posted speeds. Bernie has not looked away from the wheel. We are on the exit from the Jones Falls to the Baltimore Beltway. This puts us three exits from Owings Mills. I know I have to convince him that we need his help. "When I spoke with Karen, Scott's wife, she told me that Scott had an office in Baltimore City. He came up here about once a week. He sometime taught here, he also did research and had information on the Masonic treasures. He believed there was a treasure or information on the location of the Arc of the Covenant in a copper tube. The person I met on the river watched him find the copper tube. It was buried under a tree and the roots had grown around it. The tree fell and the cylinder was exposed. Karen believes he brought it to Baltimore."

We are an exit away from I-795. The Metro station is the first exit off of I-795. I am running out of time. "The guy with the still told me about the person behind this. He is the head of the Central Intelligence Agency covert training facility known as The Farm. He thinks Scott found something that belongs to the CIA and they killed him to get it back. Both he and the guy in the boat think the CIA has assumed Scott told me what he found. If I don't prove who killed Scott, they are setting me up to go to jail. I'm sure once I am sent to jail I will be murdered. Bernie, if you don't help me I am a dead man walking."

I see the sign for I-795 and Bernie changes lanes to get into the lane to exit the Beltway. "Where are you parked?" I tell him in front of the movie theatre. "Okay, I'm going to take you to your vehicle and then you are going to follow me. I want to put your vehicle in my garage. I believe you. This story is too strange to have made things up. We are going to have to find the address for his office. I'm not sure how we are going to do that. I'm off work for the next six days. It gives us some time to get some answers. Until then you can stay at my house. If you can handle cold cuts for dinner, we have food for the night."

I point out my Jeep in the parking lot and we get out of his car. Everything looks fine and I follow Bernie from the parking lot. Samantha watches through the back window to make sure we aren't being followed. Bernie takes meandering roads through farm fields and woods. I follow close behind him. I am worried about going straight to his house. I worry about a tracking device being put on the Jeep somewhere. I will deal with that once we get to his house. If necessary, I will take any devices for a drive. We turn onto a driveway in the woods. I'm not sure what to expect. Ahead I see a two car garage next to a small stone cottage. The door rises on one side and Bernie drives in. I wait for him to open the other door. As it rises, I see him moving a motorcycle from the second bay and rolling it behind his car. He then motions for me to drive in.

We get out of the Jeep and I pop the hood open. I want to see if anything has been tampered with. Bernie laughs. "Hey, if you are looking for tracking devices don't worry. The guy I bought this place from was paranoid. He was afraid a solar flare would destroy all the computers in the world. All the buildings are Faraday cages. Radio signals of any kind don't get in or out. It makes your cell phone completely useless in the house, but anyone looking for your vehicle will hit a dead end. They will assume you found it and removed it. We can check it in the morning. Let's get inside."

The house is small and has a comfortable lived in look. We are greeted by two cats, one a calico and the other a gray. From somewhere I hear the bark of a dog and he walks to the back door and opens it. A tall brown mixed breed comes bouncing in. He stops and looks at us before starting to growl. Bernie looks at him and tells him to go lay down. The dog grumbles before walking over to the calico cat and lays down.

Bernie gestures toward the dog "That's Max. The cats are Twilight and Coal. This is their house. I work for their food and the roof over their heads. I know they think they are in charge and allow me to serve them. The house isn't big but it serves my purpose. Here let me show you around." We follow him through the house. "I guess you can see this is the kitchen. There's beer in the fridge. If we start to run out there's a liquor store a half mile away. Bathroom is right down this hallway. Sometimes the toilet runs. If it does just jiggle the handle and it will stop. Of course we are in the living room." He walks down a hallway. "This is my bedroom. You can use one of these two bedrooms. There's a bathroom right here also. I have wifi and cable. Make yourself at home."

He excuses himself and goes into his bedroom to change clothes. He comes out dressed in jeans and a polo shirt and grabs a beer out of the refrigerator. He pops it open as he turns on the television and sits down. Samantha and I each grab a beer and join him in the living room. The early news is on the screen. We haven't seen or heard the news in a few days. We sit back to see if our pictures show up on the screen. To my relief we are not mentioned. Bernie is scanning the Richmond headlines on his laptop. "Well the good news is that you are not mentioned today. You were mentioned as a person of interest the day of the murder but your name has not come up again. I think perhaps they have lost you for the moment. Since you are at my house, I'm glad you are off their radar."

The main story is the ongoing debate over potential rigged voting machines and a claim of computer hacking by a foreign government to influence the Presidential election. One source claimed emails had been created to undermine a couple candidates and leaked by a foreign national. Unfortunately, no one will ever know the truth. The person who claimed to have the evidence died in a single car DWI accident. He was three times the legal limit when he drove into a bridge support.

In other news the popular toy of the holiday season will be in short supply because the manufacturing plant sustained catastrophic damage in a fire. Kids around the world will be disappointed and might have to wait until spring. Meanwhile, people are selling these toys online for over one thousand dollars already with prices expecting to climb as we get closer to Christmas. A few major retailers have a supply and are pulling them from their Black Friday advertisements. I watch as the head of a retail chain explains that their original advertisement listed the toy at nineteen dollars overnight on Thanksgiving. They have determined to pull the item from stock to help prevent fights in the store trying to get the toy. Instead they will take orders and arrange pick up once the price point is set on the product. The greed of Christmas at its best. Why have something they paid ten dollars for on sale at nineteen when they can get over one hundred and still look like a hero.

I shake my head and hesitate to walk outside and call John. I want to check in and let them know we are alright, but I am afraid to make unnecessary contact. Meanwhile, I know I need to walk away from the nightly news. I find myself hanging on every word and anticipating the next story might be about me.

Bernie stands up and walks to the kitchen. He takes various packages of luncheon meats, cheeses and condiments out of the refrigerator. There is a wooden bread box with various types of rolls and a tray with shredded lettuce, sliced tomatoes, onion and pickles. "My sister's anniversary party, this is the bonus of being a bachelor. People send food home with me. Of course, with all they send home for one man, you would think I eat for three. I usually share with the animals, but don't tell them that. They might stop sending them and my pets really like it. Help yourself and make a sandwich."

He carries his sandwich back into the living room. We make sandwiches and join him. "Okay, tell me what you know and suspect about this copper tube. Why kill because it was found?"

I finish chewing the sandwich in my mouth and swallow. "There are various theories. I don't know if any of them are correct. I really have no idea what the copper tube contains. Scott hoped to find the treasure of the Masons."

Bernie interrupts me. "You mentioned that before so let's begin there. Let's handle this like any other case. When did the Masons bury this and what might it contain?"

I didn't realize I was holding my breath and I let it out in a big whoosh. "The stories of the Masonic treasures go back to the age of Christ and the Magi. Whether you believe Christ as your personal savior or Christ as the father of a new religion the story begins there."

Bernie makes a time out symbol with his hands. "Time out, I am going to have to ask some questions as we go. So let's start with the difference between Christ as a Savior or the father of a new religion. I don't get that."

I was hoping I didn't have to go into too much detail. Sometimes telling too much confuses the issue in personal beliefs. "There are two very different stories. One is the well know Christian story of Christ being crucified and dying on the cross. There were people who believed in him and essentially his death lead to martyrdom and the birth of present day Christianity. That is very simplified but it is a well told story."

"The other is a bit more complicated. I will tell you what. You have five beers in the refrigerator. Tell me where the liquor store is located and I will go pick up a case."

He shakes his head. "No. I will go make a beer run and you will stay here. Consider this house arrest at the moment. I don't want you to be recognized and a shit storm coming down on my head. Nor do I want you to run. I am still not entirely convinced you didn't kill your friend. You stay here. I will be back in fifteen minutes with more beer."

Samantha and I finish eating our sandwiches while he is gone. In essence, I believe we are under house arrest. Bernie is interviewing me. I don't know if what I am saying will come back to haunt me. He had been a friend and ally when we worked on the case before. Things are different now. I am coming to him as a fugitive. I am a risk to his job and possibly his freedom. If I can be falsely accused and set up for murder, being here puts him at risk to be hunted by the CIA also. I wonder if we should leave while he is gone and find another way to locate Scott's office.

He returns before Samantha and I make a decision. He hands us each another beer and tells me to continue. I finish my first beer and open the next one. "The father of Christianity is a strange story. First you have to understand Judaism at the time of Christ. Remember Jesus was a Jew first. He was thought to be a radical rabbi with people who followed him. As a Rabbi, it was a mitzvah to have children. He would have been married. Celibacy was a Roman belief. If that is the case, the entire story that is told in Christianity is missing a vital part. That would be Mary Magellan, his wife."

I look over at Bernie who is just sitting in his chair. He looks relaxed. I'm not sure how strong his religious convictions might be, and so I am not sure how far to go with this story. "I guess I should ask you to suspend what you have been told since you were a child and listen to this alternate story. Keep in mind it doesn't mean that Christianity is wrong. I am just going to tell you Christianity according to someone other than the Romanized story we now follow."

Bernie takes a drink and tilts his head slightly to the side. "So are you going to tell me that the father of Christianity might refer to Christ fathering a child? I don't understand why if that is what happened the Romans did not tell the truth."

Samantha has been quiet until now. "That is because the pagan religions worshipped female Gods and the Romans were a patriarchal society. Men were in control and if the child born between Christ and Mary Magellan was a female she would become the direct descendant of God and therefore one to be worshipped according to the Pagans. The Romans could not risk the possibility of a male child being born either. In their beliefs, this would make this child a God. They crucified Christ because it was said he was the son of God, and therefore looked upon by his followers as a God."

I see realization beginning to set on his face. "So in order to retain control, they cut the possibility of Christ being married and having a child out of the story. They cut off the blood line with the crucifixion."

I don't know any other way to tell this story so I begin at the crucifixion. "Scholars believe the Last Supper was held on the Passover Seder. Christ and his disciples sat together and told the story of their people and the

Exodus. They broke matzah and drank wine. They asked the questions of faith and spoke of the plagues that night. The next day the Romans came and took Christ away. He was nailed to the cross next to the thieves."

I stop to take another drink of beer. Here the story begins to change from the Christian doctrine. "The Romans had rules of crucifixion. The family was not allowed to remove the body until after the person was dead and the sun went down. There was an exception for the Jews. Since they required a body be buried prior to sun down the Romans had frequently granted families the ability to take the body down prior to the person being completely dead and the sun still up in the sky. This being during the time of Passover, the Roman rules would allow the family to take the body down in the afternoon."

"A Roman soldier by the name of Longinus pierced the side of Christ with his spear. The body still bled but it was determined Christ would not survive the injuries and pain his body had sustained. People who had survived the crucifixion in the past died of infection and blood loss from this horrific act. The family was allowed to take the body of Christ down from the cross. They carried his dying body to the funeral cave of a family member, Joseph of Aramathia."

"The burial process at the time was to put the body in a cave for a year for the flesh to rot and then to place the bones in a small ossuary. The ossuary was what was buried. With all of this in mind, imagine the family taking the body to this cave. Spikes had been hammered through his ankle bones and his hands. The weight of his body had torn the flesh on his hands. His side was bleeding from the spear prick. He was in excruciating pain but he was still alive. So the family sat vigil."

"I believe those outside the cave were his uncle, Joseph of Aramathia, his wife, Mary Magdalene, his aunts Mary Salome and Mary Jacobe. In a moment of still being lucid, he tried to walk out of the cave and tell his family to go to safety. If the Romans found out he was still alive they would come. If the Romans found Mary Magdalene was pregnant they would kill her. The only way for his child to survive was to leave. He was dying. There was nothing more they could do for him but he could not rest in his death until he knew his wife and unborn child were safe. He was helped back into the cave so that he could die in peace with a promise from Joseph that he would take the women away to safety."

"So you see the story of the Crucifixion is not that much different than what you have always been told. It is just that he had a wife and unborn child, one that if the child survived would become the new son or daughter of the blood line of God. Joseph kept his word and took the women to the Camargue region of Gaul, now present day France and the town is known as Saintes Maries des La Mer. To this day there is a festival celebrated in this town commemorating the arrival of the three Mary's and Joseph of Aramathia. Lazarus, Mary Salome's brother is also credited to being with them when they arrive. Mary Salome and Mary Jacobe remained in Saintes Maries de La Mer. There are still artifacts in the church in the village. Lazarus went to Marseille to become the first Bishop. Mary Magdalene was taken to a cave by the local Roma Gypsies where she gave birth to a daughter named Sarah."

Bernie gets up to get another beer. I think the story is getting to him. When he returns, he sits down and looks at me for a moment. I am not sure if I should continue or not. "So Adam, you are telling me that the gypsies had the secret that could bring Christianity to their knees. No wonder the gypsies are hated. But, it explains a lot. The Roma gypsies will take in any child who is not wanted and protect them as their own. You are also telling me that there is a blood line of Christ. That is one hell of a secret!"

I nod my head to agree with him. "Bernie, I don't know your beliefs and I don't want to take away from them. This story is just that, a legend."

He sits forward in his chair and puts his hands on the arms of the chair. "I was born into a Catholic family and raised as an altar boy at Saint Mary's, but being a cop on the street has taught me there are always two sides to a story. Most of the time the truth is not what you want it to be, but somewhere in the middle of the two stories. So far you have not rocked my world to the core and I can accept the differences. I am curious how this ends up in a copper tube in Virginia."

I continue, "The bloodline of a family was recognized by the mother. The tradition continues with the Hebrew name of a person when used in prayer for the sick and memorializing after death. Having a daughter allowed the bloodline to continue. With this continuation of the family there was a need for protection. The secret was passed to the Cathars in France. It is believed that the crusade against the Cathars forced them to return the treasure to the caves that Mary Magdalene hid when she gave birth to Sarah. Legend has it that the treasure may have been handed over to the Knights Templar. When the church forced the death and disbanding of the knights, it is believed the Masons emerged from the secrets of the Templar's. Eventually they came to America to seek freedom. With them came the holiest articles of the Knights Templar. This includes the treasures from the Temple of King Solomon. If the legends are true, not only is there a history of the blood line of Christ, there is also the Arc of the Covenant and the Chalice of Abraham."

Bernie looks doubtful. "I don't know. I've heard stories like this before and it seems too farfetched for anyone to really believe it.

I nod my head and agree with him. "Throughout history there have been groups and individuals who searched for the child of Christ. The first of course is Julius Caesar. If you look at the path that Caesar took through Europe, he was following in the path of women who escaped. Caesar is not the most prominent. That would be Adolph Hitler and Heinrich Himmler."

"Both Himmler and Hitler were obsessed with finding the Arc of the Covenant and the Holy Grail. You can even look at the groups Hitler put into concentration camps. He imprisoned the Jews and the Roma Gypsies. Of course he imprisoned others, but the gypsies and Jews were just imprisoned for the group they were born into. It was an attempt to find and or eliminate the bloodline of Christ. Part of Hitler's agenda was to collect the art work of Europe so that he could find the treasures he was looking for, specifically, items such as the Spear of Destiny, the spear supposedly used by Longinus to pierce the side of Christ on the cross."

I know this entire story sounds insane, but this is what Scott was talking about the night he was murdered. This was what Scott believed and might have gotten him killed. I try to explain this to Bernie. I don't know why someone in the CIA would kill over this. It doesn't make sense to me, and as I hear it coming from my mouth even I think it sounds nuts.

Bernie is just absorbing what I am saying. It is hard to read what he is thinking. "So Adam, how much of this do you believe?" I tell him I'm not sure. He nods his head. At least he is thinking about the situation. "So what if the CIA knows the secret and is protecting it to do something like maintain world order? Hear me out on this. If the story is true and there is a living blood line of Christ it could be a real problem for the church. Perhaps the CIA has their headquarters in the area so that they can secretly dig for the missing scroll, but Scott found it first. If Scott had gone public with the information it might be possible for the family of the son of God to step forward. The riches of the church would be theirs. The bible as we know it would be exposed as a lie. This could cause anything from Civil War to complete chaos in the world. There is nothing to stop these people from stepping forward as the royal family of the world. We might all have to pay homage to them if they demand that. This could be to protect a secret that could destroy us all from within."

I had never thought about the repercussions of the legends being true. I had only thought of Scott's desire to dig up a historic church looking for something I doubt exists. What would it do to the world if a group of people stepped forward as someone the world should bow down and pay homage? The thought of world domination has been around for a long time. I wonder if somewhere out there a group of people might know that their family lineage goes back to Jesus Christ and Mary Magdalene. If they know this fact, what has kept them quiet all these years? They could hold the world at their feet."

Samantha breaks my train of though and I realize we have all been quiet for a few minutes. "If you knew that back in history your father was the son of God and your mother ran and hid from the world to protect his daughter, wouldn't you be afraid of the world finding out? Wouldn't the very fact of your lineage put your life in danger? I doubt the church would want to lose the foothold on the people. They exist on the donations of people wanting to please God. Having an actual person, not just a representation would stop the money flowing into the church. I don't know if the CIA would want you dead, but I can guarantee the church would want you either locked within their walls or dead. Even if the scrolls contain the information that the bloodline exists, stepping forward and claiming the bloodline would put a bull's eye on your forehead."

That is a true statement. All these years the family might have remained quiet because to speak up would have a bad outcome. This of course brings us back to the scroll Tracy witnessed him pulling from the roots of the tree. If Scott died because of this scroll, anyone who has it in their possession might die. If the killer got the information and located the scroll they hold the power of the world in their hands. This is something that in the right hands could be used for good, but in the wrong hands is nothing but pure evil.

Bernie has a lapboard on his legs and he is typing away on his computer. "I am looking up the local colleges looking for Dr. Scott Llewellyn. Where does he lecture?" I only know his Virginia office location. I have already looked and there is not a phone number or address for a Maryland office. Bernie smiles, "And here it is! Okay. He teaches at the community college. It doesn't list his office location but there is a phone number. I just entered the number into a reverse look up and I have the address. This isn't a part of the city we should go after dark. We respond to random shootings in the neighborhood a couple times a week. My other concern is that if I can find this office this quickly so can the CIA. I would rather not walk into the unknown in the dark."

Bernie is correct. We have no idea what we will find there or who might be waiting for us. We sit and watch the television for a while before Samantha and I go to bed. We plan to get up and get downtown by seven in the morning. It gives a chance to get downtown before the traffic gets too bad, be able to find a parking space, and get out before the city wakes up.

Day Four
Hunt Valley, Maryland

After spending the night sleeping in the Jeep, Samantha and I are both exhausted. I think we fell asleep as soon as we hit the bed. I hear Max crying to go out and realize it is already morning. Bernie is in the kitchen telling him to calm down and hold it for a second. I get out of bed and go to the bathroom. Samantha is still sleeping so I go out to join Bernie in the kitchen. He has started a pot of coffee and retrieves a carton of eggs and a pack of bacon out of the refrigerator. I get the pack of ham deli meat and a pack of cheese. I grab a couple pieces of green pepper, some onion and a couple tomato slices off the tray. Bernie gives me a thumbs-up and hands me a knife.

Samantha walks into the kitchen. The smell of coffee and bacon has lured her from bed. We sit down to eat and plan our trip into the city. Bernie is hoping that we can get the building superintendent or one of the maintenance people to open the door to the office so that we can look around. If that doesn't happen we have a choice to walk away and not try to find the copper tube or to break the law and break into the office. Bernie is willing to walk down the hall while I do that. He doesn't feel comfortable being part of the break in. He will provide look out though if we get to that stage.

I also want to get a throw away phone for Samantha. For now we are staying together, but, sometime in the future, we may have to break up.

Bernie decides he should also get one. We have no idea what the future might hold— we should be ready for whatever might happen.

As soon as we eat, we dress to head to the city. Bernie hands us each a football logo baseball hat and t-shirt. He mutters something about a fan appreciation day. We need to stay out of camera view and hide what we can of our faces. Most of the buildings in the city have cameras. There are also cameras on most street corners. Yesterday we hid under the hoods of sweatshirts. Today we will hide under hats and blend with the crowds.

The traffic on the Jones Falls expressway into the city is still light. We get off at the North Avenue exit and go left at the traffic light. We can see the buildings of the college of art and the rainbow painted Howard Street Bridge that crosses the Jones Falls. Bernie makes a left on a one way street and pulls along the curb a few streets down. I'm not sure what street we have parked on. Around us are old row houses. Some are boarded up, others look like private residences. Some have well-kept patches of yard along the sidewalk while others have foot tall grass littered with trash. He opens the door of the car and gets out. Samantha and I follow him.

We walk up the street to a four-story building. The bottom floor is a corner bar. We enter by a side door in the alley between the houses. Inside there is a board with names on it and office numbers. Llewellyn is on the 3rd floor office C. I hear a voice as we start up the stairs. "Can I help you?" We turn together and see a man in a security guard uniform. This is either good luck or bad luck. At this point, we just have to play nice with the man.

I walk back down the stairs to him. "Hi. I'm a friend of Dr. Llewellyn's. I was trying to get something in his office for his wife, Karen. She asked me to come get it and bring it home to her."

He looks confused. "Why isn't Scott getting it himself? I've met his wife a couple times and from what I have seen she doesn't like to come here."

This guy does not know that Scott has been murdered. I'm not happy about being the guy who has to give the bad news. "Scott Llewellyn was murdered on Friday. His wife has asked me to get a few things from the office for the viewing and funeral. I'm sorry to have to tell you this."

He looks puzzled and starts to walk up the stairs, taking them two at a time. He stops and looks back at me, "He was murdered on Friday? His office was broken into early Friday morning. The lock was broken and the office was trashed when I came to work. I called the police and they took a report but, I haven't heard anything. Here, let me unlock the door for you. Can you express my condolences to his wife? She seemed like a nice lady. I'm Stephen Koehler by the way. I've been the guard here for five years and I have seen windows shot out, I have found junkies that have OD'd in the alley. I have even kicked hookers out of the hallway but I have never had an office broken into."

Stephen Koehler seems to be a friendly guy. He looks average in his late forties. He is slightly overweight with graying temples. Other than that, he looks in pretty good shape. His shoes show signs of wear. He walks a lot on his job, which explains why his movements are swift. At the same time he looks tired. Not like he has not gotten enough sleep, but his everyday life is pulling the life out of him.

I'm surprised he didn't ask for identification but maybe because we knew the office and the name of Scott's wife he assumed we were okay. He walks down the hallway to a door. I can see pry marks on the door frame. He turns around and looks at us. "I tried to fix the door. I left a voice message for Scott about the lock. The door shuts and locks but it wouldn't take much to bust it open again. I suggested he get a carpenter to come in and replace the frame and maybe the lock." He pushes the door open. "I picked some things up and put them away. I didn't see anything missing but someone threw stuff all over the place. I guess they were in a hurry. What was it you were looking for? Maybe I saw it."

I decide to risk it and tell him a copper tube. Scott found it recently and was really excited about it. I see recognition in Stephens face. "He showed it to me when he brought it here. He was always telling me about his search for the treasure buried in Williamsburg and Jamestown. I didn't see it here after the break in. That might mean nothing though. He mentioned getting another opinion on it. You should probably speak with Billy."

I'm not sure who Billy is and why I should talk to him. Karen never mentioned a Billy. I asked Stephen about him. "See that desk against the wall? That is Billy's desk. They share this office because they share the same dream of finding that treasure. Billy's also a professor. He's a bit of a rebel but he's an interesting character. Many afternoons I have sat up here with them talking."

Samantha is looking around the office. "Are you sure the copper tube isn't here?" She opens a couple drawers and looks in a file cabinet.

Stephen looks as if it is his space that is being violated. "No. I put everything that was out of place back where it belongs. The tube was right here last week." He puts his hand on Scott's desk. Then he moves a few things on the desk top that Samantha had moved.

Karen never mentioned coming to Scott's office. This makes me wonder if Karen was right. "Scott's wife never mentioned being at this office. She acted like she wasn't sure where it was located. Are you sure the woman with him was his wife?"

Stephen has suddenly become very interested in his feet. He is looking down shuffling his feet and looking extremely uncomfortable. "At first I just assumed the woman with him was his wife. He brought her around a lot and they were—close. Then one day he showed me a picture of his wife, Karen. She was not the person he spent time with here. Some nights they spent the night here. Maybe they were just working late or all night. I could be mistaken."

He picks up picture from the top of a file cabinet. It is a picture of Scott and Karen in Egypt. "This is the woman he said was his wife Karen. I just looked the other way with the other woman. It wasn't my business. They might have been working on something together."

I feel bad for Stephen right now. This is one of the uncomfortable truths of death. The skeletons come out of the closet. For me it happened after Elizabeth was murdered. During the investigation the police uncovered emails between her and a partner at her law firm. They backed up the affair with hotel receipts and get away weekends to romantic bed and breakfasts at the beach. While I was out of town working, she lived another life with a coworker. I didn't want to know who, but it was leaked to me accidentally. This was a guy who came over to my house. He was at Elizabeth's funeral and gave me his condolences at her wake. I couldn't keep the business trips they took out of my mind. But, I was glad I didn't find this information out until after her funeral. I don't know what I would have done if I had known before then. It would have been harder to handle. At her funeral, I had no doubt she was the love of my life. A few weeks later I learned I was not the love of hers. It hurt, but it didn't stop me from mourning her or blaming myself for her death. It made me blame myself for her unhappiness as well. I don't know if I can do that to Karen. "Stephen, can you tell me what this woman looked like and what you know about her? Do you think she knew about the scroll and might she have it?"

Stephen shakes his head no. "She was young. I thought he married one of his students until I saw the picture of his wife. I'd say she was about twenty-two or three. Not much older than that. She had brown curly hair. She was a knock out Greek girl with a body that didn't stop. She lives in the Greektown section of the city. She is connected to one of the restaurants down there. Sometimes she brought me food. Her family makes a spanakopita that is memorable. She was good to look at but not that smart. I figured Scott kept her around for her physical assets. I doubt she knows anything about the scroll. She's more of the manicure and pedicure type. She dressed very designer label and was really high maintenance. Don't get me wrong, the maintenance was worth it. She was really nice to look at but I didn't talk to her much. I'm better at Klingon than designer labels."

I see Bernie looking at the window and he is getting twitchy. "Bernie, everything okay? You are looking a little nervous."

He turns around and looks at us. "Scott Llewellyn was murdered because of this copper tube. You are afraid someone is trying to kill you because of this copper tube. Stephen might know more about the copper tube than anyone else in the room. Don't you think we should tell him that he needs to pack his ass up and disappear before he wakes up dead?"

Stephen has a stapler in his hand and it drops to the floor. We all turn to look at him. "Whoa! Scott was killed because of that thing? And someone is trying to kill you? When the hell do you think it would have been a good time to tell me? You didn't see this office after the break in. They threw things around. They went through everything. These people have to know that I have access to this office. Should I get out of here? Should I leave?"

I don't want to lie. He seems like a nice guy. I also don't want to risk having blood on my hands. "I don't want you to overreact. I have been warned that the CIA might be trying to frame me for Scott's murder. I'm trying to find out who really killed him and why. Everything seems to revolve around that copper tube. If you have any vacation time coming to you, maybe this would be a good time to take it. Go somewhere that no one knows your name."

Stephen laughs, "Should I even use my name?"

I shake my head and tell him no. "If you have another name you like, I'd use it. At least until I figure out what the hell is going on with his murder and the break-in. Give Bernie your phone number and we will call you when the coast is clear."

I expected him to take this differently. He looks relieved. "You know—I get up every morning and come to this job. I see the human circus walk by here every day. I am talking about people who are certifiable. The hotel down the street is a hooker office building. Across the street—a meth lab. Half the time I look before walking up the street to make sure it hasn't blown up during the night. I have a guy that every afternoon yells and screams walking up and down the sidewalk, he likes to chase traffic. I have seen him barking like a dog running after a car. I have a guy who likes to hump the building and if that doesn't satisfy him for the day he gets off on the mailbox. I clean needles out of the alley. I deal with junkies puking on the side of the building. I just come here every day and do my job. What I really need is a new career. I'm going to take your advice. I have a couple sick days and three weeks' vacation. My brother has been asking me to move closer to him and work for him. That would require me to pack up my life. I'm too comfortable here and I'm not going anywhere. This may be the best thing that has ever happened to me. You just gave me permission to leave. Thank you."

I wish him luck. He hands me the phone number he has for Billy and locks the office. As we walk down the stairs he stops and throws the keys on the counter of the bar. "Hey Jack. I'm not feeling well. I think I'm going to take a sick day. Here are the keys. I'll see you later." He walks out behind us. "Hey guys. Thank you!"

We get back into Bernie's car and drive out of the city. He suggests we go to the grocery store and pick up food for the next couple days. I'm not sure that staying in place is a good idea. I think Samantha and I need to keep moving. I don't want to put Bernie at any more risk. He pulls over into a parking lot. "Do you think you are going to get rid of me that fast? I'm like Stephen. I see the bat-shit-crazy of the city every day. It's a damn zoo out here. I could have taken retirement a few months back, but I wanted to put in a little more time. If not I will end up talking to my dog and cats like they are human. You are going to see if you can find this Billy Gill guy. If you are leaving so am I. Give me a few minutes to throw some clothes in a bag, grab some dog food and refill the cats food and water automatic feeder. That way if I don't come back for a couple days they will be fine. My house might be being watched anyway. We don't know. Billy Gill has to live locally anyway right? Let's do this."

I look back at Samantha. She shrugs her shoulders. "We might need help. Someone riding shotgun could have our back. It might be a good idea."

I turn and look back at Bernie. "Okay. Let's get back to your house and see if we can locate Billy Gill. I'm hoping he knows something about that scroll. I just hope whoever killed Scott hasn't gotten to him."

Rather than drive home Bernie drives to a shopping center. Our first stop is to a small store selling disposable phones and cards for air time. We grab two cheap flip phones and two cards with two hundred and fifty minutes on them. We can activate these online. It is a fast in and out purchase. The clerk doesn't even blink when I pay cash for both phones and the cards. I wonder how often this happens. Phones like this are the staple of the drug and sex trades. If you worry about them being compromised they find a trash can and you purchase another cheap phone. From there we follow him into a grocery store. He looks around. There are people walking all over the store. Near us are three checkout lanes open with customers. Bernie leans on the customer service counter and turns the phone around. He pushes a line and looks at the slip of paper with Billy's phone number. Someone on the other end must have picked up. Bernie holds a finger up in the air to tell us to hold on. "Mr. Gill? You don't know me but I am a friend of a mutual friend who is recently deceased." He pauses while the person on the other end is speaking. "I was given this number by Stephen." He pauses again. "Yes, I was one of the people who just visited him. I'm glad he called you. We need to meet up with you. Where would be a safe and satisfactory location to meet?" He speaks another minute and then hangs up the phone. I am glad no one in the store came up and wanted to know why we were on their telephone.

Bernie laughs. "It is interesting. If you look like you know what you are doing and play it cool most people over look your actions. I figured I had until the person who works here either comes back or someone else in the store comes over here. By then, I hoped to get my call in. If I got caught I would flip my badge and tell them official business. Most people nod their heads and walk away thinking they are part of official police business. While we are here, let's grab some provisions for the road. We are on our way to Western Pennsylvania."

I suggest we each get a cart and grab some shelf stable stuff that we can use while on the road. Bernie also needs to grab food for the cats and the dog. We will have two vehicles and I want us to be able to be self-sufficient. We can't check into hotels and restaurants are still an at risk place. It is better to have food we can eat from a can and not worry about cooking.

My phone rings while I am in the canned soup isle. It scares me. I haven't gotten a phone call on this phone yet. Roddie, Tracy, John and Chris are the only people who have this number. I look down to see caller ID for the phone I gave to John. "Adam, where are you? Wait, don't answer that. Are you okay?"

I tell him we are fine. I can hear panic in his voice and I hope the girls are okay. "Can you get to a television?" I tell him I can in twenty minutes. He still sounds panicked, "If you are on the road stay away from large bridges, mass transit, and large interstate intersections. The shit has hit the fan buddy. All over the country, hell all over the world, things are blowing up!"

I thank him and look for Samantha and Bernie in the store. We walk to check out and I look around. Most of the people that were in the store have gotten their groceries and left. Outside most of the parking lot is now empty and in the distance I can see the highway backed up with cars. All John told me was that the shit had hit the fan. From the way people left the store, it must be a pretty big fan and a lot of shit. I am glad my kids and Christina are with John. I know he will protect them.

I watch the store employees checking their phones and texting. Normally, I suspect the store has a no cell phone policy, but whatever is happening has thrown the rules out the window. I see a woman in a cashier smock crying and hear her ask a manager to allow her leave. The manager gives in and looks around the store at the few shoppers trying to check out.

The radio in the car is giving a traffic report. There are back-ups around the area. The sun is shining and there isn't a cloud in the sky. The drive home is not long enough for us to determine what is going on, only that traffic is in gridlock and a bridge has collapsed on I-695.

As soon as we walk in the door, we turn on the television. The on air personality looks strained. "We have reports coming in of significant damage to the Fort McHenry Tunnel, the Woodrow Wilson Bridge, and Metro Center in Washington, DC." The scene cuts to a view of the spans of the Woodrow Wilson Bridge. The center of the bridge is missing. Both ends of the bridge approach are a sea of flashing lights. Below in the water there are police boats arriving on the scene. The water is filled with floating debris and twisted metal from the missing bridge span above. The camera zooms in on a person in the water. "We can see there are some survivors. Witnesses on the scene report seeing box trucks stopping on each span and exploding. A similar report is coming in from the Fort McHenry Tunnel. The tunnels of two tubes have cracked. Water is flooding the tunnels. The Maryland Transit Authority is trying to move people from their vehicles and get them out of the tunnel to safety."

The reporter stops and puts his hand on his ear. "We have an unconfirmed report that a ship carrying gasoline has exploded near the twin approach tunnels to the Chesapeake Bay Bridge. Also just coming in the San Mateo-Hayward Bridge over San Francisco Bay has suffered damage to the center span. Vehicles have plummeted into the water below. I think there is no doubt this was a coordinated terror attack. Locally, we have also heard reports a fuel tank at a gas station in Breezewood, Pennsylvania has exploded affecting traffic on both I-70 and the Pennsylvania Turnpike. A major concern is a bridge crossing the Susquehanna River near Harrisburg, Pennsylvania. The explosion was within a mile of Three Mile Island. The nuclear power plant is currently being checked for leaks."

We sit down in front of the television. The groceries are sitting in a heap on the floor. "It seems the explosions have come in two waves. The first was at noon eastern time. They have been followed by a second wave of explosions a few minutes ago. Reports are now coming in from Europe. We have confirmation that the Kings Cross Underground station has collapsed. There are people trapped in trains throughout the London Underground. In Madrid, the Alonso Martinez Metro station has suffered significant damage. They are reporting a mass casualty situation. Workers are trying to make their way to where a train may have been crushed under a collapsed tunnel."

The image on the screen changes to a street scene. Smoke is coming up through rubble on the ground. "This is a view from Gare Chatelet Les Halles Metro station in Paris. Gare Chatelet Les Halles is the world's largest underground subway station. At this time, we are being told the entire underground station has collapsed from what has been reported as multiple explosions. This collapse happened during the height of the evening rush hour. Approximately seven hundred and fifty thousand people pass through this station daily with as many as one hundred and twenty trains an hour."

"We have received word that the Baltimore, Carroll, Harford, Howard and Anne Arundel County and Baltimore City Schools will be closing at one o'clock. The school administration has asked that parents not come to the schools. Please allow the schools to release the children safely on the buses. County and state police will be escorting the buses on their designated routes. More school closings are coming in as we speak."

We are sitting in silence. I think the magnitude of the attack is overwhelming. Thousands may be trapped and dying. The screen keeps flashing from one disaster scene to the next. Survivors are beginning to appear covered in cuts and bruises. I had hoped that we would leave today and drive to Pennsylvania, but the attack has caused people to leave their offices and pack the highways. Damage to highways, bridges and tunnels have snarled traffic everywhere.

The reporter looks at a piece of paper that has been handed to him. "We have just received confirmation that the Outer Loop of the beltway is closed. A semi on the center of the triple bridges at Security Boulevard exploded. All three bridges have collapsed onto the roadway below. The Governor of the State of Maryland, Curtis Millard, has declared a state of emergency. As of three o'clock today all Maryland interstates will be close to traffic. We are asking people to shelter in place. They should stay in their homes or places of employment and shelter there until roads can be secured. Children who are on school buses will be taken home. Those who have not left school will be held at the school until the situation is under control. If you are trapped on the highway behind an accident or one of the collapses, please stay with your vehicle or get off at the next exit ramp. Please follow the directions of the police and state highways. We repeat, the Governor of the State of Maryland..."

I pick up the phone and walk outside to call John. He answers on the first ring. I tell him we are in a home and safe. He tells me Chris was on duty and picked up Alina in his police car. The school released her to him and he took her to the house. Chris is working, the rest are safe and sheltering in place. I thank him and hang up. The world has gone crazy and we are powerless to protect our family and to go home. I'm sure I am not alone feeling like this but I know telling Samantha that the kids are safe will be a relief to her.

Bernie joins me out in the yard. His phone was ringing also. "No. I'm not in the area. I put in for vacation yesterday and I'm out of town. I don't know if there is even an interstate open if I could drive home." He hangs up and smiles. "All hell has broken out in the city and they wanted me to come in for riot patrol."

I'm not sure why he is smiling, "And this is good news?"

He looks at me and winks, "Yup! I'm on vacation and hiding out from the CIA is preferable to inner city gangs rioting. You did me a favor by showing up at the harbor and needing help. Who knew all hell was about to break lose around the world. For that matter, who knew this would sound better than my current life?"

We go back inside the house. No one feels like eating but we pull out the cold cuts and sit in front of the television watching the reports from around the world. The death toll is mounting. There has not been a group accepting responsibility for the attacks yet. By the time things quiet down, there have been three waves of explosions. The first wave happened at noon eastern daylight time. This was followed by the second wave at twelve-thirty. The final wave was at one o'clock. The attacks have been primarily centered in the United States and in Europe. There have been isolated attacks in Israel and India. As the news of the attacks reach the Middle East, the people are taking to the streets with banners and shooting their rifles into the air. They are cheering and celebrating the death of innocent Americans and Europeans.

I eventually can't take the repetition of the blast sites being shown over and over on the news. I'm sure some families are watching loved ones being helped into ambulances and being pulled from debris. Others are waiting for a phone call from a family member who is unaccounted for yet. Now the cell towers are over loaded and most are down. Somehow Scott's murder seems like it was a lifetime ago. I know I still have to worry about it and catch his killer, but with roads closed and damage that might take months to repair I don't even know if I will be able to prove anything.

Max is starting to cry to go out. I offer to take him out. I take his leash off the hook next to the back door and hook it to his collar. The sun is beginning to set and the sky has turned a bright orange. A herd of horses graze at the top of the hillside across the road at a neighboring farm. They are black silhouettes against the blood orange sky. I stick my head in the door and call Bernie and Samantha. The three of us stand in the yard watching the horses graze as the sky goes from orange to gray. In a day of turmoil, there is still beauty in the world. It somehow puts everything in perspective. We are still alive.

Bernie looks at his phone, "Hey guys, the President is addressing the nation in about three minutes. We should get back inside." I pull on the leash. Max has been sniffing around and follows us back inside the house.

The view on the television has moved inside the White House. President Mike Randall and President Elect Nathan Hall are standing together at matching podiums. The two men had been meeting this morning with their transition teams at the White House.

The camera zooms in on President Randall. He looks strained. He will take a lot of heat on the bombings. In the past few months, he folded to pressure from Congress and pulled security from the airports, train stations and public transportation. Congress is claiming money was being wasted looking for a terrorist attack that wasn't happening. His opponent ran on a campaign pointing out government waste over the last fifteen years. Nathan Hall wanted to pull the scanners from the airports, removing the bomb dogs and armed agents on our rail systems and eliminate the scanners in public buildings. Over one thousand security personnel will be laid off from the federal government. He expects the state and local governments to develop their own security plans and hire those that are laid off. A slight majority of the American public bought into his plan. They like the sound of millions in tax payer money being saved.

Nathan Hall seemed like the voice of reason. He convinced the American public that we have not had a terror attack since September eleventh. He campaigned that the de-escalation of security personnel would not make us vulnerable. As it is, even with security measures in place we have fallen victim to minor attacks.

Now we have been hit with a massive attack. The current count has sixty-two individual attacks on United States soil today in sixty minutes. The people are going to be asking who was asleep at the wheel and if there was any warning that an attack was imminent. Already, the talking heads are speculating that President Randall suppressed any warnings prior to the election in an attempt to keep the news from ever getting out that he had caved to pressure. As it is, Nathan Hall won by less than one percent of the popular vote and by seven electoral votes. This was not a mandate election. The loss of security and the feeling of safety nearly divided the country in half. It was the center point of the debates. Now, I wonder if we have enough.

President Randall begins to address the nation. "My fellow Americans, tonight we come together as a nation in mourning. For only the third time in this country's history, we have been attacked on our own soil by what we believe to be foreign nationals. There is no excuse for this and I am sorry. I have failed you. In my drive to show this country is not afraid of terrorism and that we will face them head on, I allowed them to live among us. I am sorry."

"This morning, President Hall and I sat down to discuss the turnover of the White House and the transition of the country to his leadership. While we were working on this, we received the first report of an explosion. We stopped the meeting and I went with my staff immediately to the situation room. When we realized a second wave of attacks had happened, we called President Hall and his staff back to the White House. What we experienced today cannot be solved in a few weeks. It is not a task for my White House alone, but will be turned over to President Hall. We will work together. We will need to rebuild our infrastructure and mend our wounds."

"Today we began rescue and recovery of the victims of this attack. I vow to continue until we have accounted for everyone who is missing. We will not leave a man, woman or child behind. This is no small task, but it must be done."

"We will rebuild. We will repair. We will take what has been dealt to us and make a stronger America. We will not be defeated by terrorism." He slams his fist on the podium. His face is red with anger. "We will not take this act of cowardice lying down!"

"With only nine weeks left in the White House, I will begin the cleanup, but that is only the beginning. I am tasking President Hall with recovery and rebuilding." He turns and looks at Nathan Hall, "President Hall, would you like to address the nation and provide your teams plan for recovery?"

President elect Nathan Hall smiles at the camera. During the election he emerged as the golden boy. He rose up through the ranks and put in his time in the Senate. He has a sparkling record and was instantly popular with the voters. He was born in Gettysburg, Pennsylvania to a mother who taught pre-school and a father who worked for the National Park

Service. As a teen, he was a Boy Scout and rose to the rank of Eagle. In the summer he worked as a battlefield tour guide and in the winter shoveled snow for his neighbors.

He is the product of a private school education, he went to an Ivy League college where he walked on the field and made the football team. He was also the Captain of the varsity rowing team, taking his men's eights to the Olympics. Nathan Hall is the first American President to have two gold medals in the Olympics and is part of a world record holding team.

He has blonde hair, blue eyes and a dark natural tan. HIs trim muscular figure cuts a striking difference alongside President Randall's slight beer belly and pasty complexion. He is smart and well spoken. Alongside him his wife, Sarah, also a blue eyed blonde that he met in high school and their two sons and daughter. Nathan Hall is a striking figure with a commanding presence. The Hall family has already been compared to Americans second Camelot.

"Thank you President Randall. I want to assure the American people that I am not afraid to roll up my sleeves and get to work. As I traveled the country on the campaign trail, I saw families in trouble. Many are barely able to put food on the table. I saw children without school supplies or enough to eat. I saw veterans who live on the streets. I saw a country in trouble and in need of a purpose. Today through tragedy, we have been handed a purpose and a reason for being. This once great nation can rise again and like the Phoenix we can rise from our ashes."

"As a young boy when I saw something that needed to be done, I did it. I didn't wait for someone to ask me or tell me, I saw a need and filled it. Then, like now, I took the ideals that made this country great and changed my little corner of the world. Do not look at this as the destruction of our country, but of a new beginning, that we might rise from the mediocrity of our current existence and become a great and powerful nation once more."

"Tonight with searchlights we are scouring the bomb sites looking for survivors. The people who have lost their lives are being identified so that families might find closure. In the morning this work will continue. We will do so until everyone is accounted for and then we will clear away what has been destroyed and begin to rebuild. We are not going to just fix and repair, we are going to make things stronger."

"Our current unemployment is at six point two percent. By next week we will be at zero percent. Effective immediately employment centers are being established. If you do not have a job report to your nearest employment office with your resume and any licenses or certifications. There you will be given an assignment. It will be based on your abilities. If you are in purchasing, you will begin to buy the materials we need to rebuild. If you are in finance, you will be paying for them and paying our workers. Whether you are a brick layer, pipe fitter, secretary or line cook—we will have a job for you. My cabinet would rather pay you to work than to sit back and wait for the country to get better. That philosophy hasn't worked in the last thirty years. We need to stop watching reruns and expecting a new and better outcome."

"Our plan is simple. We will match people to jobs that need to be done. We will pay you for the work you are assigned to do. If you do not like it, you can apply for a new assignment. What you can't do is sit home and collect a paycheck. We have too much work to be done."

"If you are in this country illegally, be prepared to go home. You may apply to return, but you can't stay here without proof of citizenship. We have left the doors open too long. In doing so, we have blood on our hands this evening. And yes, the blood of those who were injured or died today is on our hands for allowing this to happen."

"Today we are not a country that was attacked by terrorism, we are a country that is pulling ourselves together and uniting in a cause. It is our cause. It is our country and by damn we are taking it back!"

"In closing, to those who have been affected by the events of the day. We stand by you and weep with you. You are not alone but surrounded by a country of fellow citizens who care. We are the United States and united we stand so that none shall divide us. They will only make us stronger."

When he is finished the camera lingers on him for a moment before fading to a scene of the American Flag flying over the Capitol. In the background, masses of people are standing in the National Mall. As the camera pulls out we can hear the people standing there singing the National Anthem.

A reporter comes on from the national network feed. We can still see the crowd and hear the anthem being sung. In a subdued voice he says, "The crowd of people in the mall are those who have come out of the office buildings. They are the government workers who have been trapped downtown tonight by the tragic explosion in the metro this morning. They came here to watch the President's speech on big screen televisions, which have been brought out and set up around the Capitol. No one led them to begin singing the anthem, it swelled through the crowd and is now a loud battle cry of the American people. As President Elect Nathan Hall said, 'we are the United States and united we stand so that none shall divide us.' You can see that tonight in the determination of the people. From Washington, DC, this is Brad Heitt reporting on the continued broadcast of the November twenty-fourth bombings. I now return you to the network."

We sit in silence for a moment. During the build-up to the election, Nathan Hall used his ability as a public speaker to win every debate. He speaks from the minds of Americans and says what most politicians won't say. He admits our downfalls and gives common sense resolutions. I have felt for years that unemployment checks don't work. People want a job, not an unemployment check. They want to feel purpose. The checks are meant to be a subsidy to help pay for food and shelter but they give nothing to the self-esteem of the person. They still have the label of unemployed.

I can imagine the work that must be done. The federal highway system is in shambles now. People have not fully understood the entire impact of today's events. Rail lines, roadways, tunnels and bridges have been damaged across the country. This will slow down transportation of goods and services. Prices are going to rise because goods can't get to the stores. On average most grocery stores have a 3-4 day supply of food. After that, they need a restock. Without highways, it will be difficult to move the food to the retail establishments.

My phone rings and I see Johns number on the display. I rush out the door to answer it. "Adam, I wanted to touch base with you. We are all home for the moment. Chris is going to be doing 12 on and 12 off. I'm being sent to the Bay Bridge Tunnel. Christina should be fine with the kids. I don't know if you realize the magnitude of what is happening. Are you sure you are somewhere safe and are okay?"

John is a worrier. I assure him we are fine, but I can hear something else in his voice. "Adam, do you guys have cash? You are going to need it. There were a few explosions that most people will assume were misplaced bombs. We know differently. One blew up in Philadelphia near the Liberty Bell another on a street in New York City. One in San Francisco. Banking is shut down. There is no way to access money transfers, account balances, transaction—it may take weeks to repair the trunk lines. Not only is our interstate transportation system affected, our financial system has been taken down. Whoever did this knew exactly what they were doing."

I assure him we have plenty of money but I am not sure what we will be spending it on if the stores are not open. Meanwhile, I have to get to Western Pennsylvania to talk to Billy Gill. "John, tell me about the highways. I feel really disconnected but I need to get on the interstate system soon. I need to meet with a guy and talk. What are my chances of getting to Altoona or State College?"

John laughs. "Yeah, that's not happening at least for the next 24 hours. We are being told shelter in place will hold for 24 hours. After that, the powers that be do not think the American people will listen. This has been one hell of a shock for people but they are not accustomed to being shut up in their homes. They will want to get out and see the damage. Of course, the highways are a mess. There are areas snow plows have been called in to push the twisted metal and road beds away to clear a path for emergency personnel to get to other sites."

"I have access to the current road condition maps. Where are you heading. Not specifics but general information."

Bernie has come out to join me and Samantha is standing in the doorway. They want information as bad as I do. "We will be heading north of Everett, Pennsylvania. I think it is south of Altoona."

I hear him typing. "Okay. Here's the deal. I-70 in Baltimore is toast. You can't go by the Baltimore Beltway. Take the back roads. Most cross the reservoirs, I'm not sure which if any of them have been damaged. Once you get west of Columbia you are alright for a bit. You are going to have to find a back road around Breezewood, Pennsylvania. It's a real mess there. The truck stop on the corner of I-70 and the Pennsylvania Turnpike blew. I think it is still burning. Most of the town is on fire. There are multiple gas stations in town. With people running from the explosion there wasn't anyone to hit the shut off valves and tank covers were blown off. Most of the gas tanks are burning."

"I would go pretty wide around that. There are warnings about the heat and smoke. That would put you trying to go through the road cut in the mountain on I-68. I don't know if that mess has been cleared up yet. The pedestrian bridge over the roadway was hit. That caused a multi truck pile up. I think one of the suicide bombers was driving an eighteen wheeler through there. Some pretty big rocks broke away also."

"Okay, I have a route. Before you get to Breezewood, I need you to get off on state road twenty-twenty-nine. You need to go west on it. The road will split, take SR four-twelve to Windswept Lane then to River Dell Road. This becomes Dell Road. It looks like the road dead ends into The Lincoln Highway. The Lincoln Highway will take you to Everett."

"Hey Adam, the world changed today. Maybe what happened to Scott isn't that important anymore. Maybe we can fight it together down here. I don't know if chasing windmills is a good idea now. "

I wish I could feel the same way. Eventually the world will go back to normal. I wonder what happens after that. I doubt my slate will be wiped clean. The evidence that has been planted will still be there. I will have no proof that I didn't kill him other than Samantha and Christina vouching for me being home. I still look guilty. I have a story of a treasure which might hold secrets of the bible. Scott may have found the answers to so many people's questions. All I have though is a mystery man who witnessed him finding it, a security guard who saw a copper tube in an office and legends. I don't know if there is much proof there. I either have to find his killer or find the treasure. With the country in turmoil, both seem like a long shot.

We go back inside. It seems safer behind closed doors. I fill them in on the main financial trunk lines being hit by bombs. The trunk line through

Philadelphia is a strategic line. It has to be a primary location to be repaired as soon as possible. With this communication hub down, financial transactions in the United States are at a standstill. I can understand why nothing has been mentioned on the television. If people knew the Achilles Heel of the country was part of today's attack there might be panic.

We sit for the night watching the television. The network is jumping back and forth between the regular scheduled programming and disaster recovery. I feel as soon as I get distracted by the plot of a program they go to a survivor being rescued. When they return to regular programming that show is over and we join another program already in progress. I don't want to be the first person to go to bed so I sit and endure the disjoined programming.

Finally, Samantha stands up and announces she is going to bed. Bernie and I both agree and stand up. He grabs Max's leash and I put on my coat and grab my gun. We take him out and walk him within the glow of the porch light.

Day Five
Hunt Valley, Maryland

I wake up and help Bernie take Max out for the morning. Samantha is in the kitchen making eggs. The coffee is almost done. I think about the turn of events, it is strange that two men have to walk the property armed so the dog can do its business.

I wonder how many other people feel that we have lost our innocence once again. I think about the changes to Americans after September eleventh. The first thing I noticed was how families kept each other close. It wasn't good enough to know family was away from the sites of the crashes. You had to hear them or see them to confirm in your mind that the madness of the attack had not taken them from you. For those who had family members unaccounted for there was panic and hope. Yet, there was a gripping fear that enveloped families. What if they were trapped, or dead, or too hurt to make contact? This was followed by denial, maybe not to make the entire day go away, but to calm their mind that this can't really be happening. After all, this was just something on the television. Watching the planes fly into the buildings, the collapse, the immense cloud of dust over and over made it all seem unreal. Then the faces, blood covered and gray with a caking of dust. That day the survivors all looked the same walking from Ground Zero. We were one country, one family, we all looked alike. There were no black and white, no straight and gay, we were a country attacked and trying to make sense of the horror. And we cried. I don't know if we cried for all that were feared dead or for loss of the safety we felt on September tenth because from that day forward we would never be the same.

Today, like then, there are tears this morning. As the death toll rises families and the nation are feeling the loss. Today the stories are coming out from the survivors. People who watched the suicide bombers and their vehicles exploding speak with disbelief. One woman moments earlier had looked into the window of a bomber and he smiled at her. Others are telling their story from inside metro stations. Some saw the bombers walking with backpacks through the station. They looked like college students on their way to class. These were white all American looking men. Then the explosions and being knocked down by the blast. One woman looked up to watch the roof of the train station collapse on the station floor below. She crawled from under debris and made it out. One after another there are stories of survival and struggle, also of loss and devastation. Some watched the people around them disappear in a flash

The news flips between recovery scenes. We eat breakfast watching survivors being pulled from the rubble and bodies being wrapped and removed to temporary morgues. The state of emergency still extends through the day. Local and state police are asking people to stay off the roads. Only emergency personnel are allowed to be on public streets. Stores and businesses have been asked to remain closed today. In emergency situations, there have been hotlines set up if anyone is out of prescription medicine or anyone without baby food or milk. This is only for emergency purposes. I'm sure people will abuse this, but they have stated requests would be evaluated and to please be patient. Web sites are being set up with information for families trying to locate loved ones.

I'm not sure how I feel. Watching the scenes play out on television feels so unreal. I am numb and wonder if this is a nightmare. I thought my life was upside down before this happened and now I feel lost. Samantha is our voice of reason. Her training kicks in and she begins to motivate Bernie and me. While we cannot drive to Western Pennsylvania today, we can prepare and pack. This gives us another day to plan our route and what we might need on the road.

The noon news switches to local coverage. There are looters in the city. The news crews are on foot walking the city talking to people carrying computers and cell phones. They stop one man with a shopping cart loaded with new merchandise. He tells the reporter he has to feed his family. Bernie mumbles something about "rats thinking the rest of the world is as stupid as they are. No one eats a new laptop and using acts of terrorism as an excuse to be a thief is the lowest form of humanity."

In other cities, there are fires burning. Some have found it an excuse to commit acts of civil unrest. I don't understand this mentality. I feel trapped and want to get out of the house and go to a crime scene to help investigate. Bernie wants to go to the city and bash some heads together on the looters. Samantha has become quiet. I have caught her crying a few times. When I ask her why, she tells me these were senseless deaths. These are not criminals or people who have done something wrong in their lives. No one deserved what happened. The rioters and looters are frustrated and acting out through their aggression. This all isn't going to end until everyone finds some peace.

I wonder about the mentality of someone who could load a vehicle with explosives or strap them onto their bodies. It appears all of the explosions around the world have been suicide bombers. What does it take in the mind of an individual to wake up and prepare their bomb? With the coordination of the attacks they were each assigned a time. My guess they had visited their designated location many times so that the timing was correct. I'm sure some were a minute or two ahead or behind their time, but each has been attributed to one of the three waves of bombings. I wonder if for a few days or a week before if they traveled their route and thought "this is where I will die" or if they gave no thought of death, only of pleasing the person behind the plans? What level of brainwashing had to occur that their entire sense of being was wrapping up on one glorious and horrifying act?

For me this is about getting in the mind of the criminal. The actual bombers are the pawns. They do not realize they are meaningless and expendable. They have been programmed to think they are important. In reality, they are just a device to the master mind. They are the means of transporting the bomb, nothing more and nothing less. It is all about the death and destruction brought on by the act. We are all searching for a sense of purpose, to feel like our life matters. They feel through this singular act, they are committing themselves to a greater good. I need to find out who they are martyring themselves for.

My guess from the scenes playing out in Middle Eastern countries, these bombers are connected to an Arab militant group. To my knowledge no one has stepped forward yet to claim responsibility. If it is a radicalized group, they will usually brag about the degree of destruction they caused within twenty-four hours. The news is showing the streets in some countries filled with men dancing and waving guns. They are joyous at the death of Americans. The bombers have begun to be identified but, there seems to be no unifying features. Black, White, Asian, Middle Eastern—nothing connects them. They are all from differing backgrounds, many were considered upstanding citizens, and up until this act—none of them seems particularly remarkable or out of place in everyday life. College students, Blue collar workers, Business professionals are all among the list of known attackers. Who could organize internationally and on such a large scale?

I think back to a seminar I attended on the mind of a terrorist. It was given soon after September eleventh in an effort to help profile and target potential terrorists. The FBI agent who facilitated this portion turned the lights down in the lecture hall. He stepped down from the podium and began to walk around the room. He then asked us to close our eyes. He asked us to hold our hands out in front of us and feel the controls of an airline in our hands. Then to look ahead in the distance, see the twin towers of the World Trade Center. His voice was low and calm. "Make the subtle adjustments on the controls and fly the plane closer and closer to the buildings. In your eyes, see the buildings coming closer and closer until they take up the entire field of vision. Know that there are thousands of people in the building. Know that there is over one hundred people on the plane behind you and know that you are about to kill them all. Know that you are about to kill yourself. Keep the plane steady until all you can see in the windshield of the plane are the windows of the building. Now smile. As you watch the nose of the plane crash through the side of the building, feel complete and total joy that you and everyone in the building and in the plane are about to die. You are going to the promised land to rest."

The agent quickly flipped the lights on and yelled at us to open our eyes. I could feel my heart racing. He looked around the room as we all shook off the imagery he had put in our minds. He then continued in a loud voice jolting us even more. "You cannot understand the mind of a suicide bomber until you can smile and understand his joy the instant before he dies. This is not something he planned. It is something that was planned by someone at a safe distance. The joy isn't about the act. It is about the honor they will receive after death. There is a disconnect from themselves and reality. They anticipate the praise and honor they will receive from their leader." His voice became calm and low once more. "Of course, they have been programmed to not realize once they complete their mission—they will be dead. They will not be able to enjoy the praise of their leaders. Their reward is the afterlife."

The agent paused again and walked back to the podium. He shifted some papers and looked around the room. "Do you understand them? Can you profile them? Does this help you know what they look like? Can you find the terrorist in the room? A suicide bomber is a vulnerable mind who feels they must do something to please those in control. They are the polite kid in the back of the classroom. You would never expect them to be behind such destruction. They won't all be bearded Middle Eastern men. They might be disenfranchised youth from Europe, or a housewife from the United States. A terrorist can look just like you or me. The role of a terrorist is to fit in and not be noticed until they have taken action, and by then it is too late. Understand how they can smile and be happy the moment they died. That is what makes them dangerous. Not the color of their skin, their religion, or the part of the world where they were born."

We now have a new group that needs to be understood. The reports of All-American kids with backpacks. They are people who smiled and waved at people just before they murdered those around them. These are the exact people that agent was describing. They were happy and anticipating their praise after they killed innocent lives. They go willingly into their own death.

Samantha goes into the kitchen and I hear banging. Bernie and I both head to the kitchen. She is unpacking the cans we purchased at the grocery store and sorting what we got. She has already pulled a hand can opener from a drawer and a pot from under the stove.

 She looks up at us, "I thought it would be a good idea to see what we have and divide it. If for some reason we lose one vehicle we will at least have food in the other. I see Bernie has water delivery for his water cooler. We should take the water with us. I know it is only a few hours' drive, but I don't know what we will encounter on the road or where we will stay once we get there. I don't know if there are any hotels in the area. We might need to camp."

I haven't thought about what we will do once we arrive in Western Pennsylvania. For some reason, I figured we would talk to Billy and follow whatever leads we have from there. Of course after the events of yesterday, nothing is the same. Today we are following a federally mandated shelter in place. According to the news, the travel restriction will be lifted before the Thanksgiving holiday. State and federal highways are still asking people to stay away from bridge and road collapses. Perimeters are being set up around them to keep people away from the areas and limit access. Of course curiosity has already gotten the best of people and some have crept into restricted areas to take pictures.

We spend the afternoon pulling together supplies and packing the vehicles. We hope if the travel restrictions are lifted in the morning, we can head out by the back roads and make it to the mountains and Billy's cabin.

As the sun sets for another day, we lock the house and the three of us take Max for a walk. I am amazed by the quiet. The airports are closed and there are no planes in the air. The highways are closed and there are no sounds of traffic on the roadways. The night is silent. It is eerie and unsettling. We are accustomed to the constant drone of noise and the world lacks the background sound of civilization.

I risk a quick call to John to check on things at home. We say a quick hello to Alina and AJ and tell them how much we love them. Christina tells us not to worry before telling the kids to go get ready to take their baths. She knows John and I need to talk for a moment.

As soon as they are far enough from John so that he can talk he lets me know, "Okay, they have gone down the hallway. I figure we only have a few minutes before we show up on someone's radar. Right now work is being done to rewire the financial trunks that have been blown up. The President will not remove the State of Emergency order until most of the trunk has been repaired. They are hoping to have a temporary fix in place by early morning. You need to be packed and waiting to drive as soon as the order is lifted. Traffic is going to be bad. Even though people have only been cooped up for a day, there have been a lot of problems. People want to see the damage for themselves. They are also thinking about Thanksgiving. Imagine the biggest travel day of the year combined with the actions of this week. The roads will be hell."

"The fire I mentioned has been put out. That will help you. You still have to drive around it but the detour I gave you will work. It will just be really congested if you are not on the road soon after the roads are opened. Even then expect to be in pretty heavy traffic. I would say ninety-eight percent of the population has followed directions. The other two percent have looted and destroyed whatever they can get their hands on. The cities are bad. People are using this as an excuse to create chaos. If you can, stay out of cities. Small towns are holding their own. I think because people know each other. It's harder to do something stupid when people recognize you. Avoid the traffic cameras, they are going to be watching."

"Adam, be careful. Leave early and be smart. Let us know that you are okay and have made your destination. I will keep the phone with me if you need help, call and I will try to get someone to you. Just be prepared to bunker down for a while. Take care buddy."

We say goodbye. He has not made me feel comfortable about this trip. We have to make the drive. I need to find out what Billy knows and if he has any idea why Scott was murdered. We walk back inside and lock the door. The vehicles are packed with the exception of the blankets we need for tonight. We decide to be ready to go when the sun rises. I hope the travel restrictions are lifted early in the morning.

Day Six
Hunt Valley, Maryland.

I wake up and check the news. Maryland has announced the ban on travel is being lifted at eight o'clock this morning. Dread comes over me like a wave, today is Scotts funeral. I want to be there for him. I want to be there for Karen. Instead, I am hiding out and on the run. I hear noise in the kitchen and see Bernie looking in the refrigerator. As I stand up to walk into the kitchen, I see Samantha walking in to help him. Meanwhile, Max is standing at the door crying to go out. Bernie and I take Max out for his walk while Samantha makes breakfast. Pennsylvania has not announced the ban being lifted but we hope it has by the time we get there. The federal highways will also open by eight o'clock this morning with the exception of sections that have been damaged. Detours are being put into place but there are warnings to expect delays.

We eat breakfast quickly and Samantha washes the pan. Meanwhile, Bernie checks the water for the cats and tops off their automatic feeder. He cleaned their litter boxes last night. They will be fine for a couple days. I put Max's food in Bernie's car while he walks the dog one last time before we leave. I run back into the house to get our blankets and pillows to put them in the back of the Jeep. Bernie hands me Max's leash while he puts his pillows and blankets in his car and checks to make sure the house is locked up.

It is seven thirty and we decide to take the risk and drive out the driveway. The road is empty and we make the left onto Shawan Road. We drive for five miles without seeing another car. We see our first car as we stop at the light at Reisterstown Road. I make the left and travel down Main Street. No one is stirring. This is my third time driving through downtown Reisterstown. Normally it is bustling with activity. This morning we do not see anyone.

As we drive, I see a phenomenon that was noticed after September eleventh—an American Flag is flying in front of almost every house. There was a need back then—and it appears once more—for us all to identify as Americans. Someone attacked our country and it seems when that happens the need to fly our flag and remind the world we are a proud country. Seeing home after home with a flag flying proudly in the morning light makes me feel good. President Elect Hall had said "United we stand so that none shall divide us." He was so right and it is visible this morning. It shakes me after our talks of Rome and the Christ child. Was this the cult of the Emperor? Were we all caught up in the fervor? As we travel forwards, I feel like the three of us are Mary's running to France.

We have mapped out a route taking us through the water shed and entering I-70 north of the collapsed bridge. What we hadn't anticipated was activity around the water itself. I look at the time on the dashboard. It is eight seventeen. We can legally be on the road but the bridge ahead has been blocked by police. I'm not sure if we should turn around and try another way or pull up to the officers. I decide the least suspicious is to pull up to the road block.

An officer gets out of his car and walks toward the Jeep, I put the window down and wait for him. He comes to my window, "Hi, Sir. It will be a few minutes if you want to wait. The EPA does routine water tests and they didn't get out this week because of the restrictions. As soon as they finish their sampling we will reopen the bridge."

He walks back to Bernie and tells him the same thing. Max is barking hysterically so the cop doesn't linger long at his window. We watch as two men drop something over the side of the bridge and then bring it up, take a vial from the device, write on the vial and put it in a cooler. They alternate back and forth across the bridge. It makes me glad we were drinking and cooking with bottled water and mildly concerned that we showered in this water.

Samantha taps me on the leg and I look down. She is pointing to the side. I look over and see a team of men in a boat and it appears they are doing the same thing. "Is this routine? It looks to me as if they are trying to find the source of contamination. We forget how at risk our water supply is until something happens. How hard would it have been for someone to walk along the shoreline and throw something in? Or to have tossed something while driving along the bridge? Today we are more aware of things. How aware were we last week?"

The water coming from the reservoirs are constantly tested, or at least they are supposed to be. Over the summer, an entire town got sick because an algae bloom released a toxin into the cities intake valve. If a toxin can get through, then a poison could also. It all depends on what the routine tests look for, and what is over looked. It reminds me of the fragility of society. In reality, we survive because most never dream of crossing the line. When one does, we step back in horror at the actions they committed.

The men are walking back to their vehicle and the officer moves his car. I wave thank you as we pass the officer thinking "note to self— don't drink the water."

Eldersburg is the first town we drive through after the travel ban is lifted. I see the parking lot of a fast food restaurant packed. I guess being cooped up in the house and having to deal with home cooking was too much for people. They need their fast food breakfast as soon as the road is open. Resiliency and the ability to bounce back quickly is a trait of Americans, then again so is our dependence on high fat, high salt, high sugar, high calorie, low nutrient foods.

I see a gas station that is open and I signal to pull in. I have enough gas to get to Western Pennsylvania, but I want to top off the tank. Interstate commerce will be affected for a while. Gasoline tankers have problems and in some cases can't take secondary roads. Low overhead roads and bridge weights restrict tall heavy vehicles. Interstates were designed with higher over passes and heavy weight bearing structures so that we can transport goods on them. Gasoline and food may be a problem in the coming weeks. Nothing is being said on the news but once stores begin to open the store has approximately three days' supply to restock. If a truck can't get through the store will run out of some products. Also, depending on the repairs to the financial trunk lines some transactions might not go through this morning. I am well versed on this from ice storms back in Virginia. A bad storm hit a few years back and in two days, there was no gas or food to be found. We were saved back then by the kindness of others and a quick thaw. This situation doesn't seem to have as clear of a resolution.

The gas station does not have any lines and I am glad. Bernie pulls into the pump behind us. I tell him to top off. He points at the paper sign taped on the front of the pumps "cash only." I nod and tell him I will walk in and pay for both pumps and ask him to stay with the cars and be on look out. I still don't trust cameras and most stations have cameras focused on their pumps.

The kid behind the counter yells to me as I walk in the door. "If you are getting gas you have to pay cash. For some reason the computer can't connect to the credit card company this morning. We hope to get it fixed." I tell him that's fine I have cash for both pumps. He smiles and takes the money. I signal to Bernie and he starts the pump on his car and then walks up to the Jeep and starts that pump.

I walk around the convenience store. I pick up a couple bottles of ice tea and see a sale on energy bars. I grab the entire box and walk back to the register. Both pumps have stopped and Bernie waves to me to finish paying. The kid behind the counter looks at the box of energy bars, "You really must like these. They aren't a big seller. Most people like chips. We got chips on sale too if you want them." I tell him we like the energy bars. He doesn't need to know that I buy them all the time and this is a great price. With the possibility of food shortages, these are high calorie, high protein meals. They will give you the illusion of food in your stomach and a few of them can sustain you for an entire day—it might not be a great solution, but it is fuel. With a four hour drive still ahead of us, these seem like a sound lunch and saves our cash reserves.

Outside Bernie and I discuss which option we should take. We can make the turn out of the gas station and go to I-70 or we can stay on this road and drive through the small towns. Both will get us to Frederick,

Maryland. The traffic in small towns is light so far. I do not know what the traffic looks like on the interstate. I also don't know what the police presence will be like on them. The farther we stay from police the better we might be. I don't need my tag run. That might trigger the identification of our location. I still doubt the chaos will shake the CIA from our trail, if anything they have more resources to track us now. We are also a threat to national security. I want to get to Billy without being detected. We decide to stay on the back roads.

Traffic builds as we get closer to Frederick, but it is still moving. As we enter town, traffic becomes start and stop. I was afraid this would happen and we work our way to the exit for I-70. It looks packed with traffic. An electronic sign flashes to tune the radio to the state highways channel. I tune to get the information.

> "...all traffic will have to exit I-68 prior to the Sideling Hill road cut. Traffic is being diverted onto I-40. Current restrictions to non-commercial vehicles in the Sideling Hill detour is being limited so that commercial traffic that has been held can continue on. Expect delays. Traffic heading west and northwest should expect delays from Town Hill to the Breezewood Bypass. Vehicular traffic is forbidden within the town of Breezewood. Travelers heading west on the Pennsylvania Turnpike expect delays. The exit at Breezewood is closed until further notice. The Pennsylvania Turnpike can be reached by following the Lincoln Highway, route thirty to Bedford..."

I change the channel back to a country station. Our route is taking us straight into the congested area. There is not much we can do so we drive on. Ahead, I watch people jockeying for position. They keep changing lanes further delaying the cars behind the lane jockeys as people have to slam on brakes to let them in. Now and then a car speeds by us on the shoulder. I always love the special people who feel they are too good or too important to sit in line with the rest of us. As we reach each entrance traffic slows to let cars onto the already packed road.

I wonder where everyone is going. It is the day before Thanksgiving and I don't know if they are driving to get away or to see damage. It is hard to tell. Some vehicles, like ours, appear to be packed. Maybe people are getting away from the chaos in the cities to cabins in the mountains or traveling to help family who got caught in this mess. The need to get away might be safer than sitting in your home as looters smash the windows out of local stores to pillage.

As I drive I wish I could turn on my GPS. Normally, I would rely on it to give me a route around a backup. I try to listen to the music and stay calm instead. Once clear of the town of Frederick the speed picks up for a few miles. I see the signs for Washington Monument State Park/Gathland. It seems an eternity since we spent the night there.

As we crest South Mountain, I look out across the valley. We are driving down the west side of the Appalachian Mountains. Ahead I see the Blue Ridge. From there we need to drive into the Allegheny Mountains. The highway is a constant ribbon of cars. Off in the distance I see the distinct cut in the mountain that is called Sideling Hill. The sunlight is hitting the bands of rock that make up the syncline that was exposed when the rock was blasted away so that the road passes between the mountains rather than over it.

I point out the rock pattern to Samantha. "Do you see how the rock layers are a smooth downward curve? Try to imagine if that was the downward curve how high the upward curve went. Geology has always fascinated me. The fold in that rock tells a story. It's one that can't be denied about the history of the earth. First you have to consider that rock is formed by layers of dirt, sand, or volcanic material laid down over the millennia. As the dirt and sand is compressed over thousands of years, it fuses and creates rock. One of the veins of rock in that formation holds marine fossils. So we know at that point this area was under water. There are clams and small sea creatures forever molded in the fossiliferous shale so we know it was a shallow portion of a sea. On top of that is a fine layer of sandstone. So the ocean receded and became a beach. After thousands of years something happened. This area is known as the Ridge and Valley region. The mountain chains are not volcanic, so there was force put on the rock. So much force in fact that the ground was thrust upward forming the mountain chains we have today. But the story doesn't end there because we see the roll of the rock was declining, known as a syncline. Geologists have modeled what these mountains looked like prior to erosion by wind and water. Using the width of each band of rock they got a picture of a mountain taller than the Rocky Mountains. Most of these rocks are made of softer rock material and they eroded away so that today's mountains were the valleys a million years ago."

The explanation helps pass time in the back up and Samantha listens with interest. She has remained quiet. I know she is thinking about something. She finally speaks, "You know how I try to see the other side of a story? I was just thinking about the fossils that were found when we initially blasted the rock to make the road cut. What if we didn't curve the road and cut it twenty feet in another direction? There were large rocks taken off the wall during the bombing. Wouldn't it be amazing if those rocks reveal a dinosaur skeleton imbedded in the rock? The world around us changed, but maybe it was meant to be. Maybe there was something better that the bombing exposed. Many of the world's greatest discoveries happened by accident. I am hoping they can happen by an act of terrorism also. While you are thinking of what we need to do today, my mind works on tomorrow. There are so many people who will need to heal. Not just those who lost a family member in the bombings, but also people who have been traumatized by the images on the television. I need to find the good so that I can pull people away from the horror they faced. I have to find the positive to convince people to continue on in life. The stages of grieving are necessary but some never pass into acceptance and recovery. They linger and it takes someone to make them see the sun still rises and brings a new day."

I glance over and she is looking out the window. "I am thinking about Karen also. I'm worried about her. She has to deal with the murder of her husband and she was blaming herself for the infertility. She is taking blame for their marriage being on the brink of collapse. And then, just like that, he was murdered. If we can bring that person to justice, it will give her some closure and she can hopefully begin to build a new life. Yet, I wonder about how the bombings will affect her. She is internalizing Scotts murder and may begin to internalize the bombings as well. She could be internalizing everything that has happened. I hope because they cannot reach me her family has reached out to another professional and she is getting help."

There is little we can do for her until we talk to Billy Gill. I hope he has some answers for us. I glance at the time on the dash. We have been on the road for four hours already and we are not to the halfway point of the trip yet.

I feel Samantha's hand on my thigh, "Remember I'm here for you also. When the time comes and you need to talk to someone—you have Scott, your job, the attack and being framed for the murder, it's a lot Adam."

I nod and drive on. I'm not even sure how to verbalize the thoughts in my head. For so many years my life has been about my job and protecting the country, and now, when the country needs me to help—it has turned its back on me. The FBI was my home and mistress. I lived my job and slept in my office. At a time that I need the FBI, it is distancing itself from me. Elizabeth died and my job was my life. Now, Elizabeth's and Scotts deaths feel like they are rolling into one tragic series of events. It has become bigger than me and more than I can handle. The only thing that kept me sane and gave me the lifeline to hold onto after Elizabeth has recoiled from me. I feel like I am a split second from tumbling over a cliff.

I take a deep breath and remind myself that I have to hold it together. Right now I am guilty of a murder I didn't commit. In the midst of this chaos, I have to control my thoughts and make it through another day. The only way I can prove my innocence is to prove the government I trusted has betrayed me.

My phone rings and I see Bernie's number. Samantha answers it. She responds "me too" and hangs up. "We have to make a bathroom stop soon. We are getting close to Hagerstown. Bernie suggests we head for the outlet mall. I hope they are open. It is also lunch time. I think we should try to stop, use the restrooms and get some food before we continue on. I am hoping they have one of those local attraction magazines with a local highway map on it. At the pace we are going, we will need to drive into the state game region and look for a dirt driveway in the dark. That is not something I want to do after the sun goes down."

We inch our way toward Hagerstown and eventually get off the exit ramp. Traffic is heavy. I think the people who were not on the highway must have come to the outlet mall. Most stores have signs about cash only so we do not see many people walking with shopping bags. People are using the time to window shop and reassure themselves that the world has continued to spin on. I see parents with children walking in groups. This is a return to something normal. I understand why they are all here.

The food court is packed and we work our way around the crowd to the rest rooms. We can't find a table so we get sandwiches to go and walk outside. The sun is shining and the temperature has gotten warmer than the last few days. It is pleasant to be outside. Samantha finds a bench and we all sit to eat lunch. Bernie points out the number of American Flag tee shirts and sweaters. Like the houses people are sending a message that we are Americans.

Somewhere in the parking lot a car backfires. People scream and grab their children while ducking behind the corner of buildings or behind bushes. Someone says, "I think it was a truck backfire". People give an uneasy laugh and come out of hiding. The fear is still on the surface. The mall police are trying to move a man who is preaching in front of a store. He is screaming about the end of times. I think to myself this guy is a couple days late. Two men walk by in Marine uniforms. They have brochures about the Marines. These are the guys banking on fear. After September eleventh, there was a rush on the military, police and fire. People found an outlet for their anger by joining up and going to protect the people. Some regretted their decision when months later they were sent to Iraq and Afghanistan. Mothers protested that this was not what their sons and daughters signed up for. I think they forgot the part about signing up to protect people. They were thinking it sounded good at the time.

Samantha takes a couple free travel magazines at the information booth and is looking through them. On the back of one she finds a map that is helpful. She keeps searching until she finds a brochure for a cavern that complements her map needs.

I see her flipping back and forth between the two until she looks up and smiles at me. "Move in close guys. I have a route. If we leave here and drive through town to Interstate 81 it will take us to the Lincoln Highway, route 30. We need to take 30 west. Before we get to Breezewood traffic will probably be a nightmare since the town is blocked off but I found a detour that is on 30 way before Breezewood. We can take route 915 to route 26 near Riddlesburg. Then we have to take route 36 to Loysburg. At Loysburg, we need to find route 869 and take that over to highway 99/220 toward Altoona. Before we get to Tyrone we need to find the exit for Tipton. That is State Road 4023. It will take us directly into State Gaming Land 159. Somewhere on the right side of the road, we should see the dirt road that leads to Billy's cabin. He said it was near an upland lake. There is a body of water right here on the map. My guess is that the road is somewhere in these trees. Once we get on the dirt road, we have to follow the directions Billy gave Bernie. I suggest he leads from that point or Bernie, you can give them to me and I will give the directions to Adam as he drives."

Bernie and I both nod and he suggests Samantha take over the directions. She has become our navigator. I look around and no one is close to us. No one seems to be giving us any attention. I hope we are still alone and not being followed. I have had the feeling of eyes on us, but this could be due to everyone watching everyone else. I think in the back of people's minds there is a suicide bomber out there ready to break the safety and security we feel today.

We stop by the restroom again and walk to the car. I look up and realize I haven't noticed planes in the air. The travel ban lifting did not extend to airlines and trains. I guess most forms of mass transit are not running today. This area relies heavily on their personal vehicles and rarely on mass transit. Things in the downtown areas and inner cities will have more pedestrian traffic today unless city buses are running. The normal daily chaos will be compounded downtown by the civil unrest that has been sweeping the metropolitan areas since yesterday. The biggest impact will be to people who had planned to fly for Thanksgiving. The ban will change many family plans. In turn, it will put a strain on the grocery stores.

People who would not be cooking for Thanksgiving because of travel plans might find themselves obligated to produce a meal. That compounded with people being cooped inside for a couple days might cause the run on the stores to be profound. Rather than the 2-3 day supply of food, my guess is that store shelves and storage rooms will be empty by tonight. Most stores will be closed tomorrow for the holiday. Friday will be the day panic begins to set in. If commerce can't find a way to get the resupply into the stores by Friday morning panic could lead to civil unrest by the weekend. People are herd animals, whether they like to admit it or not, they get spooked and do things that put themselves and others at risk in a vague attempt to protect themselves.

As we drive out of the outlet mall, I see a gas station and pull in. I have used a quarter of a tank sitting in traffic. Bernie pulls into the pump behind me and Samantha jumps out with money for both vehicles. She also yells that she's going to get more drinks for the road. Once again, I wave to her to go to the cashier and get our change. She comes out with a drink for each of us and bags of candy for later. She hands two sugar free bags of candy to Bernie and tells him these are for later, when he needs to pick his spirits up.

I follow the signs to interstate 81 and head north. This is a north/south interstate that in this area cuts through some rural areas. The traffic is not congested and we are able to drive at highway speeds. The cars we see are also loaded with gear. This confirms my theory that families are leaving their urban homes and heading to rural safe houses or family away from the cities.

I think about my house. John has the animals and the kids. There is no reason for anyone to be around my house or property. I wonder if it will be ransacked when we get home. How do I prove it was someone looking for a copper scroll and not someone looting? I remind myself I have full liability and replacement on everything in the house. If we come home to a ransacked mess, I am going to call the insurance company and move into a hotel until they have it cleaned up, repaired and replaced what is needed. As long as my family remains safe and I do not go to jail for a murder—everything will be fine.

I see a sign for the Historic Lincoln Highway. I have driven on parts of the Lincoln Highway in the past. It is an interesting highway completed and dedicated in 1913. The official road designation is interstate US 30. It was the first transcontinental highway in the country. It begins in New Jersey and ends in California. It parallels both Interstate 70 and Interstate 40. They are the small, medium, and large of the transcontinental highways. Interstate 30 started it all and was designed to carry car traffic. It was the original path of the wagon trains and became the Model T highway. The hills and valleys of the Lincoln Highway were taxing on trucks filled with goods so interstate 40 was built to address interstate commerce. Trucks got bigger and the birth of the interstate commerce system was merged with the interstate highway system and the defense highway system. This created the need for interstate 70. According to the map that Samantha picked up, we stay on the Lincoln Highway for a while. I would have loved to take it past Everett.

Ironically, one of the maps she found with the roads we need to travel, is the map to the Flight 93 Memorial in Shanksville, Pennsylvania. The entrance to the National Park that now encompasses the crash site is located off of the Lincoln Highway. September 11, 2001 was the day that America lost its innocence. Being near the crash site of one of the 9/11 planes feels like déjà vu. Terrorism has come full circle and we spent yesterday looking at senseless destruction and murder. I'm sure those in New York City and near the Pentagon feel the same way. Those three sites have sat for years as America's home of terrorism. For many, terrorism was an east coast thing. People on the west coast watched in horror at what happened, but they were removed from it. They didn't detour around the crater of the World Trade Center for a couple years as the ruins were removed and the monument built. This week terrorism came home to the entire country, every state was touched in some way.

In Shanksville, the owner of the property opened the site quickly to people wanting to see for themselves. Then a group of people raised money and purchased the land to turn it into a park. It was donated to the National Park Service. Plans were drawn up and construction started. I have been to Shanksville and visited the park a couple times. Flight 93 is quiet. At Ground Zero, the hustle and bustle of the city still rages around you. The fountain helps drown out the noise and life of the city, but it isn't the silence of Flight 93. It is an open area of parkland with a solemn wall. On each panel of the wall there is a name of a passenger. One panel lists a mother and her unborn child. The monument is noticeably stark and plain. The area where the plane crashed is marked, nothing elaborate. For many years the site of the crash was marked with a bale of straw and an American flag. When you visit you are reminded this is a place where people died. The ground where the plane crashed is protected. The only people allowed to walk in the crash area are grounds crews with the park service and with advanced notice and permission, the families of the people who died there. Remains were found but complete bodies were not found for some. This is foremost a gravesite. To the family members, this is the place their loved ones died, and where part of them still remains.

I respect the ideals behind the Flight 93 Memorial. It wasn't made into a tourist location. People come to see the site with their own eyes, but walk away feeling that they have just paid their last respects. Not visiting today is something I will regret, but it is too dangerous for us to stop.

The road stretches in front of us. Once we crest one of the rolling hills we see the road ahead running down and back up the next. I think about the challenge these must have been for the low powered engines of the early automobiles. I also understand why the road cuts and detours around mountains made the later interstates favorable to commerce. I feel as if I am driving a car on a roller coaster.

The scenery out the window is small town and rural farms of America. During the early days towns sprung up to cater to the traveler. Someone who got on this highway was driving a distance and that was an exciting adventure. There were restaurants, amusement sites, picnic areas, motels and overnight travel parks. Depending on what you could afford there were themed hotels or a wooded lot to park your car and sleep inside it for the night. I see many of these places still standing. Some falling apart along the road, while others still grasp at travelers trying to stay alive one more year.

I begin to see signs for Breezewood. I have been through this location before. I don't want to call it a town because I am not sure if anyone actually lives within the limits of the town, or whether they live on the outskirts. If you have ever traveled Interstates 30, 70 or the Pennsylvania Turnpike, you have passed through Breezewood. It is a truck stop, gas station, fast food, bathroom break or overnight stay on your way to where you are going. This is the intersection of the three roads, nothing more.

Breezewood and places like it are American icons. Our grandparents stopped at these places to use the restroom and grab a drink. Our parents stopped to let us kids out of the car for a few minutes. Moms always yelling to the kids to use the toilet before getting back in the car. They stop because it is a tradition. There are interstate rest stops now with toilets and fast food places, but they aren't destinations like the original tourist traps on the highway.

I'm sure this location was bombed because of this junction of roads. The bombing was a message of control. Meanwhile, many people have sentimental value connected to this place. It has become a meeting place for travelers. Many times I have heard, "I will meet you at Breezewood and we can get a cup of coffee." No one asks where it is, how to get there or whether it is in their travels. It is a destination on the highway.

I hear Samantha say, "Oh Adam, I just saw a sign. We need to make a left in a mile." As we approach, I see where someone has stacked a pile of rocks. The stack is about fifteen feet high and at the top is a flag pole holding the American Flag. I wonder if someone put it there as a land mark years ago or if this is something that was erected in the last day to make a statement?

We are now starting to drive up through the mountains. The road takes us through the valley and through some natural road cuts. In other places the road snakes through hairpin turns and switchbacks. At times the road ahead is ten or twelve feet above our heads on the mountainside above. At each of the hairpin turns there is a runaway truck cut off in case trucks lose their brakes coming downhill. Through the trees we see houses back in the wood. Smoke from their chimneys drift through the hollows. It is like a place caught in history. If it weren't for a modern home here or there, you would think this could have been any time from 1800s to present day. In these woods, you lose a sense of when or where you are.

I slow down when I see a field full of deer. They are grazing alongside some cows. It is quiet and peaceful here. I almost feel guilty leaving the fear and panic in the urban areas. I hear Max barking in Bernie's car and the deer look up. I decide before we cause them to panic and run, I should drive on.

The sign along the road said that Riddlesburg is three miles ahead. We see the sign for route 26 and the sign for Loysburg. We are driving through the valley. The mountains tower above us. We are back to driving through more road cuts and switchbacks. My ears pop as we drive up and down the mountains. Samantha offers a piece of gum. She chews gum when we fly to help with her ears popping. I take a piece and begin to chew it.

Soon we are on route 869 and follow that to highway 99/220. On the left we can see windmills lining the top of the mountains. They are amazing. The windmills are the primary power source for the small communities in the mountains. We see solar panels on the overhead signs along the highway. This area is a silent enclave of green technology. This is a divided highway and I expected to see heavy traffic but very few people are on the road. People here seem to be staying at home. Small towns, self-sufficient and living on their own grid.

I have worked a case in this area before and remembered this is an interesting group of people with tight knit families. Tucked in and around the mountains are machinists and engineers. The military has mountain training areas and most towns have at least one business with a defense contract. The big names in the defense industry have large offices and manufacturing in the area. There is also a large facility that is building the turbines and blades for the windmills. To the average person driving through, this looks like a rural farming community. Instead, the silent wheels of the machines turn and produce some of our most advanced technologies.

The signs for Altoona exits begin to appear. Traffic continues to move smoothly. Most people driving through this area would think the people in the homes tucked in the mountains were unintelligent rednecks. Instead, I would put my money on these people being the ones who are smart enough to hunker down and survive just about anything. Coming here was a good choice for us. I don't know if Billy chose this area for that reason also—I hope to find out soon. The sun is beginning to fall behind the Western rim of the Alleghenies. Soon it will be dark and we have not quite reached our destination. I try to speed up a little so that we don't get caught in the woods looking for an unmarked dirt road.

As I look ahead, it appears that we are driving straight into the side of a mountain. Then the road turns and we follow the ribbon of blacktop as it winds through sheer cut rock walls cut to ease the grade for traffic.

North of Altoona we see the sign for the Tipton exit, State Road 4023. The road once again begins to weave up a mountain. This is state gaming land. People have cabins and camps in these mountains for hunting. It appears that we are heading for Billy Gill's hunting camp.

We are on the east side of the mountain in the woods and dark shadows are creeping onto the road. The headlights automatically come on at dusk. My Jeep has sensed nightfall and turned the lights on. There are a couple dirt roads. Most have wire across the road with no trespassing and no hunting signs. We are looking for a dirt road on the right. Billy told us to look for a bear totem pole along the road. His driveway is next to the bear. I am driving slowly. I know we are near a lake. Billy mentioned the lake when Bernie spoke to him.

Samantha spots the bear. It is one of the totems that are cut with a chain saw. It was carved from a large tree and has incredible detail. I stop and get out unhooking the wire that blocks the driveway from the road. The wire is about two inches in diameter and heavy. A lock is looped through a metal eye in a wooden post. It appears to be locked but on inspection it is just looped through the wire and eye hook. I get back in the Jeep and pull into the driveway far enough for Bernie to get inside the wire. He gets out with me and we drag the wire back across the driveway and put the lock back through the eye hook.

It is dark as we drive down the dirt road. It is just a path through the woods. The trees hug the side forming a natural guard rail. The Jeep bounces as we drive across a washed out portion. On the side of the trees we pass no trespassing signs. I look back in the mirror to see how Bernie's car is handling the ruts in the road. He is driving slowly and picking his way around. My Jeep is high enough to take the road in stride but I know it has to be tough on him.

I expect to break into a clearing. Instead, I drive up to a metal gate. Behind that I see stacks of metal storage containers. I stop the Jeep. I am not sure what to do now. A voice from somewhere inside the compound asks me to state my business. I open the door and get out with my hands in the air, "I am looking for Billy Gill. I was told I could find him here."

The voice asks again, "State your business with him. I have a gun pointed at you. You need to start talking."

We are in the woods somewhere north of Altoona in a state hunting area. Bernie is parked behind me. There is no way for us to back out of this road and there is no place to turn around. I have no doubt the person inside the fence has a gun pointed at me. "My name is Adam Clay. Billy spoke with my associate Bernie Moll two days ago. He is in the car behind me. My wife is in my car with me. We do not mean any harm. I just need to speak with Billy Gill."

I hear leaves crunching as someone walks toward us. Out of the darkness I see a figure. He is dressed in black. He walks to the gate and I hear him pulling a chain. Something clicks and I assume it is a lock. He opens the gate wide enough for us to drive in. He walks in front of my jeep. In the headlights, I see his rifle slung over his back.

He indicates for me to stop and park and points at Bernie and indicates for him to park next to me. He then walks back to the gate and I hear it lock. We are now locked inside the compound. Samantha and I open our doors and get out. Max is barking in the car. Billy yells to Bernie to get out and shut the dog up. Bernie complies and pulls Max by the leash out of the car.

The first thing Max does is run to a tree and start to pee. This gives me an opportunity to look at Billy Gill. He has long graying hair that hangs down his back in waves. He looks in his early fifties. He has a trim figure and looks athletic. I see a handgun strapped to his hip where a sword might be attached. He is prepared and I have no doubt if he doesn't trust us he will shoot us.

He walks across the grass to Bernie and Max. I am surprised when he reaches his hand to Max. Max smells his hand and steps toward him. Billy starts to pet the dog. "I can tell a lot about a man by his dog. My little girls, Sophie and Dee Dee, stay in my pod. I will let you keep him in the guest pod. Just make sure he doesn't hurt Sophie and Dee Dee. I will shoot him." Bernie assures him Max lives with two cats and gets along well with other animals. Billy nods and says "Good. Welcome."

He turns and walks toward the metal containers. Samantha is looking around "Are these shipping containers? How did you get them back here in the woods?"

He walks in through an opening between containers. The storage containers look like a giant building blocks. They are stacked two high. We walk into a center compound. The bottom row is two containers long on all four sides. The second story consists of one in the center and the back with three on each side. There is a front and back exit. The center has a small well surrounded by the remains of a vegetable garden and an herb garden. There are doors cut into the sides of the containers.

Billy walks toward a door on the side. "Have you eaten dinner?" I tell him no, but we have supplies in our vehicles. He nods and turns around. "You should probably get any food and beverages out of there before it gets too late. I have had a bear that has dropped down into the compound before and I don't want to invite them in again. But first, let me tell you where you can put your stuff and sleep tonight."

He opens a door and turns on a light. "There are bunks in here and you can store your stuff under the bottom bunks. Once you put your stuff in here come on over to the green box. That is my living space. I'm going to start some dinner. I didn't know when or if you were coming so give me a few minutes."

We go to the vehicles and carry the bedding inside. It takes us three trips to get everything in the storage container. I look around. The floor has been carpeted. The bunks are custom built. At the end of the container is a desk and entertainment system with a flat screen television. The two storage containers have been locked together. I turn on the light and walk through the inside of the containers. There is a living room set up and at the end is a bathroom with a shower. There is a stairway going up to the upper level storage containers. The stairs have been designed as storage. Inside are towels, pillows and blankets. Upstairs the inside walls are covered with shelving. One rack has medical supplies. Inside a refrigerator, I see vials of medicines, mostly antibiotics. The next rack contains heirloom vegetable seeds. In the next refrigerator, I find more seeds. Bernie sticks his head up the stairs, "We should probably get across the compound before he comes looking for us. I don't know if he wants us poking around up here."

He's correct and I go back downstairs. We leave Max in the bunk room and go to the green container directly across the compound. Billy is in a kitchen. He is cooking a pot of spaghetti noodles, "I hope you guys like spaghetti. I wasn't sure what to cook that was fast and filling. This came to mind."

A table is set with four places and we go to the table as Billy walks behind us with a big bowl of spaghetti and sauce, "Have a seat we have a lot to talk about."

We sit down and he passes the bowl around. We help ourselves and start to eat. Billy has gotten up to grab four beers. "These okay for everyone?" He opens the first beer and gives it to Samantha "ladies first."

I raise my beer "To our host. Thank you for agreeing to meet with us and allow us to stay here tonight. You have quite an impressive compound. I take it these are your preps? I took the liberty of checking out the second floor over the bunk room. You have a good supply of medical supplies and quite a seed vault."

Billy looks as if he has stepped out of the crusades. I could easily see him dressed in chainmail with a sword in his hand. I look into his eyes and they are serious and penetrating. His movements and the way he carries himself speaks Special Forces and his hair yells rebelling after getting out. I didn't mention the gun slits that I saw on the outer wall. My guess the entire perimeter can be guarded from the second floor. I am surprised that he is here alone. It would take a minimum of four or more, maybe up to eight people on guard duty to protect the compound.

Billy sits back and looks at us, "Thank you. And yes, these are my preps. If you stick around I will show you the rest. Now, can we address the elephant in the room? Why are you here? What do you know about Scott?"

I put my beer down and look at Bernie and Samantha and then at Billy. "I assume you know that Scott was murdered and found lying on the Palace Green in Williamsburg." He nods yes. "I have been accused of his murder. I didn't kill him. I want you to know that I did not shoot him."

Billy nods again, "I know. I never suspected you as his killer, but do you know why he was killed?"

I shake my head, "No. I have been told that he found a copper tube in the roots of a fallen tree that was about three hundred and fifty years old. If it had been there all that time that might make the tube part of the fabled map to the Masonic Treasure. I have also been told that an individual connected to the Farm might want whatever is inside that copper tube. More than one individual has told me that the CIA killed him and they are framing me."

Billy is listening intently. "I cannot confirm the CIA connection. That is a new twist to me. I can confirm the existence of the copper tube. Now besides being accused of his murder, tell me your connection to Scott. I have heard your name before and I know who you are. I know your background, but I want to hear it from you. Give me details so that I can confirm you are who you say you are. Then tell me why I should believe you? Convince me why I need to put my life on the line."

Our eyes lock. He doesn't play around. He has built a fortified shelter in the woods. My guess he knew we were coming the moment we stopped on the road. He is smart and prepared to deal with whatever comes his way. I appreciate his hospitality and his openness to work with us. I also understand his caution and concern. If I say the wrong thing, the three of us might find ourselves out on the road tonight possibly stripped of our supplies. "Throughout college Scott and I talked about searching for the Masonic Treasure. It was a challenge and something exciting. We saw ourselves as modern day explorers. For a while Scott's family lived near Oak Island. It is an area fabled to be a potential treasure site. One summer he and I went to the island for two weeks. We poked around and hoped we didn't get caught. Everything we read about the island and the exploration of the well made us believe it held some secret. We worked on finding out who we knew who were Masons and found someone to sponsor us. We thought if we joined the craft they would tell us the secrets. He and I worked like hell to get to the top degree. At each level of initiate, we thought they would tell us something we needed to know. We both made it to the top and know no more about whether there was an actual treasure, and if it is the Arc of the Covenant or the Holy Grail, than we did at nineteen."

This is not something I have ever told Samantha. It was a boyhood dream that carried into adulthood. After I met her it became a thing of the past. My love of history and my need to uncover the secrets of the country's history has always been connected to finding the lost treasure. Samantha's face shows shock and interest. I'm sure tonight I will have to answer some questions about this. Bernie looks interested also. Maybe the thought of treasure hunting and exploring exists in us all. "Our senior year in college we got the opportunity to be laborers on an Oak Island dig. It wasn't working in the well. By then it had already refilled with water. This expedition was looking for the hidden channels around the island. We found a couple. This was definitely a well-planned spot. Of course the well wasn't a natural occurrence, but neither were these water inlet tunnels. Considering they were constructed prior to the eighteen hundreds there was some serious thought and engineering put into them. The well is estimated to go down a couple hundred feet. No one ever got to the bottom. As they were digging down into the well, every ten feet or so, the excavation team hit wooden timbers. These timbers were dated back before the area was known to be inhabited. Then one day they hit wood again. They stopped for the night. By morning the well was filled with water. They tried pumping it out but the water kept coming in from somewhere. Later along the shoreline an intake tunnel was found. They would have had to pump the Atlantic Ocean dry in order to get to the bottom of the well."

"The summer before we were hired as laborers, an attempt was made to block off that intake tunnel and pump the well. The dam around the tunnel held but water kept flooding in. That summer we discovered the ground under the island is riddled with tunnels leading out to the water. They were dug down and layers of rocks put in so that they remained ready and available to run water into the bottom of the well. After a back breaking summer, we came home with nothing more than new found muscles. We looked great. I had a great tan and six pack abs. What I really wanted was to see what was hidden at the bottom of this very well planned puzzle. Now I think unless they have it sealed in something very water tight, whatever was there has long ago become victim to the water. Once the well flooded it destroyed what had been kept buried for so long."

"That was when Scott and I turned to something closer to my home. The Williamsburg treasure site. It was always believed that there were copper scrolls buried in Williamsburg. These scrolls did not hold the treasure itself but an explanation of the treasure and directions to the treasure. Whoever found these scrolls had the secrets which were brought over here to keep them safe."

Billy has been sitting here quietly absorbing what I have told him. He is stroking his beard and seems lost in thought. "This is similar to what Scott told me. He and I connected because I am a scholar of Nathaniel Bacon. Not for the Masonic Treasure, but I would like to find truth in Shakespeare. I believe he was a hack who never wrote the stories attributed to him. To me the real treasure are the words of Bacon and proof that he was the bard. Scott and I had mutual ground and interests, so we teamed up. One of our thoughts was that when Jamestown was abandoned some or all of the scrolls were left behind. So many had died from the initial group of colonists and from both the first and second resupply that something could have been lost. Scott was digging in an area that was outside the fort. Everyone else had always assumed if something was buried it would be within the fort. It didn't make sense to us. There were too many eyes and if the men running from the crown were Templar's they still had secrets to keep. Scott went to an area that was said to be good hunting area for the Jamestown colonists. A few men with guns going out for the hunt could easily have hidden something in the woods. Scott had been walking through the woods looking for clues. One day he saw this big white pine. It looked old and dead. He guesses hurricane Sandy knocked it over. He saw a Masonic symbol carved into the tree. It had been there for years. He started to walk around it and he told me there in the roots he saw something. He dug in the sand around it and eventually pulled out a copper cylinder."

Billy pauses and looks at each of us. "Scott died because of this thing. Do you really want me to go on?"

We all say "yes" at the same time. He runs his hand through his hair and then puts it over his mouth, tugging slightly on his beard. Finally he looks up into my eyes. "I have the copper cylinder." He looks down as if he is ashamed. When he looks back up, he has a defiant look in his eyes, "Just to be clear, I didn't kill Scott either. He called me the day before his death and asked me to put the scroll somewhere safe. He had been approached by a man with a very pointy gun in his rib cage. The man asked about the copper tube and if he had opened it. Scott told me that this happened in the men's room at the gym and someone else walked in. The gunman put the gun back into his pocket and Scott said he got the hell out of there. He felt sure that this was the real thing after that. That's why he asked you to join him for dinner. He wanted your help in protecting the cylinder."

I ask Billy if he has the scroll here. He looks over at Bernie, "I'm not ready for that yet. I know who Samantha is and you, but I don't know anything about Bernie. I can still shoot him if I need to and the cylinder will still be safe. It's time for him to talk."

I start to say something but Billy holds up his hand to me. Bernie had been sitting there quietly listening. Now he sits up in his seat and locks his eyes with Billy. "My name is Bernie Moll. I am US Air Force Retired, currently in the employment of the Baltimore City Police. You have a gun and I have a gun. We have mutual distrust." He raises his hand from under the table displaying a 9mm with a four inch barrel. It is tight, compact and obviously easy to conceal. "I am a friend of Adam. We have worked together on a case and I am running shotgun for him on this little adventure. We have two choices right now. The first is the most sensible and we put our toys away. I suggest we hand them to a neutral party, let's say Samantha. The second option is that we shoot at each other. This is very close range. We will have no problem hitting the other. Besides the gunshot we will each receive, the sound inside this metal box will deafen all of us temporarily. No one will be making a 911 call. So you and I both bleed to death here leaving Adam and Samantha to ransack the containers until they find what they are looking for. All those stores you have hidden away for survival will be for nothing because you will not live to see tomorrow."

Billy nods in agreement and turns his gun around and hands it to Samantha. Bernie does the same thing. I finally let my breath out. I didn't even know I had been holding it. Samantha now sits at the table with a gun under each hand. She looks at each of us, "Okay, does anyone else have a gun, knife, hand grenade, whatever it may be while sitting at this table? Every male at this table is going to stand up and fucking disarm. I get all the toys, than we are all going to sit down and eat our dinner like normal human beings." The three of us stand up.

I reach down and pull my gun out of my ankle holster and put it in front of Samantha. Then I reach down and get my knife from my boot sheath. I pull my second knife from my pocket. Billy is unstrapped a gun from each ankle and stops to comment on the knife I pulled from my boot. Bernie leans down and pulls a gun from his boot as well. Billy looks at Samantha, "what about you? Are you armed?"

She looks at the pile of guns and knives in front of her. "I wasn't but I am now. Sit down and eat. It's getting cold." Billy begins to walk away from the table and she spins to look at him. "Where the hell do you think you are going?"

He reaches up behind a box on the wall and pulls out the copper cylinder. "I am bringing the elephant in the room to the table." He walks back and puts it on the center of the table and sits down.

I think I expected something more impressive. It is a plain copper cylinder capped at both ends. I don't see where it is threaded or how the ends come off. It appears they are welded together. It is not large, maybe seven or eight inches and less than two inches in diameter. It is hard to imagine Scott died because of this plain little tube. I wonder if Billy has thrown a red herring on the table.

We are all staring at it. Samantha breaks the ice. "That's it? A container that holds information that could change the world should be something magnificent, not a crummy piece of pipe with end caps! What is inside it? Did you open it? How do you open it?"

I don't see any way to open it. This was intended for one use. It was sealed and buried. The person to open it would have to cut through the cylinder to get the information inside. I look over at Billy, "Why didn't you cut it open?"

He shrugs his shoulders. "I got the cylinder and went back to my Baltimore apartment. I didn't have the tools there to cut into it. In the morning, I got an email from the university that Scott had been found murdered. I went to the office to get some things and the place was ransacked. I went back to my apartment and packed my things and got the hell out of there before whoever killed him and trashed our office found out about me. I rode my bike up here. Then bombs started exploding and I ran out to get a few more supplies. I thought this might not end well. I'm still not sure how it is going to end. I knew you would eventually come and I figured I needed your information on the Masonic Treasures to make any sense out of what might be inside here. So I waited. Bad shit has happened since this was removed from the ground. Who knows, I might cut this open and all of us will be cursed and die."

I can feel my heart beating and trying to get out of my chest. Before me on the table may be the secret to the Masonic Treasure. The location of the Ark of the Covenant may be a few feet away from me. Many times at night, Scott and I had talked about the person who finds this information. "It is said only those pure at heart and spirit may look upon the Ark. If the directions are there to its location who at this table can go to it? I can't. While I have tried to live a good life, I have sinned. I murdered a man in cold blood. He was a serial killer. He liked to kill women. He would sexually abuse them for days before he cut out their genitalia and watched them bleed to death. John and I walked in on him masturbating over a fresh kill. He turned around and looked at us. He begged me not to shoot him, but I did. I killed the bastard. John and I covered it up. We both swore he had the knife in his hands and he came toward me. He did lunge toward me but it was his dick in his hands, not a knife. It went down as a clean kill."

The other three look around the table. Samantha looks at Billy, "I was a hooker. I sold my body. I have no idea how many men I have had sex with in my life. I laughed in Gods face and spit on a Nun after my new born daughter and I were thrown out of a halfway house. The nun was trying to help me but I liked the money I could get from spreading my legs. So I broke the rules and went back to working the streets. She told me to leave, so I spit in her face and told her she didn't know how good sex felt. She would rip that habit off and beg for sex if she knew what an orgasm felt like. I think that seals my fate, I'm not pure."

He looks back at her and throws his arms in the air. "Well I'm the one who probably got Scott killed!" I look at him. My mouth is open in shock at his announcement. "Two days before his death, the phone rang in the office. The man identified himself as someone from Virginia Antiquities and wanted to talk to Scott. I told him that Scott was in Williamsburg at the conference. He asked me where the object was that Scott found. I played stupid for a moment. He said something about a copper tube and I told him Scott had it with him at the conference. He asked if Scott had opened it and I told him yes. In his closing speech, Scott was going to reveal what he found in the cylinder. Scott was murdered the night before he was due to give the concluding remarks!"

Bernie stands up, "Well don't look at me. As a kid, I was picked up for shop lifting a couple times. My dad was a cop. He beat my ass every time. I don't know why I did it. I just wanted some candy and we didn't have the money. So, I stole it."

Samantha starts to laugh. "The murderer, the betrayer, the prostitute and the thief sitting around having supper together. What we are missing would be Jesus and a couple disciples. Do we know any?"

Billy gets up and we all turn to watch him, "I think if we are sitting around for what may be our last supper this calls for wine—and a hack saw, what do you think?"

I look at Samantha and Bernie. Neither seems to have cared about my revelation of killing that guy. I killed a man in cold blood. He was the scum of the earth but I have no right to be his judge and executioner. "I guess Jesus would have been Scott. He was the one without sin."

Samantha is shaking her head, "No. He was the one who committed adultery. Karen told us that he had a mistress in Baltimore. He looked to Adam to be the one without sin. We all did." She looks at me. "Not that you have fallen from grace. I probably would have shot the guy myself." Bernie is nodding his head in agreement. "When Karen started to talk about the infertility treatments and the sex on a schedule, I knew it pushed Scott away, so did she. Women know when the men in their lives cheat. It is painted on their face like a scarlet letter."

Billy returns with the bottle of wine, some glasses and a cork screw. "Her name was Kathryn. We worked with her at the university." He sits down and exhales loudly. "Scott didn't know Karen knew about the affair. He told her he slept at the office. You saw that place. Besides the obvious that there wasn't a bed, who would be able to close their eyes in that neighborhood. The bar stays open until two and the drunks and junkies take over the night. The traffic for the meth house is heavy after the sun goes down and next door to that is a crack den in the abandoned house. Samantha, when you talk about hookers, we have some dirty skanks on that street. They are cheap, but you pay for what you get. They are strung out druggies. If the heroin doesn't kill them, AIDs will. It's a sad place but one that we can hide out away from the university. They will claim your work if you make any break through. Some work from their homes to keep the university out of the loop. Scott asked me if I wanted to share an off campus office with him after his thing with Kathryn started. It gave him a reason to spend the night in Baltimore."

Samantha sprinkles the top of her spaghetti with cheese and gets up to put her plate in the microwave to heat it. . After starting it, she turns around to look at the group, "Did Kathryn know about the cylinder? I am not a fan of telling Karen her suspicion was correct. Is there any way Kathryn could be involved in Scott's death? Maybe you didn't betray him, perhaps she told someone first and they confirmed it with you."

Billy shakes his head, "When I say work with I don't mean she was another professor. She's a student and not a good one. She came to Scott's office to see if there was anything she could do to improve her grade. Before he came up with an idea, she was on her knees under his desk performing some extra credit work. That was two years ago. She's a history major now and wants to become a teacher. I feel bad for any kid she gets in a classroom. She couldn't pass a history test if her life depended on it. She's got great tits and a nice ass but she passed by looking at the tests in advance with the answer key. Even then she barely got a "C" on the exams. Scott gave her good grades for classroom work and her extra credit assignments. I'm sure his wife didn't know that he liked to be tied up and spanked. Kathryn got very good grades in S and M."

"She also fed us well. She would bring food from her family's restaurant. I had to watch the baklava. I could have eaten it all day. The Spanakopita was delicious too. The girl could cook and I heard she was amazing in bed. Scott was no saint. I don't mean to speak ill of the dead, but it might be better if his wife didn't know about Kathryn. He said he lost the ability to get it up with his wife, but the kink with Kathryn brought him back to life."

The microwave beeps and Samantha gets her plate out. "Anyone else need me to heat theirs with some cheese? We need to eat." I hand her my plate. She stands by the microwave with her plate and fork eating her spaghetti. "Okay, so Kathryn was his dominatrix? I worked with girls like that. While they liked to dominate men, they were also very protective of them. They were almost like bad children. You love them and these girls loved to punish them. If that is the case, she would not actually harm him. They also didn't talk much about his work. It wasn't the pillow talk type of relationship." The microwave beeps and she takes my plate out and hands it to me. Billy's is next and she pushes the button for another minute.

I don't understand why Scott was murdered. Seeing the cylinder doesn't help explain it. "I think we need to see inside this tube."

Billy nods, "Agreed." Samantha hands him his plate and takes Bernie's. I start to eat. As soon as we finish eating, we can get a saw and answer some questions. I didn't realize how hungry I was until I started to gulp down my food. I look around the table. The others are shoveling food in their mouths also. We are about to open something that has possibly been sealed for more than three hundred and fifty years. We are all excited to get the tube open.

Billy stands up and dumps his plate in the sink. He walks down the hallway and I hear two small dogs bark. These must be Sophie and Dee Dee. We have yet to see them but occasionally I have heard them. He comes back with a saw in his hands. "We have to be careful with this. I cut rebar with it. Copper is soft and I don't think we should saw all the way through and possibly damage what is inside." He hands the saw to me. "Here, you saw and I will hold the cylinder and turn it."

The saw digs into the copper. Every two strokes Billy turns the tube. It seems like an eternity but eventually the end cap begins to come off onto Billy's hand. I stop and he makes the final twist and bends the end cap backwards revealing papers inside. I reach in to pull them out and Bernie yells. "Wait! Shouldn't we say a prayer or something? I mean if this says, Mary Magdalene, wife of Jesus traveled to France and gave birth to their daughter, I think we should say a prayer."

Samantha is wringing her hands and looking in the tube, "Maybe he's right. I mean it wouldn't hurt, right?"

I look at Bernie, "Okay, go ahead and say something. We will wait."

He looks back at me shaking his head. "I think I flunked out of Altar Boy school at eight. I think maybe Samantha should say something."

She is quick to jump in, "Don't look at me. John and Adam had to convince me that I wasn't going to spontaneously combust in a church. I have no idea what to say! What is the prayer for opening a cylinder and reading the scroll inside that might change the world?"

Billy is shaking his head, "You people are just unprepared at everything aren't you? No real survival gear, no safe place to go and if this had been judgment you would have been waving at everyone ascending! Okay let's put everything down on the table and join hands." I feel a little ridiculous but I comply, "Heavenly father, we ask that you join with us and protect us as we open this scroll. Guide us in the path to take as we help fulfill the prophecies and unlock the treasures to your kingdom. In Jesus name, we pray. Amen."

I carefully unroll the first parchment scroll and flatten it out on the table. The writing is small and I sit down to take a better look. Billy and Bernie do also. Samantha leans over my shoulder. In my ear I hear her say, "that's not English."

She is correct. For some reason in my mind the Masonic Scrolls would have been written in English, maybe old English but not this. I'm not even sure what language it might be. I don't recognize any of the characters and can only speculate that it is Aramaic or Arabic. Samantha walks back to the other side of the table and sits down. I look through the three sheets of paper. Nothing is in English.

I feel let down. I expected to open this and read it. It would reveal the secrets of the world and we would be shocked and amazed. Bernie gets up and walks around. When he comes back to the table he looks back down at the paper. "Now what? Can anyone read Hebrew or Ancient Aramaic or whatever that is written in?"

I have no clue what language it is, but I might know someone who can help us. I pull out my phone to make a call. Billy points out the door. I realize we are in a metal box so the reception won't be very good. I walk out the door with them following me. Roddie Clark answers on the second ring, "Adam. It is good to hear from you. I assume all are alive and well? If you are calling it is because you have hit a problem. What is it?"

"We are fine and you are correct. We have hit a snag. I have a piece of parchment and it is written in a language I don't recognize. No one with me can decipher it."

He is silent on the other end for a moment. "Describe the writing. Are they standard alphabet and you don't recognize the words or is it Middle Eastern?" I tell him definitely Middle Eastern. "Does it look like Hebrew? Is it boxy?" I tell him no. It is squigglier than print Hebrew. "It could be Hebrew script or a number of other languages. If I was to send my associate from the boat, in which direction should I send him?" I tell him north to north west. "And approximately how many hours should he drive from here until he contacts you? I tell him about eight and a half. "You visited the office I assume? Am I also to assume this is northwest of the office? A highway with a seven, a four or a three?" I tell him three hours and any of the above. "Very good. Your friend from the boat will be there in the morning. He will be meeting another associate on the road. They will call you from a big bang so that you might talk them in." I tell him that is a great idea. And hang up the phone.

Tracy will be here in the morning. With him will be another man. With nothing else to do for the night we have to wait until morning. We go back inside and finish off the wine. The scroll is rolled back up inside the tube and is back in its location on the shelf.

Billy stands up and announces "Since you will be staying the night, and we will have guests in the morning, I should probably show you around. Come follow me." We stand up and follow him. "About ten years ago, I found out about shipping containers from a prepper network. I thought they were a pretty good idea. At the time, I had a hunting camp here. It wasn't much. Just an old beat up travel trailer. It gave me a place to cook some dinner and sleep during hunting season. You can't see them all but I had twenty-four containers delivered to this lot. My original plan was to bury all of them and make an underground bunker. I got two in the ground and realized I was not a fan of living like a rabbit. So I laid out this compound. You have the twenty visible containers stacked around my center courtyard. On each side I have two underground units. They are storage. The containers are water tight and will take up to a fifty caliber bullet. It took me a while to cut the doors and weld what I wanted. The downstairs compartments are linked together on the individual sides. The front and back doors are in thick well casing. Nothing is coming through that. The doors also open outward. It's good to know if we need to bug out. Push the door out, not in. The iron rods in the ground go down nine feet and are in cement footers. They are not moving."

"You found the stairs to the medical and seed vaults. I wanted to make sure this stuff stayed dry. I'm sure you also noticed the slits in the outer wall and understand the need to be able to observe from all sides. The entire upstairs is connected. The inner wall contains supplies, food mostly and of course the armory. I can feed and house ten people for about three years." We are following him downstairs to one of the underground bunkers. "This was the find of a lifetime. While I was digging the hole to put this container in the ground. I hit something. At first I thought my construction was over and I would have to find a new location. I took a flashlight and looked down. I could see bottom so I dropped a rope down inside the hole." He walks over to a spot on the floor. He pushes a table and reveals a handle that lifts out of the floor. He turns on a light switch on the wall and I see lights come on in a stairway. "I put these stairs in afterward. I knew this entire region was full of caverns. Back in the old days some of the farmers used them for cold storage. It is a constant fifty two degrees down here. Be careful and watch your step. This is not a show cave. It is still very much a wild cave. Also while it is hard to resist, please don't touch anything. Keep your hands in your pockets if you can. The rocks are alive in here. The stalactites and stalagmites are still growing. The oil from your hands will repel the water and they will stop growing. I try not to come down here unless I have to. I have explored the cave and found an escape route. It is marked in the event we need it. We will come out about two miles from here. I also have a natural stream that flows through here. The water is pure and good to drink. This was a great find. I just wanted to show you in case we need to bug out. I plan on using this only if I cannot defend my ground."

We turn around and go back up the steps. "The last thing I wanted to make sure you have seen are the stairs to the upper level. I put in roof access. Sometimes it is nice to sit up on the roof and watch the world go by. It's been really quiet with the planes being grounded. I am far enough away from everything that the view at night is unbelievable." We follow him up the stairs. He has welded panels to the top of the containers that serve as a fence and a defensive area to shoot from. I'm sure during the day there is visibility through the woods in all directions. Billy brought us up to the roof right now was to look out at the heavens. I have never seen so many stars. Even when we drove through Texas the sky did not look this filled with lights. From our vantage point he points north, "That is State College and to the south of us is Altoona. Off to the west you can see a slight glow. That is Ebensburg. We are on the top of the Allegheny Highlands and the stars in the sky allow you to reach up and touch the Gods. I'm going to go back inside where it is warm but feel welcome to sit up here all night if you want. You just can't find this view anymore."

I agree and sit down to look out. As he is heading down the stairs, I yell to stop him, "Hey Billy, Do we need to sit watch or anything?" He laughs and tells me no. The woods are bugged. He has heat signals on every animal that lives around here. He sees everything for a couple miles and knows its movement. If something is here that doesn't belong it sets off an alarm. "Okay, then good night."

Samantha looks at me after the door to Billy's container closes, "Should we stand guard tonight? They got through our security system." I shake my head no. My guess is that Billy doesn't have the standard alarm system on the market.

We are all exhausted and go downstairs to get ready for bed. I offer to take Max out into the compound. As I am walking, I hear Billy, "Hey Adam." I turn and look. He is walking into the outer courtyard with his head down and his hands in his pockets. "I don't know any other way to tell you this. I got an email from Kathryn. Scott's funeral has been postponed and she is planning on taking their son to say goodbye to his daddy. I emailed her back that I don't think this is a good idea. I mean Scott loved his son, but it isn't right for his widow. She may find out about him, but Friday is not the day for that."

I feel like my entire world has been turned upside down, "What is his name?"

I know before he says it, but I want to hear it spoken out loud. "Scott Raymond Llewellyn the third. Scott named him after himself and his grandfather. His parents know. They flew in after Scottie was born. They also set up a trust fund for him. I hope Kathryn stays home, but I doubt she will. I thought I should tell you. I know you can't make it to the funeral but I think you should know." He turns around and goes back inside leaving me to cry for the loss of my friend.

Day Seven,
The Allegheny Highlands, Western Pennsylvania

With the lights off it is dark in the bunk room. I roll over and look at my phone. It is six thirty in the morning. It has been six days since my phone rang and I got the news that Scott was dead.

Samantha is still sleeping and I lay in bed looking up at the bottom of the bunk over me. So much has happened in the last week. The world changed and I am on the run. I am looking forward to Tracy arriving. Not only because he or the person with him will be able to decipher the scroll but to also get word from home. John, Chris and Christina have been interviewed about where I am. They have been told my running has made me look guilty. They have not been told if there is a warrant out for my arrest. John is afraid to dig into the case. There is a blanket order in my office to stay out of the investigation unless the police need to talk to them. If anyone knows, either Roddie or Tracy will know the status.

Bernie is still asleep so I put Max on the leash. As soon as I walk outside I see that I have a missed call with a voicemail. I hit play and hear Tracy's voice. "Okay, where the hell are you? We passed the burned out truck stop and have stopped at a fast food place in Everett. According to your friend John, who happens to have the second phone we gave you! You were heading north of Everett. Now if I don't hear from you by the time we finish eating, we are going to go north to the town that can be bought. I don't want to go much farther until after I hear from you. Call me back!"

I walk to the Green container and smell coffee. Billy is up so I knock on the door. He yells, "it's open." As I walk in he points to the coffee pot. I make a cup and Max lies down at my feet.

"My associates have called and I must not have gotten the call because of the metal box." He nods in agreement. "He told me they were driving to the town that could be bought, any idea where that might be?"

Billy is laughing. "I like this guy already! A couple years ago a filmmaker went around to a bunch of big corporations and solicited money. He was looking for a couple million dollars as backing for a movie. The guarantee was that if you were a sponsor you company wouldn't just be shown in the credits. Your company logo would be used throughout the movie. After getting a bunch of sponsors he put something out that he was looking for a town that would sell their name for a few months. In return, they would get a couple million dollars. The object of the movie was to show that America has been sold to the highest bidder."

"Altoona was nearly broke. This was a small mountain city once based on the railroad and coal mining. Neither one was real strong in the early two thousands so they stepped forward. The rules were that they would change their name. Not just on paper but put up street signs, become the Sold Fire Department, the Sold Police Department and so on. The city council knew how important this money would be to the town. It would save it, so they agreed. Even the highway signs were changed. The movie was filmed. The film crews left and the town went back to being Altoona. The big difference was they were no longer poor, nearly bankrupt Altoona. The film crew spent a lot of money in town, plus the millions dropped into the municipal budget after the filming was completed. They were a town with a price tag and the movie bought them."

"Most people don't remember it. You know how people are, once the signs come down they don't remember any more. So, I like your friend. He seems to get it. The message of sold America was very clear. We have all fallen victim to corporate sponsorship. Come on. Let's go out and call him so that I can figure out exactly where he is and how to get him from bought and sold to found in the state game lands."

I walk out the door and call him back. First, I apologize for not receiving the call. I explain that the walls are metal and we are in a survival compound. I ask if he would like to speak with the owner who is willing to give him directions to the site. I hand the phone to Billy and he immediately smiles, "Yes it is a secure site. We can take up to a fifty round blast and stand up to it. I hear you are friends with Adam, so I am willing to give you directions in. Now how many of you are there and what are you driving." He pauses to listen and then nods his head. "Great. You are about twenty minutes from us. Here's what I need you to do. Get back on 99/220 heading toward Tyrone…"

I go back inside to wake up Samantha and Bernie. They will want to be awake when our guests arrive. Samantha gets up and goes into the shower. She comes out dressed in a black sweater and jeans. Bernie gets up and gets into the shower. I warn them it is cold outside and we had a light snow. Samantha grabs her jacket and heads out the door into the courtyard.

In the distance, I hear a motorcycle. Billy calls for me to come verify that I recognize something about either of the riders. They are both wearing leathers and helmets. It is hard to tell, but one has the same build as Tracy. They stop at the bear and turn in. "Well, I guess this must be them." He throws me an M16. "I assume you know how to use one of these things?"

I click the safety off of the gun and sling it over my shoulder. "Yup. Let's go meet our guests." We walk to the outer gate. I follow Billy's lead and raise my gun and aim mid chest as they pull up.

Bernie walks up beside me with his gun out as well. "Take your helmets off please gentlemen." Tracy is the lead rider. The second rider is taller. He's about six foot two. He has graying in his temples. Even under the leathers I can tell he has a muscular build. I had thought Tracy was the brawn but this guy is built like a brick. He does not look like one I want to piss off or, for the moment, turn my back on, "Tracy, would you like to introduce us to your friend?"

The other rider shuffles on his bike and glares at me. Tracy looks over at him, "this guy? I believe you called Roddie looking for someone to read some bubble gum wrapper that you found? This guy can read anything ever written in the Middle East. Let me introduce Talmadge Bowdein. I'm just here to deliver him and watch his back. He's very important to our operation. Now open the damn gate and let us in!"

I look him in the eye, "your operation? When did this become an operation? When did it become your operation? I'm tired of the games and I am not playing. You need to satisfy this gentleman's requirements." I lean my head indicating Billy. "This is his compound and his operation. I'm just the hired gun backing him up right now."

Talmadge shifts on his bike. He looks uncomfortable. "We drove all the way up here. Are you going to let us in or should we ride home? To be honest I have been riding all night and I would like to get a little shut eye."

Bernie looks at me "I can shoot him. I have wanted to shoot someone for a couple days now." I tell him no, not yet. I look over at Billy and tell him I know one of the men. I guess it's alright to open the gate.

Billy unlocks the outer gate and the two ride into the compound and Billy points to where he wants them to park. I notice he has not lowered his gun. Bernie walks over and closes the gate. I hear the lock click as it locks us back inside the compound. I note to myself that we can get in, but Billy holds the key that lets us out. At this point, I trust Billy and he has not given me reason to lose trust in him. Times have changed in my life and trust is becoming something hard to accept. Something about Talmadge Bowdein puts me on edge. I am not going to trust him until he proves to me he deserves my trust.

We walk toward the bunk container. Billy walks by the container we are in and opens the next box. Here, you can throw your gear here. Leave your guns and weapons. You are inside the compound and don't need it here.

Tracy cocks his head to the side and looks at Billy. "Now, what if we get attacked? We need to be armed to defend ourselves. Things have gotten a little hairy out there in the last two days. With cash only sales and store shelves running low, things are becoming more dog eat dog. Haven't you been watching the news?"

Billy shakes his head and walks away. "Why would I need the news? There is nothing there that I need to know right now. My computer told me we were attacked and I looked at news from outside the country. I'm not into half-truths and full lies. They tell the American people what they want to hear and water down the truth. You and I both know why it is cash only and the shelves are going bare. The financial trunk is down and stores have three days in stock. After that why do I need to know more?"

Talmadge is following after him, "What about the weather? There's a winter storm warning for tonight. Would you have left us sit outside the gate on motorcycles if you knew there was the possibility of a foot of snow falling by morning?"

Billy reaches up to a rock tied on a string outside the green container. "Do you see this? It is my weather rock. If it is wet I know it is raining. If it is warm and dry I know it's a hot sunny day.

If I walk out my door and it is swinging so hard it hits me in the head I know to go back inside and stay there. It is actually a simple but very accurate tool."

Talmadge is standing in the center of the compound next to the well. His hands are on his hips and he has a smile on his face, "Yes, but did you know it was going to snow tonight?"

Billy smiles back and walks over to the well. "Indeed I did. First look up and see the heaviness of the clouds. I know it will precipitate sometime today. Those clouds are full of mist which will eventually get heavy and fall to the ground." Billy looks around at all of us standing in the compounds, "Let me give you all an education. This was taught to me by my grandfathers, one was Comanche and the other Choctaw. Take a good look at the clouds. What you might not know is that those are giant snow banks floating over your head. See how they tower up in the sky and are flattened out on the bottom? That tells a story to you. Right now it is really cold up at the top of the cloud and there is warm air flowing up from the planet surface. It has melted the frozen mist on the bottom side of the cloud but up above is still light and airy. As long as the lower level temperatures stay above freezing there is only a chance of rain, but let the temperatures drop and the weight of the clouds get too much for the air it will start to fall. The wind is very strong up there and can rip pieces apart. When that happens it begins to fall. A warm air layer will turn it to rain, a cold layer could turn it back to sleet but if it stays cold—we get snow. The rock is pretty cold today so if it falls, I'd say we are going to get snow."

Talmadge starts to laugh and walks over to him and reaches up to touch the rock. "Well now I see it! You see I am Assateague Nanticoke and North Carolina Cherokee Nation. Being from hurricane country we learned to read the clouds by the tropical bands. The outer bands are no big deal. You get stuff done when you see blue sky and head back inside when the band crosses over. Now when the bands get tight you need to worry because tight bands make a tight eye in the storm. Once that storm brews an eye it becomes a mighty beast and aims itself at land to commit destruction."

Tracy joins the group, "we didn't use a rock. I am Chickamauga, Cherokee and Creek. A wet rock signified the rocks along the trail of tears. They weep for my people. We have always just been smart enough to get out of the rain while your tribes were trying to hold a conversation with clouds to determine their intent." All three men begin to laugh.

Billy laughs, "You guys have been on the road all night. Come on it. Coffee is on and we can get breakfast started." Samantha, Bernie and I follow them into the green container that Billy calls home.

It appears the three of them have become instant friends. Something about Talmadge seems familiar. I don't know why but I have seen him before today. He is sitting at the table trying to steal glances at Samantha. He stands up and walks over to her, holding out his hand. "We have not been formally introduced. I'm Talmadge Bowdein and you must be Dr. Samantha Callahan Clay."

She cocks her head to the side and looks puzzled, "I know you. You were one of the DC Agents who escorted Christina and Alina to Fredericksburg. You followed them as protection." She pulls her gun out of the back of her jeans. "Sit down. What are you really doing here?" Talmadge sits in a chair and puts his hands up on the table.

I look over and Bernie has pulled his gun out and is pointing it at Talmadge as well. He motions with his gun for Tracy to move over next to Talmadge. He moves over and sits down at the table. Billy stops cooking and turns around. "Adam, pat them down and make sure they are really unarmed. I will finish cooking. We will all put our guns away and eat breakfast. While we do, those two have some explaining to do. You say you know the one. I was willing to allow them in here. Now I need some information."

Talmadge is glaring at Samantha. "Yes, I am an FBI agent but I am on your side. Can we listen to the man over there and put the guns down? I don't work well with a gun pointed at my head."

Samantha lowers her gun and slips it back into the back of her jeans. Bernie leans against the wall but keeps his gun in his hand. "I will just withhold judgment for a while."

Billy puts a bowl of scrambled eggs on the table and follows that with a plate of sausage. "Everyone sit the hell down and let's discuss this like adults." He looks over at Talmadge. "Just know this is a big woods and I have friends who will help me hide the bodies. Fuck up and you never made it here. Do we understand each other?"

Talmadge and Tracy nod their heads. Samantha pulls out a chair and sits down at the table. "To be honest Billy, I am not happy about sitting down with these two right now. I don't know either one of them, but I recognize that one as an FBI agent. As far as we know, Adam is wanted for murder. How do we know he is not here to bring him in? Adam's partner, John, is the only person who knows exactly where we were. John hasn't called us to say the FBI was sending someone to help. Unless something has happened to John, in which case something has happened to my kids. That doesn't create a friendly circumstance."

Talmadge interrupts her, "woman can I speak? I am on your side! I'm trying to find out why John Wake has put out a hit on your husband! In the middle of the bombings NSA was watching chatter and Adams name came across the radar! We know Joseph Callan killed Scott Llewellyn on behalf of Wake. We just don't know why. You aren't wanted for murder but someone wants to murder you, so you are better staying here."

She reaches across the table and spoons some eggs on her plate. "Keep going. Give me something that will prove what you are saying. It seems like a crock of bull shit. Why would the head of the CIA covert training want to kill my husband and a history professor?"

He takes the bowl from her hand and spoons some onto his plate. "That's why I'm here. We snagged your computer from your house and forensics backed our way into Roddie Clarks little network. From what I heard, he has firewalls that put the FBI to shame. Originally, the forensic programmer thought this was a hack by the Chinese. Instead, it led to a geocache site. We found an Easter egg and opened it with your name. That led us to Roddie Clark. After a call from Director Macon, Mr. Clark became cooperative."

My mind is spinning. I was shocked that there was a hit out on my life. I figured the CIA had killed Scott but the Director of the FBI getting involved in this is way over my head. Talmadge pushes a cell phone over to me. "Do you see the phone number? Do you recognize it?"

The phone number is to the Washington, DC field office. Talmadge taps the phone. "Go ahead. Make the call."

I take the phone and walk out the door. I push the button and make the call. Someone on the other end answers "FBI Office Washington. How may I direct your call?" I ask for Director Thomas Macon. The voice asks the reason for my call. I tell her Talmadge Bowdein has directed me to call.

A moment later, I hear the voice of the Director of the FBI on the other end. "Adam Clay I presume. I'm glad I came in early today. I take it Agent Bowdein has arrived at your destination?" I tell him yes. "Agent Clay, this is a need to know situation, I do not need to know your location. I assume by now you know that Agent Bowdein is there to help you. He is under my direction and reports to me and only me. Tracy Davis can also be trusted. He works for Roddie Clark. They are both former agents who have been working undercover independently. They have filled in many of our questions and we are working with them. Agent Clay, we need to know why the CIA is killing people. I think Scott Llewellyn found something that started this. We need to get to the bottom of it. We work inside the country, their job is outside the country."

I thank him for the information and walk back inside. Everyone stops eating as I enter. "He's legitimate, so is Tracy. The great news is that I am not wanted for murder. The bad news is that John Wake wants to kill me."

I put some food on a plate and sit down with the group. "Okay, where do we start? I assume you want to get some sleep first?"

Talmadge has a mouth full of egg and motions as he chews to hold on. "I'm sorry. I was starving. As long as the coffee keeps coming, I am good for a little bit longer. I want to take a look at both the cylinder and the scrolls."

Billy stands up and gets it off the shelf. He lays it in front of Billy. "So can you really read it or is that a half-truth to get inside my gate?"

He chews, swallows and takes a sip of coffee. "I can read anything out of the Middle East, old or new." He wipes his hands on his jeans and slips a finger inside the tube. He pulls out the papers and flattens them out on the table. He looks at the next page. It is hard to read his face, but confusion is one of the expressions.

I can't wait any longer, "Is it Hebrew Script? Aramaic? What is it and what does it say?"

He looks up and looks around the table. "Is this all there was in the scroll?" We nod our heads. "Wow. This is strange. It looks like someone buried a stack of lists written in Arabic. This top page is a list of Christian schools." He holds the next page up, "This lists people's names, addresses and their children's names." He sorts through and holds up another sheet. "This is a list that includes Congressmen and Senators with their home and district office addresses. I have one sheet that appears to have the names of seventy-three Muslim men." He stops and reads one of the sheets. "This is the strangest of them all. It is an essay on Adolph Hitler's plan of the master race and the Aryan people. I need to check but I think it is a word for word copy of some of his descriptions. Why would someone write all of this down in Arabic, put it in a copper tube, seal both ends with welds and bury it under a tree in Jamestown? This does not make any sense."

He puts his head in his hands and sits for a moment. "Maybe I am just tired. Let me get some sleep and then I will need some paper and a pencil to translate all of this. Maybe after I do that we can sit down together and make sense out of some of this. I just don't know what I am looking at right now. It may be a hit list. If so why store it in this tube? It makes no sense!"

I tell him to get some sleep. Maybe a fresh mind will find an answer. I had hoped for a map to the treasure that could justify Scott's death. He would have died a man who unlocked the key to a treasure, maybe even identified the family of Jesus Christ. Instead he died for a stack of lists and the words of Adolph Hitler.

It has started to snow. Billy goes to his private area and comes back with Sophie and Dee Dee on their leashes. "I want to take the girls for a walk before the snow gets too deep for them. In the morning, I will have to shovel a path for them." The dogs are small and he has put little quilted winter coats on them. This is a little unexpected but I understand. They are shivering while wearing the coats. This weather would be too cold for them to go out. I think about Doughnut. I miss my fur ball. I know he, Ebenezer and Chaucer are better off with John but I still wish I could be with them.

When he returns, Billy takes out a deck of cards. "You guys play poker?" We sit down and he starts dealing. We have time to kill while Talmadge and Tracy get some sleep. He fans his cards out in his hand and moves a few. Then folds them and puts them face down on the table. "Part of building a place like this is anticipating the day all hell breaks out. I spend a lot of time up here. Usually I play solitaire. It's just me, you know. Going to the city and working with Scott reminded me what I hate about the city. I know preppers are thought to be nuts by some, but look where we are now? The cities have looting and fires. People are yelling on the streets for answers. Meanwhile, we are safe with full stomachs, sitting down to play poker."

I tell him I will take two and he slips me two cards. A pair of Aces queen high is not a bad place to be sitting. Samantha folds. Bernie is sorting his cards back and forth before folding also. Billy winks at me and takes one. He's either got a great hand or he's a master bull shitter. I am about to call his hand when a gunshot rings out.

I grab the rifle against the door. Samantha pulls the gun from her holster. Bernie and Billy grab rifles against the back wall. Bernie, Samantha and I hit the ground crouching under the table. Billy looks under the table at us. "Remember, we can take a fifty caliber round. Wait to go out the door and look first. We are good here, just stay low when we go outside."

I open the door a crack and look out. Tracy is standing on the roof of the bunk container. He is turning to come down the ladder. If someone just shot at him he seems calm. He's wearing his gun behind his back. I open the door wider and ask him if everything is alright. He looks over his shoulder and shouts, "Yeah. I just took down an eight point buck. Come help me drag him in."

Billy shakes his head muttering to himself and walks toward the door to the compound. He puts his hands on his hips and turns around to look at Tracy. "Dude, next time you want to go hunting you might want to warn the rest of us. If you look around you will see a whole lot of weapons." Tracy looks down and sees Talmadge standing in the doorway of the container with a gun also. The world is on edge and we are all ready to shoot at someone or something. Tracy almost started a shootout over a trophy buck.

Samantha stays inside the compound as we go out to get the deer. He's a big boy and Talmadge helps drag it into the outer compound. Tracy pulls a rope from his saddle bag and ties it around the back legs of the deer. "Anyone want to help field dress this?"

Billy shakes his head and says "No, but I will be glad to cook a pot roast for dinner if you get it butchered." The idea of a venison pot roast sounds delicious. Samantha is making a face but I know she will like it if she tries it.

We leave Tracy to butcher the deer and return to the green container. Talmadge follows us and sits down. He has given up on getting some sleep or the nap he got was enough for him to be able to decipher the scrolls. He sits at the table with a legal pad and a pencil.

He begins with the list of families with their names and addresses. I sit across the table and read what he is writing. This list is just men and women with their children and home addresses. There are two hundred and twenty families on the list. They are in alphabetic order but there appears to be families living in clusters around the country.

Once he finishes with the families list he begins to translate list of Christian schools. The list consists of the school's name and address, the Education Director, grades taught and notes on the school curriculum.

He passes the list of schools to Samantha and me. We begin to look for some connection between the two lists. Meanwhile,

Talmadge translates the list of politicians. He is making faces as he works. I don't think he likes some of the politicians on the list.

Tracy walks in with a large chunk of deer and Billy holds a pot out for him to put it in. Tracy goes back out to his butchering while Billy puts water in the pot and turns on a burner. Soon onions are being chopped and spices are being added to the water. Everyone in the compound is busy working on projects.

Samantha gets another legal pad from Billy and begins to group names into cities and states. The families seem to be located in twelve states. Most within a state live relatively near each other.

I look at the schools in relationship to the groups on the list. There are schools in the same region as the groups of families. Other than that, we cannot find any connection. Talmadge hands me the third list. This consists of Senators and Congressmen. As I skim the list two names pop out, President Elect Nathan Hall and Vice President Elect Michael Morris. This makes the contents of the tube much more interesting.

It takes Talmadge a little longer to translate the final sheet. About one quarter of the way down the page he pauses and exclaims, "Someone loves the Fuehrer a little too much! This is not what I expected to read in Arabic. It is the eugenics Lebensborn program. What the hell?" He continues translating the sheet.

Samantha has a puzzled look on her face. Billy has turned around and is looking at Talmadge. I decide to allow him to continue and explain to them, "The Nazi Lebensborn program was a breeding program using selective genetics in order to breed children of the perfect race. For the Third Reich, this was a group of men and women who were blue-eyed, blonds, with pure Nordic genetics, trim physical build, in perfect physical condition with no illnesses and men at least six feet in height. Those over six feet six inches were considered to be the ultimate physical specimens. This height and above got you immediately promoted to officer with a special designation. Men close to seven feet though were not the Master Race and many of these men were sterilized because this was gigantism and therefore not perfect specimens. The program paid woman and captured women who were the perfect Aryan specimens to breed them with SS personnel. The program was ended in nineteen forty-four and it is estimated it produced more than forty-two thousand babies of pure Aryan descent."

"The Germans also kidnapped children from neighboring countries. I know in Poland alone over two hundred thousand children who were blue-eyed, blonds were kidnapped and raised as part of the Master Race. When they reached maturity they were put into the breeding program as well."

"The whole perfect Aryan race was the reason some people were put into camps. It was said Jews, Roma gypsies, the handicapped, the sick, and homosexual were not perfect and therefore destined for sterilization or death."

I can see Samantha is trying to wrap her thoughts around this. "So Hitler, who wasn't Aryan, wanted to kill everyone who wasn't perfect. But, if he was following the path of Mary Magdalene looking for the blood line of Christ, wouldn't he have killed the descendants?"

Billy turns the heat down on the pot roast and sits down at the table in order to be part of the conversation. Talmadge has stopped writing and is looking at us intently, "Samantha, the best way to explain the mind of Adolph Hitler is a contradiction Things like the Master Race required to be Christian, and not tainted by the Catholic Church. Jews were bad, but Hitler's mother was Jewish. He himself was not Aryan and would have been put into the camps."

Talmadge puts his pen down and begins to talk with his hands as he explains, "I have never seen this theory published but I have thought a lot about the mind of Hitler and why he did what he did. We know he wanted to kill the Jews and anyone with Jewish ancestry. He was fixated with Christian holy relics. What if he saw himself as a direct descendant of Christ? If he thought he could trace his ancestry back to Mary Magdalene— he would have thought of himself closer to God than most. If he killed off all the Jews and everyone with Jewish descent, he would be the last of the possible blood lines. He and his children could be rulers of the world if they wanted to be. But first, he had to get rid of the competition. The gypsies were as much of a threat as the Jews because Mary hid among the Roma Gypsies. Her daughter could have grown up among the gypsies and married one. Then her children would have gypsy blood. Plus the Roma hid the three Mary's and gave them sanctuary. To a man obsessed with power, these people may know the very secrets he did not. Because of that, no gypsy could live. As for gays and people who were sick or handicapped, they got in the way of the perfect race. They could pass on their affliction to a child and taint the gene pool in his mind. He was making the gene pool pure by removing the impurities and creating a breeding program of perfect Aryan descendants."

Billy has been quiet absorbing all of this, "So what you are saying is that Adolph Hitler was drawn to power to answer his own questions about his ancestry and to eliminate all that stood between him and his own perfection. I have heard similar explanations but none adding the part about Mary Magdalene being pregnant and having a child. With this added twist, if Hitler had found the answer to the bloodline of Christ and that he could prove to the world he was the sole descendant he would become the son of God by default. By eliminating all who might be able to provide a similar claim, he made himself the sole survivor. As for the Catholic Church, it is believed they have the truth, and therefore the proof, hidden away in their archives. The contents of the archives could prove he was not the bloodline of Christ."

He gets up and checks on the pot roast before continuing, "So what does that have to do with what we have now?"

Talmadge has been writing. I thought he was copying the rest of the scroll. Instead he has written his thoughts onto the page. He crosses something out and writes something over it. "Let's try this. The eugenics scroll mentions breeding a perfect male. Mating him with the perfect female and creating a superior race, one that no one can deny is far superior and far more desirable than common man who walks the earth."

"I have wondered why this was written in Arabic, but perhaps that is easily answered. The Knights Templar are thought to have removed the Ark of the Covenant from the Temple Mount during the Roman invasion. What if the Ark did not make it out and in building the Mosque in Jerusalem the Muslims found the Ark and hid it away? Now with all of the clashes between Jews, Christians and Muslim going on in the world, the Muslims want to come out with a God that cannot be denied by any of the three major religions. What if they bring forth the perfect man? One that is Jewish but pure Aryan appearing, has the bloodline of Christ and is a Muslim? The trifecta of holiness? He's a Jew by birth, he's the son of Christ, and he worships Mohammed."

The thought is intriguing. If the final scroll holds the key, then the contents revolve around eugenics. During Nazi Germany it was a concept used by a group of men who most would think were mad. Imagine women volunteering to have sex, and become pregnant with the children of men who were judged as perfect specimens. This was not a time of artificial insemination. Women applied for the job of broad mare for the Nazi party. People always concentrate on the Shoah. They focus on the horrors of the concentration camp but few know about the Lebensborn and the children bred by the Third Reich. They and the hundreds of thousands of kidnapped children went on to represent the Master Race. "So what if this breeding program continues?"

Talmadge stops translating and looks up at us, "Well, from what I am reading, this is exactly what has happened:

Herr Fuehrer gave the broad mares of Mother Land safe haven to take to seclusion and bare the children of the Ubermenschen. To supplement the broad mares, they kidnapped children and raised them as cattle to breed and produce more Ubermenschen. The dream is of perfection in the eyes of Herr Fuehrer.

The analysis of Americans shows a higher respect for a male who is tall, has tanned skin and is muscular. They find the athletic figure to be the most desired and will overlook dissenting thoughts and ideals if they person is attractive. In males, blond to light brown hair is considered to be more sexually appealing. A chiseled face with a day's growth of beard is sensual. The female voters appreciated a male build that has a medium to large frame. The smaller slighter men are viewed as impotent. In many ways, the female voters look at a potential candidate for their breeding potential, not for their ability to lead. The male voters are slightly different. They appreciate an athletic build and a history of sports participation. They scored a day's growth of facial hair as unclean. Males want other males in power positions to be clean shaven.

The target American female is short to medium in height. Women over six feet are usually viewed as undesirable. There is a contrast between the views on models. Fashion models tend to be angular with rib cages evident in swimwear. Nude models for pornography have a more rounded appearance with a hint of hip bone showing under a thin layer of fat but not the rib cage. Large breasted women are the most desirable. Males tend to fantasize about blondes and red heads. Darker hair is not viewed as attractive. Wider hips are preferred over an athletic build. Women are viewed for their breeding potential making wider hips and larger breasts the most desirable traits.

The target breeding stock will be males with blond to light brown hair. There must be a family history of having athletics and muscular frames. The average male height should be over six feet tall. They should be Anglo Saxon ancestry. Latino or African ancestry is frowned on by a portion of the population, while the overall female population finds the olive and darker skin tones to be appealing.

Care should be taken also in vetting both male and female candidates in the breeding stock. While the female population finds bald men to be appealing, the male population will not vote for a bald man. The genetic thread for baldness passes down the maternal line.

If allowed to continue, the Lebensborn Program would have created the perfect gene pool. There would be a proud race now that is undeniably a superior human. Borrowing the ideals of eugenics and applying them long term will create the perfect candidate.

The description is followed by a check list of education requirements, suggested sports, social activities and affiliations. "Someone has put together a plan that expands the Nazi breeding program and adapted it to America. What I don't know is why."

Samantha is looking at the lists and lays them side by side on the table. "At first, I thought these were hit lists. Something possibly connected to the schools. I think maybe the parents teach at the schools and or the children attend the schools. I think we need to look at these Congressmen and Senators and see if their voting records either all support funding for church based schools or if they voted against church based schools. I don't understand the relationship to the breeding program. That is unless someone has selected these families to breed children for some purpose."

Talmadge sits across from her and turns the politician list around, "Maybe you are on to something. If these families are connected to a breeding program and the schools, then the politicians would either support or be against the schools. It makes perfect sense—at least on the surface. I just don't understand why."

I stand up and walk to the bunk room to get our new tablets. Bernie and Talmadge join me in retrieving tablets. Billy has brought his to the table. When I get back, I remind Samantha to not sign on to any of her known users. We need to surf anonymously.

We split the list of politicians and family names so that we can get through the lists faster without duplication. Billy has brought legal pads and pencils to the table so that we can all take notes.

We are looking for connections between the politicians on the list to each other, to the schools, and to the names on the list of families. Hopefully, something will pop up and we will find a connection between all of the people on the lists.

Samantha has taken the lists of schools and is looking for a connection between them. She is also making notes on the names of people on the board of directors, educators and teachers in relation to the list of people.

I have the beginning of the list of politicians. I'm not sure what I am looking for. The first one I pull up has been in the Senate for over twenty years. I look at his reelection web page to see what platform he ran under. He is a fundamentalist Christian who is pro-life, pro-family, and against universal healthcare. He spoke about a child's right to be born, even under circumstances such as rape. He is an advocate for adoption and thinks the unwanted babies should be adopted, rather than aborted.

In his local area he was very vocal about a young woman who was addicted to drugs and her baby was in danger of being born addicted to heroin. He led the charge to imprison her and force her to clear her body of the drugs. The young woman died during detoxification from a heart attack. The family of the young woman tried to sue the Senator for murder of both the young woman and the child. I remember the publicity on this case. I believe it is still ongoing.

The next politician I search has a very similar background. One thing that stands out from his campaign was a controversial statement against daycare and preschool. Many women's rights groups were up in arms about his stand against universal Pre – K. During a debate he stated "children belong at home with their mothers, not being housed during the day in centers." He went on to say that women belong at home with their children, and not in the work place. Women's rights advocates held signs outside of polling places protesting these comments. On Election Day, it appeared he was in a dead tie with his opponent. It took a week to validate the election and the counting of all mail in ballots in his district.

One after the other, the politicians are for God and family. Universally, they are against abortion and in favor of Christian family values. A few spoke about traditional roles for women in the workplace. There were comments about women on birth control being whores and prostitutes woven throughout their campaigns. Many feel that birth control is against Gods will and women murder the unborn by taking it. They stand behind a religious organizations right to not include birth control on their prescription formularies.

I can imagine each of the politicians on the list is in line with the teachings of the Christian schools. The incoming President and Vice President ran on a platform of returning the country to Christian values and the inherent evil that had swept this country. His campaign slogan was, "A vote against Nathan Hall was a vote against God. Together we stand with God and return this great country to him."

I wonder if the families on the list are major donors to either the schools or to the politicians. That thought makes me pause for a moment, why is this written in Arabic?

I do not know any other way to work a case other than timeline the clues. "Samantha, help me timeline this case. I need to see it." She taps a few things on her tablet and tells me to start. The others take a seat around the table. "First Scott found the scroll on James Island. Tracy, you witnessed this." He responds "yes". "He then takes it to Baltimore and puts it in the office with you, Billy. You and Scott try to find a way to open the scroll but you see no way other than to cut it. Is that correct?"

Billy nods his head, "Yes, we discussed bringing tools and cutting it open after his seminar in Williamsburg. He never made it back up to get it open."

I continue. "The only other person to know about the scroll were Stephen Koehler and Kathryn. I don't see him as one to spread that information around. He also had limited knowledge of the scroll. Kathryn is an unknown to me, but she has a son to protect. Scott came back to Virginia and was at the conference for most of the week. On the night he was murdered, his office was ransacked—but Billy, you had taken the scroll from the office to your home. Why?"

"Scott asked me to. He said I had the tools here and with everything that goes on outside the door to our office it was safer to have it with me. He was going to come here after the conference to open the scroll." Billy has the copper tube in his hand turning it over and over. I know he feels guilty about Scott's death also, even though there was nothing any of us could have done to stop the murder.

"On the day Scott was killed, someone turned off the alarm system and entered my house. They went to my gun safe, opened it and took my service revolver out of the case. Then put everything back, exited my house, turned the alarm back on and left. They then waited until we left the tavern and killed Scott. My guess, they used a silencer. I also feel they kept him alive for a while to get information out of him about the scroll. When he wouldn't talk, they killed him. That is pure speculation, but since Billy has not had a visit from these people, Scott did not release the location. He may have told them the office in Baltimore, but it was gone before they got there." I see Samantha typing away. I am hoping this paints a picture of the crime because I have no idea what direction to go with the case.

"After Scott's body was found, the police notified Karen, who told them Samantha and I had dinner with them that night and that Scott and I argued. This made me a person of interest in Scott's murder. The next event is the autopsy coming back and ballistics matching my service revolver to the bullet that killed Scott. Which prompted the return of the police to the house with a search warrant for my gun."

Samantha interjects, "Don't forget we drove to Fredericksburg to see Karen and the reporters have already been tipped off you are a person of interest. Also Christina saw the man turning the alarms off as he walked through the yard."

I shake my head. I can't forget that they made an attempt to return the gun. Tracy interrupts, "I think Roddie got the job at your pizza place and we had the pizza delivered about this time. Roddie needed to talk to you because he thought John Wake was framing you for the murder. We figured this out when we saw Joseph Callan creeping through your yard. Those two are in bed together and where you find one up to something, you find the other."

Samantha yells, "Wait a minute! Did you say Joseph Callan? I have a Joseph and Marie Callan on my list. He's an insurance salesman from Buffalo, New York. They have two children, Joseph Junior and Michael. When I pulled their online profile I saw pictures of the family at the Academy of Buffalo Christians. It was for a turkey dinner for charity." She pulls up the picture from a social media site. "Is this him?"

She turns it around and Tracy looks at the picture, "That's the same Joseph Callan but he's no insurance salesman. The 'Company of Independent Agents', yes, but actual insurance, no. That very well may be a picture of his family. I know he splits his time between being at The Farm and being up north somewhere. So—is the Academy of Buffalo Christians on the list of schools?"

Billy runs his finger down the list and stops at a name. "ABC, Buffalo, New York. A Christian Academy of forty students allowing one on one education. Money for the school is obtained from tuition, donations and fundraisers."

Tracy smiles, "I think we have a spook, to family, to school confirmation." He turns his tablet around. On the screen is ABC, Academy of Buffalo Christians, private education with one on one instruction.

This is interesting. Maybe the scrolls are connected to The Farm. This would explain why they are written in Arabic. The language was chosen because few in the area can read it. It would make sense that the covert branch of the CIA has individuals who can read and write Arabic. Maybe we are getting somewhere. "Okay, let's see what we can find out about John Wake."

Tracy gestures a time out with his hands, "His name is John Wake now, it wasn't that in his early life. That is a name he may have assigned himself at some point. I did some digging into his background because he didn't seem to be who he was on paper. His real name is Craig Willet. I found this by pure accident. I was researching John Wake for a military record. His name came up as a restricted file so I put in a borrowed identity and got passed the fire wall. It redirected me to Craig Willet. It seems Craig was born in the Midwest and went into the foster care system early in life. There doesn't seem to be a father in the picture and his mother was a drug addict. She ended up an attempted overdose on the street and little Craig was put into foster care. His first foster family was military. When they moved, he was transferred to another military family so that he could stay in the same school. His mother got him back briefly until she was picked up for distribution of controlled substances. This put him back into the system.

The same military family asked for him back. He spent a couple years bouncing between his mother and this family. She would get out and get him back, then bounce back into jail. Her last act was to shoot too much heroin. Little Craig was four at the time and spent close to a week alone in the house with his dead mother. He was put back into the foster care system. Military families seemed to work for him. His mother had no discipline and he liked having the comfort of having rules. He ended up in the home of the Commander of an elite Army recon division. At eighteen, he graduated from high school and entered the Army. From there he was on to Fayetteville, North Carolina for Special Forces Training."

"Vietnam was going full strength at the time and Craig's unit went from Fayetteville to Cat Lai, Vietnam. Pretty soon he was detached to the five oh one military intelligence and recruited into the CIA. He was key recon with Operation Phoenix. He was part of a five man hit squad that jumped into remote villages and took out targets. They were quite successful and have a five digit kill count. After the war they had a problem on their hands. His name was Craig Willet. He was a trained assassin who liked his job way too much. For twelve years, we kept him out of the country. He would go where we needed to kill someone and take care of the problem."

"Finally in the nineteen eighties, we decided to bring him home. He was sent to The Farm where it was thought they could fix him. Roddie encountered him there, but by then his name had been changed to John Wake. Roddie can't prove it, but in the early years of him being John Wake he was still out of control. Occasionally, tourists disappeared on the Colonial Parkway. Roddie found a spot in the woods to watch for a while and witnessed John Wake killing a couple. That sealed the deal for him. He leaked the information to the press that the serial killer was a rogue

CIA agent. Once people began to ask questions, the Farm put tighter controls on him and the killings stopped."

"Wake worked his way up from instructor to eventually becoming the head of Covert Operations at the Farm. I think because our country could not risk allowing him to walk free. If he doesn't like someone or something—he has impulse control issues. He kills them or destroys it."

This is a lot to take in. If this cylinder belongs to John Wake either he or his henchman Joseph Callan killed Scott. Samantha has been sitting patiently tapping her pencil on her note pad. I can tell by the look on her face she has something important. "I have pay dirt. I searched for the history of Fayetteville Special Forces and they have a very nice virtual museum. In it I found the past commanders of the units and came across the name of General Forest Parker. I cross references it with our list of names and found a Mister and Misses Forest Parker in Fayetteville, North Carolina. Her name was Millie and their son is listed as Craig. From here, I looked at schools and found Country Estates Christian School in Fayetteville, North Carolina. Here on their alumni charity campaign Gala page is a captioned photo— 'General and Misses Forest Parker and their son, Craig'. For confirmation I went to the CIAs web page and searched for John Wake. We either have twins or a man with two or three names. I have seen Craig referred to as Craig Forest on the Country Estates Alumni page."

This is getting interesting. "Now we might be on to something. Let's assume all the names on the list have these connections. Let's play the game with President Elect Nathan Hall. He's on the politician page. First up we know he is a third generation American. His grandmother and mother came here to escape Nazi Germany. He made that part of his talking points. Even as a victim of the war his family struggled to come to this country legally. I believe his grandfather was killed in the war."

I look over at Talmadge. He is paging through something on his tablet. He is lost in thought and I think we may have triggered something. As part of the Washington, DC field office, he would have been working on background reports for the incoming White House staff. Each person working in the White House must have a background check performed. This includes everyone from the President down. In order to have access to the White House unaccompanied, the person must pass the background. If they have not completed their background they are issued a restricted badge and must be accompanied outside of their office. This can for some include trips to the rest room. With an incoming President there is always a mad dash after the election to get everyone checked and credentialed before the inauguration. "Talmadge, please tell me you have information from the background checks on both the President and Vice President."

He looks at me for a moment and smiles, "Yes I do and I have found what I am looking for. President Hall put his grandfather as unknown. I didn't make the connection at first but the story we were given was that his grandmother was a Polish peasant who was taken prisoner by the Nazi's. She was held in a prison and her daughter was the result of a rape by an SS officer. Her daughter was still with her when the facility she was held in was liberated. As a prisoner of war, she and her daughter were granted immigration to the United States. She arrived in New York and was immediately transferred to a church run school in Pennsylvania. Her background as a teacher got her a faculty position. She and her daughter lived at the Gettysburg Christian School. His grandmother died a few years ago, still living on the campus of the school. His mother stayed there until her wedding day. She didn't go far. She and her husband met at the school and bought a house a few miles away. Hall graduated from that school before going to college in Boston."

"His grandmother never admitted it, but she may have been one of the Polish children kidnapped by the SS and bred to the Ubermenschen. His mother may be a Lebensborn child. He fits the criteria. He's six foot two, blond hair, blue eyes; he's physically fit, and athletic. The picture of him rowing in the Potomac with his shirt off turned up everywhere on social media and in the press during the election. 'President Ripped-Abs' and 'President Hunk' were thrown around as much as the return of Camelot reference of his family."

"Who knows, Nathan Hall may have been Adolph Hitler's dream. The scroll mentions breeding to please the voters. Perhaps this is something that happened by accident, but with his name written in these scrolls I have to wonder if he is the product of a breeding program."

We are all silent when Talmadge finishes speaking. Bernie asks the question we are all thinking, "Was Nathan Hall bred to be the President of the United States—and who now has control over the leader of the free world?"

Samantha stands up and gets another cup of coffee. She walks over to the pot roast and looks into the pot. Billy asks her to stir it for him while she is up. She then announces she is going to go use the rest room. I stand up and get my coat and offer to go with her. As soon as we get outside she stops, "Adam, I looked at the names on that list. Besides the incoming President and Vice President—there are other names I recognized on the family list. I'm sure Talmadge has made the connection also. I mean it lists the parents with their children, but those are not infants. Most of Nathan Hall's cabinet are children from the same families. One thing they all have in common is their looks. They are all blue or brown eyed blonds with muscular builds. They are all six feet to six feet six. You've seen pictures of them. I bet if we start to cross reference them we will find they have been grade school friends from private Christian schools. My question is why? Why is this connected to the head of the Farm and why were these lists written in Arabic?"

I wish I could answer her questions. I don't know if we should trust Talmadge. I want to trust him, Tracy and Roddie but they walked into our lives. They haven't done anything to lose my trust but I don't know if I trust them. I'm not sure who I can anymore other than my immediate family and friends.

I hear a door open and Billy walks out, "We seem to all have to go to the rest room. I guess the power of thought huh? Are you going to the rest rooms or just going to stand out here?" We walk into the bunk room. Billy follows us. "Tracy and Talmadge do not know that I have a toilet in my container. I wanted to talk for a moment. What is your take on this?"

I wish I had an answer for him. He goes in and uses the toilet and comes back out. "As I see it, the President and the Vice President that are about to be sworn into office in six weeks are connected to a rogue CIA agent who murdered Scott because he found the cylinder containing information about their birth and education. Why does that information warrant a man's death? Did this rogue individual kill to protect the President or to protect himself?"

Samantha uses the toilet while Billy and I walk outside. Bernie has walked out of the green container and walks over to us. "I guess we are all asking the million dollar question. What exactly is going on here? Is the CIA breeding Presidential candidates?"

Samantha joins us and we all return to the green container and pull chairs back to the table. She pushes the button and wakes up her tablet. "This looks a lot like one of Alina's math problems in school. You know the 'if all gnips and gnops are gnaps and gnaps can be either gnips or gnops, how many gnops are there who are not gnaps?" My initial answer was forty-two but I didn't expect Alina to get the joke and I think the teacher was serious in asking the question. It took a while to come up with the correct answer."

All of the men at the table are looking at her confused. Samantha starts to laugh, "Zero. If all gnops are gnaps there cannot be a gnop who is not a gnap. They use the words to confuse you. Maybe we are getting tied up in the words also. We have a list of families, a list of politicians and a list of schools. We know some politicians belong to the list of families, we know every family we have checked is associated with one of the schools. We also know the politicians are connected to the schools. We have a manifesto on breeding the perfect man to run for political office and we can see the politicians on the list fit the description of the manifesto. They are gnips, gnops and gnaps. They are each a subset of the other with the school being the central circle in the diagram."

This makes sense and I think she may be on the right track. "So let's set aside the lists of people and concentrate on the list of schools and the manifesto. Do we think the schools are a breeding ground? Has the concept of the Lebensborn been brought to the United States to create a master race that takes over the United States government?"

This statement stops my thoughts in their track. If someone is breeding people to take over the country the election of Nathan Hall was a success. "If this is the case, than the discovery of these documents is a reason to kill. Scott died because he found the breeding program that led to the election of the new President of the United States!"

The only sound in the room is coming from the stove. The pot roast is bubbling and the noise has become deafening. Billy gets up and walks to the stove to stir it. Scott being killed because someone deliberately bred a man to become President sounds insane. Then again, use personal preferences to choose a partner, is this any different?

Raising children in a small select environment with families who have like interests and beliefs seems to be a reasonable way to meet a spouse and raise children. We always want the best for our kids and for them to marry someone who fits in with the family. A Christian family would want their children and grandchildren to be Christian. Why then does this feel menacing?

We are all lost in thought until Samantha says, "The writing is the anomaly. Someone presumably in the United States felt more comfortable writing these lists in Arabic script. I have always seen Arabic printed, because I doubt many in this country can hand write it. Look at the writing—it flows and isn't broken. It was written by someone who is comfortable with the words and Arabic."

She is right. Someone went to extremes and not only hand wrote in Arabic but wrote German words in Arabic as well. I had assumed this was a German, possibly skin head plot. Something Neo-Nazi and related to racism, but in the text it mentions borrowing from the Lebensborn Program, not an extension of or continuing it. I put the thought out in the open to the group, "Who has the connections to the lists and can write in Arabic to the point they are comfortable?"

Talmadge suddenly stands up. His chair falls backwards and crashes onto the floor. "Shit! John Wake! He started in the Russian block while they were breaking up. When that region began to settle down, he was transferred to the Middle East. He went native, grew the beard, wore the garb, and talked the talk. He would have coffee and toke on a hookah in the morning with a group of men and slit one of their throats in the afternoon."

He is standing there running his hands through his hair and rubbing his forehead. He finally bends down and picks up his chair. He turns it around so that the back of the chair touches the table. He straddles the chair and sits down. He leans his elbows on the table and rests his hand over his mouth, "Okay, here's the deal. I think I need to go outside and call my boss. We need to get this to Washington, DC. If John Wake killed Scott Llewellyn to protect the breeding program that produced Nathan Hall and Michael Morris the Director needs to know. Hopefully someone has the answers to the plan behind this group. If not, Nathan Hall and Michael Morris may have to answer some questions between now and January twentieth."

I stop him, "Wait! If we decide to turn this over to someone, I have lost any proof to protect myself. I know this isn't much but it gives doubt. I need something sent to me in writing that I get some protection. Here I am safe. Once I leave here and enter into DC, I could face anything from arrest to assassination."

Talmadge agrees and promises me that Samantha and I will get protection. He walks outside to make the call. Everyone grabs their coats and follows him. Bernie walks over to the bunk container and puts a leash on Max to walk him.

It is peaceful outside. The snow is falling and I can hear it lightly hitting the ground. The leaves and grass in the center of the compound are completely covered. The herbs around the well are still visible but they are slowly beginning to slip beneath the snow. If this had been any other time, I would have enjoyed the view. Instead, I look around wondering what I might have to deal with ahead.

Talmadge is on his phone. From his responses it does not look as if the conversation is going as well as he had hoped. I notice when he gets frustrated he paces and runs his hand through his hair. He stops and puts his hand on his hip and then goes back to pacing. He finally turns around and looks at us standing together. "We have a little complication. Virginia State Police are insisting on issuing a fugitive arrest warrant. They released the information to the media. Your picture is all over the news right now. You are wanted for questioning and for fleeing the state during an active investigation. Hopefully, the news will remain local, but it puts a complication in our trip into DC."

I turn around to walk back inside. Talmadge yells to me, "Adam wait! We've got a plan. I need the cooperation of everyone here." He looks around the courtyard, "If everyone agrees we can do this. What the director suggested will work—if we all work together."

Samantha is looking at me. I can see she wants this over. We both want to be home with our kids. I don't want to live my life looking over my shoulder. At the same time since my name and picture have been released to the media, I am now going to be convicted by the court of public opinion. I have seen it before when someone is targeted by the media. They sensationalize the issue and spend their time speculating about a situation. They do it for the ratings but the damage they do cannot be repaired. Public opinion is turned against the person and no one will believe the truth. It is part of the dumbing down of our society. If the television tells us something is true we believe it. We could have the actual truth handed to us and many will still not believe it. The idiot box has lived up to its nickname. I will now be known as a murderer.

We walk back into the green container. Billy reaches up and turns on the television and checks the pot roast. He opens a canister and soups out some corn starch. After mixing it with water he slowly stirs it into the pot. "It's almost ready if someone wants to get some plates. We can spoon this out."

Samantha gets up from the table and helps Billy with the food. I have lost my appetite. I know I have to eat but I no longer have the desire. I feel like a ruined man. Until now, I thought I could fight this and beat it. Now, I know it is over.

Once we are all sitting at the table with food Talmadge begins; "Here is the plan. We all need to get a good night's rest. In the morning, we need to get up and get packed to head out. Our goal will be to enter Washington, DC after dark tomorrow night. Adam, I am going to drive your car. Billy, I am either going to have to leave my bike here or someone else has to ride it. We are going to have to alter Adam's tag or switch it out with someone's. Bernie, I am going to need you to follow close behind. I don't want a vehicle to be able to get between us. Tracy I'm going to need you to ride your bike and stay to the side or in front of Adam. Billy, I need you to either switch off the front or stay on the side. We are going to box the Jeep in as inconspicuously as possible. Adam and Samantha, you are going to have to stay in the back of the Jeep under cover.

At least once we get into populated areas. I need you down in the back and under a blanket. Any questions so far?"

Billy taps the table a couple times and offers to ride Tallmadge's bike. "I'd rather ride the bike. It gives me more maneuverability. I also have a set of truck tags we can put on the Jeep. Throw the real tags inside. Make the Jeep dirty and no one will notice it."

Tracy looks over at Bernie, "how is your driving? You mentioned you ride a bike. I rode the bike to make it through backups with Talmadge. I'm not a big fan and its Talmadge's other bike. So do you want to take shotgun on the bike and I will drive your car. Don't worry. I will only wreck your car if we need to protect Adam and Samantha. You have insurance right?"

Bernie smiles back, "Sure, I will ride the bike. If you want to hand over a sixty-five thousand dollar Italian motorcycle to me. I am not going to turn down the opportunity."

Talmadge looks around the table, "Speaking of riding shotgun. I think everyone should be armed. Obviously, on the bikes you are going to have to have handguns. In the vehicles, I think we need to ride with handguns and rifles. We have to travel as witness protection at this point. There is an active hit on Adam and the people we are dealing with are professional hitmen. I cannot stress this any other way. The intelligence has indicated that John Wake, or someone in his office, has issued a hit on him by the country's top snipers. It could get dicey. Are you up to this Samantha and do you feel comfortable with a gun?" She nods her head and looks over at me.

This sounds insane. I feel as if we are driving into a trap. "I understand we are going to Washington but where exactly? It's a big city. What protection do I have once I get there?"

Talmadge pulls out his tablet and clicks on a link. He turns the tablet around so that we can all see the map. "Our destination is MacArthur Boulevard North West, specifically the Grand Lodge. We will take I-70 to I-270. It's pretty straight forward. Once we hit Northwest DC, we take the Cabin John to Clara Barton. That's a straight shot to MacArthur. It is mostly open interstate. I want to wait until the sun goes down. We won't have police support, we are on our own until we hit DC. We need to keep it to the speed limit and not get the police attention. We can't risk having a pull over. We pick up the FBI escort at a location that will be relayed to me by the Director on approach. Nothing is going to be broadcast on official channels."

Samantha interrupts him, "Why the Grand Lodge?"

Talmadge looks at each of us around the table before speaking. "I don't know the entire story, but we are dealing with a coup to take over the United States government. The information I sent from the scrolls has been compared to chatter and it appears Nathan Hall is a plant. There has been chatter for weeks about a coup somewhere in the world. It wasn't known the country at risk but all world leaders have been on alert. No one expected it to be the United States. The chatter was about the overthrow of the government and the conversion to Sharia Law."

He looks uncomfortable talking about this to the group; "This is sensitive material. It is top secret but I think everyone here has a stake in what is happening. Some of the people on the scroll have been on a terrorist watch list. There have been some fairly radical ideas filtering out to the public. We had thought they were part of an Islamic cell. The connection had not been made to the schools. This gave us a much broader picture and it's not good. This was the final piece to the puzzle."

He pulls something up on his tablet and turns it around for the group. "This was sent to me while I was on the phone to the field office." The picture show a group of women dressed in burkas and men in habibs. "This shot was taken in Baltimore City last summer. There was a conference at the convention center—"

Bernie interrupts him, "There is a new Muslim conference center in Baltimore. We see people dressed like that all the time at the inner harbor. We have been told hands off of them."

Talmadge nods his head in agreement, "Yes, but look closely at the men." He points at one of the men. "That is Nathan Hall and this woman is his wife."

We sit stunned for a moment. No one ever expected to see the future President of the United States dressed in traditional Muslim garb. Talmadge lets this news sink in for a few seconds before he continues. "A Mason walking into the lodge is given the right to speak and his brothers will listen. They will also do what is needed to protect a brother Mason. There is no other place in this country that houses more Masons who can make decisions and control this country than the Grand Lodge. It is the home Lodge of Presidents, Congressmen, Senators and Supreme Court Judges. If you are a Mason in Washington, DC, you belong to this lodge. What has to be done isn't something we can do alone. We need their help."

Samantha shakes her head, "I can't go into the inter-sanctum. What am I going to do, stand in the lobby?"

Talmadge is shaking his head, "No, there will be a dinner tomorrow night in a banquet room. It is by invitation only and the participants are being told this is a meeting of the upmost importance and discretion is mandated. After the meeting, we will take a stairway that leads to the catacombs. I can't tell you more about where we will go but we will be entering the Masonic tunnels under the city. We will be safe and our vehicles will be stored."

Bernie raises his hand. Talmadge looks in his direction. "What about the animals. We can't leave the dogs here."

"Provisions have been made. They can enter the lodge and will wait in safety in the catacombs until we join them. Someone will be with them until we retrieve them. They will be staying with us at our destination for the night." Talmadge looks around the table again. "Does anyone have any other questions? If not we should finish eating and try to get some rest. I'm exhausted and tomorrow will be an intense day."

I'm not sure what else there is to say. I am still trying to sort facts out in my head. The story seems too strange to be real. Could Scott have accidentally found a storage site for a coup against the country? Why would someone hide something like this? Unless of course it was for proof to be leveraged as protection if things went wrong.

I look around the table at everyone. They are sitting there with untouched plates of food. I wonder what John and the kids are doing right now. It is Thanksgiving night. I saw on the news that the parade in New York had been canceled. The professional football games have been postponed because teams did not get a chance to travel to out of town destinations. The fate of the college games are in question for this weekend.

I wonder if families across the country are sitting down to turkey dinners. Is there normalcy and the traditional family meal is going on in homes across the nation? Karen is facing Scott's funeral in the morning. I wish I could stop her from potentially meeting Scott's son and namesake along with his lover.

What a screwed up world we now live in. I am suspended from my job and wanted for questioning in a murder. I am being framed by the CIA, who it seems has a rogue agent that is involved in a coup to take over the country. And my question is why?

I look down at my plate. I have been moving hunks of venison, potatoes and carrots around the plate. The gravy is beginning to get a film on top as it cools. Tradition—that would have me sitting at a table surrounded by my family. In front of me would be a huge turkey. The table would be filled with stuffing, cranberry sauce, green beans, mashed potatoes, corn bread—everything that makes it a Thanksgiving dinner.

The house would smell of roasted turkey mingled with pumpkin pie that would be sitting just out of the oven and cooling for dessert. Samantha would be sitting next to AJ trying to get him to eat dinner and not wear most of it. Doughnut would be under the table waiting for food to fall from AJ onto the floor.

I smile thinking about Alina. This child lights up a room. She would be dressed in her prettiest dress. My guess the red velvet one. It's her favorite. It's getting too small for her but she still wiggles herself into it. We bought it for her last year to get her picture taken for Christmas. Her blond curls would be pulled back in the front and held down on top her head with a big red bow. Samantha has started to put Alina's hair like that to keep it out of her face. It looks so adorable on her.

Christina would be sitting next to Alina. Her job would be to make sure Alina eats something other than cranberry sauce and corn bread. She would have AJ on her other side and helping Samantha poke food in his mouth. In many ways, Christina has become Samantha's sister. They share everything including raising our kids.

John and Chris would be sitting at the table. Chris would be keeping us entertained with his stories of tourist traffic pullovers and crazy things he has caught people doing in and around the historic triangle. John would be smiling from ear to ear. John is my best friend. I do love him like a brother. In many ways as Scott and I drifted apart, John filled in the space in my life.

Tomorrow night we would pile into the cars and do another family tradition. The holiday light celebration opens tomorrow night. Well, I guess it still opens tomorrow night. Maybe that too has been delayed because of the insanity that has happened to this country. The tradition originally started with Elizabeth and me. After her death, I stopped going but it started again when my buddy allowed Samantha and I to go in one night before it opened to the public. They were putting the last few finishing touches on and all the lights were burning as we walked through and they checked each display. Just before the end of the trail, I proposed to Samantha and put her engagement ring on her finger.

Instead of the traditions that I love and the family that I miss, I am sitting at a table mostly surrounded by strangers. Turkey has been replaced by venison. There is no holiday laugher. Just people sitting at a table eating in silence.

My mind drifts to America before Thanksgiving. Unlike the Pilgrims, life in Virginia was tough. The people of Jamestown eventually made an agreement with the Powhatten Indians and the killing stopped. They branched out from the protection of Jamestown and established Middle Plantation. It was still a time of famine. The colonists began to farm and establish the colonial capital of Virginia known as Williamsburg. A venison dinner like this was a standard meal for those who lived off the land in the new world.

Last week Scott was talking about the early settlers of Jamestown and the transition from living on the early frontier to the Colonist in Middle Plantation. Eventually, it became a city overseen by a Colonial Governor living the life of English gentry. In a few short years, the area went from survival of the fittest to pianoforte concerts and balls at the Governors Palace. Then the world changed and the fledgling Colony stood up to their government and became a country into their own.

Ironically, Scott thought he had found the words of the early settlers admitting to rumored treasure. Instead, it appears he found the notes of a group who are trying to change the government once again. He died for his find.

I force myself to eat my dinner. Tomorrow is going to be a long day and one that I might not live through. Hiding in the woods is safe. Leaving the security of this shelter feels like a mistake, but I can't keep running.

We leave Billy and return to the bunk containers. Tomorrow will bring what it brings. Tonight we all try to get some rest. In the morning, we prepare our route and pack what we need.

I know I have to sleep but as I go to bed my mind is spinning. I can't get the parallel to the Last Supper out of my mind. It once again fueled the struggle in my mind on Samantha. Since I met her, I have had a constant struggle between my love for her and her past. It has never bothered me that she has had sex with many men when she was a prostitute. She has been open and honest about her past life. She has not tried to hide anything.

Throughout our relationship we have talked. She has no idea how many men she has had sex with and doesn't even know their names. She had no love for any of them. Some were regulars and she knew their first names. With those she has a friendship but sex with them remained a job.

She was young when she ended up on the street. Sex was a way to eat and to pay for a place to sleep. She was fifteen when she gave birth to Kali, yet, she never saw Kali as a mistake. She was a bi-product of her job.

I have always been a guy who dedicated myself to one woman. I feel I owe the women in my life my full attention. Now I know Scott had an affair. I can put a name to the woman and to Scott's son. I don't know how I feel about Scott's parents keeping the affair and illegitimate son to themselves. If Kathryn goes to Scott's funeral with her son, his son, Karen will become a victim again. Her body let her down and he found a woman who could give him what he wanted. To Scott and his family this child justified the affair.

I wonder if Scott saw me as the one without sin. Did he come to me to convince me to be there when the tube was opened? Did he think I was the one who could look upon the Ark of the Covenant?

Samantha has fallen into a restless sleep. She is moaning and thrashing around the bed in her sleep. I guess she is dealing with her own demons and fears for tomorrow. I try to put my arms around her for comfort. I wonder if Scott saw her as the repentant whore. Was she my Mary Magdalene? She fits the description. She is a loyal disciple who stands her ground next to me. She went from inmate to FBI profiler from my recommendation. She is mother, nurturer and devoted wife. In many ways she is a modern day Mary Magdalene in my life. I close my eyes and will myself to go to sleep, knowing my night will be just as restless as Samantha's.

Day Eight,
The Allegheny Highlands, Western Pennsylvania

I wake up to voices in the center compound. Talmadge is cussing someone out. I jump out of bed and grab my gun. Through the crack in the door I see him on his phone pacing back and forth. I still have trust issues with him and I stand by the door and listen for a moment.

I'm not sure who is on the other end but Talmadge is pissed that we are being told to stay here for the day. He wants to get on the road and get this resolved. The person on the other end seems to not be accommodating to the idea. He pushes the button to end the call and stands in the middle of the compound. He runs his hand through his hair and bows his head. I watch him take a few deep breaths before he walks over and punches Billy's weather rock.

I walk out the door as he is standing there rubbing his knuckles. I see one is bleeding slightly. He looks over at me and gives me a slight grin, "I guess you just saw that? Sorry. I tried the breathing technique and it wasn't working. I needed to punch something. I didn't want to piss Billy off by punching his walls."

I understand that feeling all too well. "I take it we have trouble?" He nods his head. "Should I wake the troops?"

He shakes his head, "No, let them sleep. We are in a holding pattern. Commerce has kept crews working twenty-four/seven to get temporary trunk lines run and patched in to get banking back online. They have a temporary patch that will allow them to open stores. Originally, the big boxes were crying to be able to open last night but there was no way to provide security. We have no idea if this is over yet. What do we do if that was just stage one? How do we know malls aren't a secondary target? Can you imagine a big mall being blown up on Black Friday?"

I had forgotten about the shopping frenzy that normally happens today. Talmadge is standing there shaking his head. "As it is, there have been people camped in front of stores since before the bombing in order to get Black Friday deals. They aren't moving until they get their wide screen TVs. That is at least from the places that haven't been looted. It appears the big box stores ended up being protected in most places by the Black Friday campers. They stood in the way of looters and pushed them back. It is an impressive indication of capitalism at its best. People were fighting for the right to shop. Last night shoppers arrived at the stores expecting to get in. Commerce worked fast and worked out a deal. Stores are going to open at ten this morning. Meanwhile, malls and big box stores are being scanned for bombs. People are being told on the news and at the stores that there will be security checks. Some locations have rolled out portable X-ray scanners. They have been pulled from schools and government buildings. Those locations will remain closed next week in order for us to return to some normalcy. Malls and stores will have controlled access. This will piss a couple people off. They can't walk in just any door and there will be lines to get in. Hell, there are lines that have been forming since last weekend, so they might have to learn to be patient to shop."

The door opens to our container and Samantha walks out with her backpack in her hand. I shake my head at her. "Babe, we aren't heading out today." Bernie and Max come out behind her. Samantha throws her bag in the door and walks over to us.

The door to the green container opens and Tracy sticks his head out. "Coffees on and bacon is cooking. Y'all might as well get out of the cold. We can talk in here."

Max finishes his morning business and Bernie lets him run around inside the center compound for a while. He is enjoying himself digging and snooping around in the snow. Billy is sitting at the table with a cup of coffee when we walk in. His laptop is open and he is scanning the news. "It looks like all hell has broken out in the shopper's paradise. The idiots are chanting outside malls to let them in. Women with minivans have swarmed the malls and circled stores with shopping carts. I think it might be a new national sport! Do you think they have forgotten we just had a terror attack?"

Samantha helps mix up and make pancakes while everyone else gathers around the table watching the news. Someone from Homeland Security is explaining the X-ray scanners and the procedures everyone will have to follow to get into the malls today. Some doors will remain locked with guards posted at them. These doors are for emergency exit only. No one else will be allowed to enter or exit from there. The National Guard has been activated in most areas to either assist with the bomb clean up or maintain order at the malls. The fact that order needs to be maintained at malls amazes me.

Tracy puts the plate of bacon on the table as Samantha puts the plate of pancakes down. We all start to fill our plates. Billy is still buried in his laptop. I'm not sure what he's looking for or what he is doing. He seems to be intent on something. We start to eat allowing him to be lost in his thoughts.

I am almost finished when he looks up from his screen. "Who is up for some recon today? This shopping thing has made me curious and the only way to answer the question is to leave the compound. We can lock it down and it will be secure if everyone is getting cabin fever. Plus this might be interesting."

Samantha looks happy at the prospect of getting out from behind the walls of the compound. Talmadge and Tracy don't look as happy with the idea. Talmadge looks over at Billy, "What is your idea? Adam is a marked man. I don't think it's a good idea for him to leave the protection of the compound. He's safe here. Out there, I have no idea if anyone knows we are here. What about Scott's girlfriend. Does she know? You said Stephen Koehler knows somewhere in Western Pennsylvania. So does Adam's partner. Going out opens the door for us to get attacked and Adam taken out."

Samantha give me a worried look. I feel like we are cut off. I want to see how things are going for myself without the sanitized control of the government on news broadcasts. I'm not ready to go to a mall and deal with the Black Friday frenzy, but I would like to see what is going on outside of the woods.

Billy looks around the table. "Okay, here's the deal. Those who want to go do some recon can come with me. Those who don't can guard the compound. I have a few locations that I want to check out. We have a serious supply chain issue in the country. With interstates down or limited, I need to see if commerce is moving. The stores open for Black Friday deals have stock in shipping containers in their parking lots. People will expect them to run out of the special deals. What people won't be anticipating will be shortages in food and gasoline. I have a stockpile of both, but if we wait too long to bug out moving on the highway could put us at risk. There is a golden hour for these things. Go too fast and we are at risk. Wait too long and we are at risk. This time not just from a hitman, but John and Jane Doe who have run out of food and gas."

I think there has always been a little bit of prepper in me. I have items stored and ready to wait things out. Most people don't seem to be able to make it through a tropical storm or snow storm without wiping the grocery stores out of food. Billy is right. If we wait too long the possibility of an ambush rises as things become scarcer. I tell him I am in. Samantha also agrees to go.

Talmadge and Tracy stand their ground. They think it is a mistake to leave the compound and by leaving we might bring a shit storm down on ourselves. Everyone looks at Bernie. He has been sitting there quietly eating. "I'm with Billy and Adam. I want to see what is going on out there. I'm a cop. I know how crazy people can get. The cities went nuts the day of the bombings. I don't know what we will be driving into once we leave here without testing the water. I'm going."

Billy looks around the table again, "Okay, it's settled. Tracy and Talmadge you stay here and guard the compound. I will give you the keys to the outer and inner gates. When we head out lock it down and don't unlock it until we return. If someone comes too close— fire a warning shot. If they still keep coming, kill them and we will deal with the bodies when we get back. Samantha, Adam, Bernie— let's saddle up. Carry concealed. My guess most around here will be. I'm going to put a couple rifles behind the seat in case we need them. Take a couple extra clips as well. I don't want to be hunkered down waiting for someone to reload while I'm getting my ass shot at."

Behind the compound I hear an engine start up and Billy pulls around in an old king cab pickup. It looks like it has seen better days. The bed and sides of the back of the truck have been made out of landscaping timbers. There is a six by six wooden timber replacing the front bumper also.

I open the passenger side door and see the door panels have been replaced with steel well casing. Billy smiles as I tap the glass. "Yup, this redneck ole boy has got himself bullet proof glass windows and reinforced steel interior. Pennsylvania state inspection won't let me do much to the exterior of the body but I can reinforce the interior. I did the same thing to the engine compartment. The tires are run flats. This baby is an urban survival tank. It is just registered as and looks like a beat up old pickup truck. Hop in."

Billy starts to drive as soon as I close the door. I tighten my seat belt and reach for the handle on the roof. He is driving straight out the driveway ignoring the craters and washout spots. We are bouncing around the truck. Samantha is in the backseat of the cab and is holding on to the roll bar with both hands.

He stops at the wire along the road and gets out to unhook it. I notice he is doing something at the bear totem pole.

He gets back in, leaving the door open and pulls forward far enough to be able to put the wire back on the hook. I notice he locks the lock before he gets back in.

He has a smirk on his face and winks at Samantha and I as he puts the truck in gear. "I take it you have turned some sort of security system on when we left. Anything I should know?"

Billy reaches in his shirt pocket and hands me a smart phone. The screen is divided into sixteen blocks. I can see Talmadge and Tracy in their bunks, various positions inside containers, the center courtyard and views of the exterior. "This will ping if anything moves in or out of view. Those guys have seemed straight up, but I'm still not sure that I trust them. I want to make sure nothing comes in or goes out of the compound while we are away. It will also notify me if any radio waves change. If they bug the place, turn on any remote control or tracking devices—well, I will know and I have something that will jam the signal."

I appreciate his foresight in security. Like him, I trust them to a point. This will show their real intention. No one is there to watch them. If they are going to do something or double cross us, we will know in advance.

Billy is laughing and I look over at him. "They also don't know about the cavern and the trap door. If they set up a trap I can always come in the back door and remind them whose house they are dealing with."

We have hit 99/220. Traffic is heavy but not as bad as I envisioned. Most people are heading toward the shopping areas in Altoona or heading north to State College. The cars are not packed with blankets and pillows like I saw on Wednesday. It looks like people are getting out of the house after being cooped up and they are spending the day as a family.

I am curious about our destination. Billy seems to have some place specific in mind. When I ask I am surprised at his answer, "I want to visit a couple tourist sites. The road tells me people are venturing out, but you will notice we have not seen an eighteen wheeler. Where are the trucks? This tells me they aren't moving fast. There is one other method, the railroad. That is my destination. Most people do not know how important the railroad was to the growth and development of Pennsylvania, nor to the country."

He takes an exit south of Altoona. The scenery is beautiful. To our left I see what looks like a series of lochs. The water has a skim of ice across the entire surface, it is beautiful and reminds me how cold it is outside. It takes a while for a large body of water to freeze over like that. It doesn't look thick enough to hold someone and is probably very dangerous right now. I know it has felt very cold while we have been here. This confirms we have stayed below freezing.

To the right is the rise of the Allegheny Mountains. The road follows the contour of the base of the mountain and we wind in and around the lochs. He pulls into a parking lot with three cars parked. There is a building and some train cars both in the front yard and up on the mountainside.

The gift shop is closed but a couple people have walked up the long set of steps to the top of the railroad platform. Billy starts up the steps. "You don't have to come up if you don't want to. These stairs are pretty steep and you are walking up the side of the mountain. I just want to talk to a couple people and see what they have to say."

I'm curious and we follow him up the steps. The stairs looked long from the bottom. They feel as if they are getting longer the farther up the stairway we walk. By the time we get to the top, Samantha is holding onto the railing and rubbing her knee. I put an arm around her and ask if she's okay. She nods her head and we follow Billy onto the train platform.

Horseshoe Curve is magnificent. From the platform I can look out across the water to Altoona. The train tracks follow the contour of the mountain in a crescent shape. There are three tracks laid side by side. I can imagine the thrill of watching trains pass each other on this tight turn. I notice someone has a sheet of paper and he is standing with a group talking. Billy walks over to them and we follow.

There is a set schedule of trains that pass through the curve. The railroad publishes a list daily with approximate times. People come here to watch the trains and take pictures of them going by. It sounds strange that people would do this over and over but I feel a thrill anticipating the next train.

A man in a train hat walks over to Samantha and me. "So this is your first time to the Horseshoe Curve? Your friend over there said you were tourists from out of town. Bad time to get stuck in Altoona isn't it?"

I play along with the tourist thing, "Yes, we are up here visiting friends. We're from North Carolina. Its beautiful country but it was a hell of a time getting stuck here through this."

The man seems pleased with himself. "My name is Craig Wolf. I'm a regular here. To be honest as soon as I thought it was safe to come out, I drove on down here. I live about twenty minutes north. I serve as sort of a volunteer tour guide. I thought more people would have come out today. So what do you know about this place?"

I look at Samantha and we both shrug at him. I have never heard of Horseshoe Curve before today. It looks like an amazing place. The curve of the track looks as if it might be at the tightest angle for a train track.

He smiles at us and I can see his roll of tour guide setting in. "In front of you is the famous Horseshoe Curve. The curve is about two thousand three hundred and seventy-five feet long and one thousand three hundred feet in diameter. It was completed in 1854 by the Pennsylvania Railroad as a way to lessen the uphill grade of the Allegheny Mountains. Before the Curve was built, the railroad used portage lakes to float the trains across the mountains."

Samantha stops him, "What is a portage lake?"

Her question brings a big smile to his face. "I am so glad you asked. The portage lake was an ingenious invention. The grade of the Alleghenies was too much for a loaded train heading west. Before the portage lakes train cars had to be disconnected and each car hooked to a cable and pulled up the incline. Imagine riding on a train and being forced to get off the train and walk up the side of a mountain. Next to you was a railroad track and a cable about the width of a man's wrist connected to the front of the railcar. Occasionally, the cables would snap and whip over into the group of people walking up the mountain. When that happened people were maimed or killed. At the top of the mountain, the train was reassembled and people were able to return to their seats for the downhill portion of the ride. At the valley, they had to get back off the train and walk up the mountain on the other side. It wasn't pleasant."

He stops for a moment and points over to a bench. "Would you like to go sit down? I haven't seen a train yet and we might as well make ourselves comfortable." We walk to the bench and sit down before he continues. "Someone got the idea to put earthwork dams in the valleys and flood them. A barge was designed with train tracks across the deck. A car was disconnected and rolled onto a barge and floated across the lake. On the other side it was hooked back to the locomotive and continued its way west. Imagine if you will the advancement to rail passengers. They no longer had to walk up the side of the mountains on foot."

He pauses and looks at his watch, "Still nothing. We should have had three trains this hour alone. I think today may be a waste. Anyway, back to the railroad. There is one famous portage lake that many people have heard from history. The dam in South Fork. Well, actually the town of Saint Michael. After the railroad moved away from portage dams and the Curve was up and running they sold off the land. A couple of Robber Barons purchased the portage lake known as Lake Conemaugh and turned it into an exclusive hunting and fishing club. The richest of the rich built summer houses along the lake. They stocked it with fish and it was the place to see and be seen back in the 1880s. They made what they thought was improvements to the dam. Two of those improvements led to a fatal dam collapse. The first was to remove the metal drain pipes because they were ugly and rusty. The second was to shave off the top of the dam and lower it so that two horse draw carriages could pass on top of the dam. Keep in mind this was an earthwork dam. There were rocks mixed with mud and repair was made with straw and manure. You can tell it wasn't built with hardy substantial building materials."

"Memorial weekend 1889 turned into the perfect storm. There were some severe thunderstorms and a nor'easter'. Without the ability to drain water from the dam, the levels hit a critical point. With an earthwork dam, the water is maintained by the pressure of the water against the dam. All is fine until the top is breeched. Once that happens, the flowing water will quickly erode the dam. When the dam broke the twenty million tons of Lake Conemaugh flowed down through the valley taking houses, animals, trains and people in its path. Fourteen miles away was the town of Johnstown. The telegraph lines had been taken out by the flood. Fifty-Seven minutes after the dam collapsed the sixty foot tall wave of water hit the town. It killed over two thousand people. Much of the debris were caught under a stone arch bridge. When that caught on fire, people could hear those who had not drown screaming in pain as they burned to death. Until September 11, 2001 the Johnstown Flood was the highest single day death toll in the United States."

I have heard of the Johnstown Flood. I think we studied it in school. I don't think we were ever told why it happened. I have found in history it is never politically correct to point blame at the richest people in society. In this case, over two thousand people died because the richest families in the country couldn't wait a moment while another carriage crossed a dam.

Off in the distance we hear a screeching sound. Craig looks at his watch. "Well at least there is something moving on the track. I will wait to see it but that should be the Pennsylvania Railroad excursion train out of the railroad museum. Why don't we walk up to the fence so that you can enjoy the full experience of the curve?"

We stand up and walk to the black cast iron fence. In front of us I can see the three sets of train tracks. The screeching sound is getting louder but it is still off in the distance. Craig continues on his explanation of the Horse Shoe Curve. "The Curve was and remains an important part of rail transportation through Pennsylvania. So important that during World War Two the Nazi's tried to blow it up as part of Operation Pastorius. Eight men landed in U-boats on Long Island with the intent of blowing up locations in the United States. The commerce flowing through Horseshoe Curve was so significant even the Nazi's knew of its importance."

We can now see the distinct brick red and gold engine of the Pennsylvania Railroad. It is pulling three passenger cars painted in the same distinct colors. The sound of the engine and the screech of the metal wheels on the steel track is deafening. I can feel the vibration of the approaching train in my feet. It is thrilling. I feel like a kid watching the train pass. It is belching out black smoke and the smell of burning coal is in the air.

I look at both Samantha and Billy. They are both smiling. For a brief moment we have forgotten what has happened in the country and the threats I currently face. Unfortunately, I come back to reality and suggest we head back to the car. There were people on the train looking out the windows smiling and waving at the people standing around the fence. Someone may have seen us and recognized me.

We walk back down the stairs and across the front of the gift shop to the parking lot. Billy suggests we head to another location to see if anyone has seen a train moving on the tracks other than the tourist excursion.

He takes back roads and weaves in and around the mountain. We pull into a parking lot of a railroad museum. The museum has a closed sign out front and the parking lot has two cars parked on it near the road. I see a few men standing along a railing on a bridge. Billy opens his door and points over to the group of men. "I am heading over there. You can come if you want. I want to see if they have seen anything moving here."

Samantha asks, "Where are we and why is this important?"

Billy points to the bridge. "That is the observation platform for the Gallitzin Tunnels. Here the trains pass through the Mountain. The Gallitzin Tunnel is used by the commuter trains. I want to see if they are running. These tunnels aren't tall enough for commerce trains. They can't accommodate two containers stacked on top each other so they are mostly used for human transport. I want to see if any rail traffic is moving. It was halted for a few days but something was on the news about being back to normal. I have my doubts and that the rail lines heading west have been unaffected. If that is the case, it is impossible to move commerce or people around the country right now. Shortages will be severe."

We follow him out of the truck. As we walk along the road, I look down and see a commuter train parked on the tracks. The engine isn't running and it doesn't appear to be occupied. Billy walks over to the group of men standing there and points at the train, "What's up with this? Did they just park a train here?"

One of the men shakes his head. "Right after the bombings started this train was stopped here. It was full of people at the time. A couple hours later some tour buses arrived and everyone was taken off the train and driven to a hotel in

Altoona. I guess some have been there since. Maybe others had family drive to get them on Wednesday when the roads opened up again. You can imagine how full the trains were right before Thanksgiving. They were packed with holiday travelers and kids coming home from college. I have never seen anything like this. This train has just been abandoned on the tracks. I guess there are problems between here and Altoona. That's the only explanation I can think of for them to put the passengers in tour buses to drive them."

This leads me to believe the damage is more extensive than what is being reported. The rail lines between here and Altoona are remote. They pass through small mountain towns. If there is a track problem here, terrorism has entered the most rural areas.

Billy thanks the men for the information and we walk back to the truck. Billy looks around before getting inside. "One of those guys was looking a little too close at you and Samantha. I think we need to get back to the protection of the compound. I'm feeling a little exposed. We have the information we need. It appears both truck and rail transportation have been taken out."

He takes the interstates to drive back to the compound. It only takes a few minutes to drive back into the mountain and to his driveway. Everything is exactly how we left it. Both Talmadge and Tracy are sleeping in their bunks. It makes me gain more trust in them.

Tracy and Talmadge join us in the green container when they hear us return. Everyone has their tablets out at the table. I know Talmadge and Tracy have been waiting for news.

Bernie has been quiet the entire time we have been gone. He has been the cop observing his surroundings. I look over at his tablet. He has pulled up a satellite map of the area. The screen has been enlarged to show the path of the railroad tracks through the mountains. "Bernie, you have been quiet today. What are you thinking?"

He has distant look for a moment. Then he points at his tablet. "I have been looking at known locations that had road and bridge destruction. They have all been very populated areas with access to interstates. If there are attacks to the rail lines between here and Altoona it leads me to believe there are more attacks than those that are reported. That doesn't surprise me. I don't expect full disclosure but this could be really serious. I have been thinking of the implications. We have not seen truck traffic. This is because the interstates are damaged. We are not seeing rail commerce either. I have sat in on Homeland Security meetings about this. Right now we have split the task of the National Guard between clearing the highways and guarding the malls so that people can shop. What are we doing about Monday? The grocery stores should be able to hold their ground through the weekend, but by Monday they will need fresh produce, meat and dairy. If there is a stop/hold on commerce this means perishable food is sitting in refrigerator trucks and on rail cars. You have to keep the refrigerator units running to keep the food cold. If trucks are being held at truck stops, they can refuel and keep them running. Trains sitting on a siding are another story. Plus that stuff has a limited shelf life. We have food rotting in containers right now, and by Monday we will have shelves that are starting to be empty. This is a bad situation that will only get worse the longer it takes to get things moving. It also hasn't been mentioned to the general public. Most have no idea that by the middle of next week they will not be able to go to their local grocery store and get fresh food."

Billy is sitting in his seat nodding his head. "Bernie, you are absolutely correct. Most people will live off their left overs for the weekend. Monday will be another story. They might still have some left overs but they will be ready to eat something other than Thanksgiving dinner for the fifth straight night. The problem will be the shortages. Homeland Security will have to retask the National Guard to get the food supply moving."

This information makes our need to travel as soon as possible more important. If shortages begin to be noticed the possibility of civil unrest increases. The cities are already on edge. The lack of food will make the situation worse.

We eat leftover venison for dinner. The group is quiet and lost in their own thoughts. For me, it means facing a hitman or jail time for a murder I didn't commit. For the rest, it means trying to keep me alive and out of jail. On top of that we have to stop the two men who have been elected President and Vice President of the United States from taking office. There is also the problem of how we will eat come next week. My main question still remains why? What is to be gained by this coup?

Day Nine,
The Allegheny Highlands, Western Pennsylvania

I hear Bernie taking Max out to walk him and put my coat. More snow fell overnight. It is beautiful in the Allegheny Highlands. I look through the trees and see the windmills turning. Up and down the ridge line as far as I can see there are clusters of them. Each group supports a small town. I look at them as the calm before the storm.

We all meet for breakfast and go over the route. Communication will be kept to a minimum. We each have a disposable phone for emergencies. We also load each vehicle with a loaded rifle and a box of ammunition. Everyone checks their handgun and supply of bullets. Billy takes my tags off and puts them in the back floor and puts a Pennsylvania tag on the back.

The seat in the back folds down and I pack our backpacks against the front seats. Samantha and I try to make the back as comfortable as possible with pillows and blankets. We have decided Max will help with our cover and keep prying eyes away from the back. People see a dog and ignore all else about the vehicle. Also, he is large and has a good bark if someone gets too close. Sophie and Dee Dee will be in Bernie's car with Tracy. They will bark but not as intimidating. My big concern is Max getting excited about something and stepping on us. While it won't cause permanent damage—it is going to hurt.

Billy yells over for some help carrying a barrel. I'm not sure what he's planning on doing with it. It is filled with fireplace ash. It takes both of us to rock it back and forth to get it over to the Jeep. He takes his garden hose and squirts down my Jeep. With a scoop he begins to throw ash into the air as he walks around it. Soon it is covered in a coating of ash. Once he finishes the Jeep he does the same thing to Bernie's car. As it dries it appears both vehicles have a layer of road salt on them. It's a great camouflage. It is hard to see the color of the vehicles under the dirt.

We are packed and ready to go at one o'clock. Billy suggests we eat lunch and then begin our journey. If we take roads avoiding traffic cameras for most of the trip it will take us approximately four hours to drive to the heart of Washington, DC. Our goal is to leave after two. This will get us there at approximately six o'clock. The sun will have gone down completely just prior to us entering the city.

Talmadge makes a final call to the director. He has arranged for Maryland State highways to take down the highway traffic camera system for maintenance between two and four. This is done routinely in areas to reboot the system and do any needed computer maintenance. An outage on a Saturday will not be considered unusual.

I am not enthusiastic about having to lay under a blanket for the next four hours. Luckily Max decides to sit in the passenger seat leaving the back to Samantha and me. We can't see anything but clouds. Occasionally Talmadge lets us know we are about to be passed by an SUV or motor home and we pull the blanket over our heads. I can hear the motorcycles moving around the Jeep. Sometimes they are in front of us, sometimes I notice to one of the other sides. I have no idea where we are or how much progress we have made. Time seems to have stood still. I begin to understand how a hostage feels. I have the same sense of isolation and distortion of location. I concentrate on the speed I feel and how bumpy the road is. I can hear and feel where the road has been grooved for construction. I notice the feel of exit ramps and when the tires run onto the grooved side of a single lane road.

Samantha has fallen asleep. I continue to try to remember the characteristics of the road. It keeps my mind busy and may be useful one day if I have another victim locked in the trunk of a vehicle. Talmadge has the windows open a little. It is cold and the blanket feels good. The change in the sound of the wind helps me determine the noise of traffic going under bridges and over passes. There are distinct sounds. I notice traffic is getting heavier. We have slowed down. From my view of the sky, I see that the sun is going down. We must be encountering traffic outside the city. This means the traffic cameras have come back on. We have now become visible, but we are a small fish in stop and go traffic.

Talmadge stays in one lane. I hear the motorcycles behind us. This means Tracy must be in front of us. The bikes can maneuver traffic better than the car. During our planning meeting we had determined when we reach four ninety-five Tracy would take the lead vehicle with the bikes in the back. Whenever possible Talmadge will be in the right lane allowing us to use the shoulder as an open get away. The bikes will be able to watch the left side from the rear. It is safer to ride two bikes across through traffic making them more visible.

I feel another exit ramp. This should be the Cabin John. Outside the sky is a dark blue and I am beginning to see stars in the sky. Talmadge is on the phone again. He lets us know we will be picking up the FBI escort in a few seconds. He confirms with the director that he can see the two unmarked cars along the highway. We slow down and he confirms the lead vehicle has gotten on the highway in front of Tracy. The sound of the bikes is more distant and he confirms the tail vehicle has made it on the highway. I hear the bikes getting closer again as they move up along the tail vehicle and take their position behind us again.

I feel a lump in my throat. The FBI vehicles joining our convoy has handed over trust and protection to people I don't know if I can trust. The line between friend and foe has been blurred. Right now someone in the security detail to protect my life may be here to kill me.

Traffic is inching along and is stop and go. We are turning again. This should be the Clara Barton. We are almost there. I hear other motorcycles and can't tell which ones are our group and which are someone else. Talmadge lets me know they are all ours. They have taken position on the side. We are in full traffic cameras and if someone has located us we are around buildings easily accessed by snipers. He tells us to hang on. He can see the sign for MacArthur Boulevard.

I can hear my heart pounding and feel Samantha reach over and take my hand. We know there are hitmen in the area who are being paid to kill me. The snipers have the full access to the CIA. We may have been tracked the entire way by satellite. If so, we are in an area of no escape. Traffic has boxed us in. The road is a box canyon of houses, offices and shops. The motorcycles are looking for other motorcycles and motor scooters. In Europe, these are the mobile hit vehicles. They can ride up a sidewalk or shoot between cars to fire and get away.

I feel the Jeep pulling over. Through the window I see the spotlight bathed frieze and cornice of the Grand Lodge. It is impressive against the now darkened sky. We have reached our destination. I have never visited the lodge before but from my vantage point it is magnificent. In 1811, the Masons erected a monument to themselves. It is befitting of the other buildings and monuments they had already created and the corner stone of the buildings to come.

Talmadge tells us to stay low. We are waiting for confirmation of a few things before we move. I look back over at the lodge. The façade has a plain high wall from the sidewalk up to stories tall Corinthian columns supporting an elaborate frieze and cornice. The columns are lighted at the base by spotlights making the white marble glow in the night. It is a traditional Greek style exterior. I raise my head slightly and can see the white marble grand staircase leading from the sidewalk and passing between two lions lying in waiting to pounce from their perches.

Director Macon walks up to the driver's side window and Talmadge puts it down halfway. Four other men have walked forward with him. He looks in the window and speaks softly. "Bring what you need for the night and weapons if you have them on your person. These agents are going to take the vehicles and motorcycles to a safe location for the night. We have food and a place for you as a safe house for the night. We need everyone to be ready to travel light. After dinner and the meeting we will be going on foot for about three miles. We need to be able to move quickly and if necessary evade anything we encounter. We will be going through the underground."

I notice another group of men approaching. I am surprised to see John, Chip and Morgan from my office in the group. It is good to see familiar faces. I watch as they take up positions along the sidewalk and the steps. I see other men standing farther up the steps and near the door. I see movement from behind the columns and the director assures me they are our men.

The director is looking around and making sure everyone is in place. He checks something on his ear piece and tells them we will hold for the signal. "Are you ready? When we get the signal get out and go to the left side of the sidewalk. The steps are shallow. I'm telling you this because we will be moving in total darkness. In fifteen seconds, this street will experience a one minute power outage. Everything is going dark for us to get you up, out of the back of the Jeep, up the steps and inside the door. One of the hitmen we suspect Wake has hired was confirmed on traffic camera entering by the Woodrow Wilson bridge this afternoon. We lost him when he abandoned his car in a parking garage. We have not been able to find him on camera since then. Facial recognition software located Joseph Callan entering the city through the subway system. We assume he had a high powered rifle disassembled in his back pack. Okay, I have confirmation from the power company in five, four, three, two— let's move!"

The back hatch of the Jeep opens. Talmadge exits the vehicle with Max on his leash. Someone helps pull Samantha and me out of the back. It feels good to stand after being in the back for so long but I am not given the luxury to stretch. We are being ushered over the sidewalk and up the steps. I hear the bikes start up and the vehicles drive away.

At this moment, the entire North West side of Washington, DC has gone black. Bernie has taken the leash for Max away from Talmadge and is running him up the stairs. It is dark and I am glad the stairs are even. I don't want to trip and fall. Tracy has the leashes for Sophie and Dee Dee. He picks up Dee Dee and Billy grabs Sophie to get them up the stairs quickly. We have reached a porch area. I can barely make out a figure pushing the big bronze door open. We step inside and I hear the door close behind us with a bang. It sounds heavy and solid. I hear a click signifying the latch has been thrown on the lock.

The only light comes from a green exit sign over the door behind us and one ahead of us. We are standing in the foyer. I hear a voice in the darkness, "Welcome to the Grand Lodge of Washington, DC. If you wait a moment the electric company will bring the lights back on in the city. We of course apologize to the good people of the city who just experienced this slight inconvenienced but the head of the power company is a fellow Mason and understands the necessity of our momentary need for the discretion of darkness."

I hear a pop as the lights come back on. After being in darkness the light is blinding for a second. I look around and see John walking toward us. He gives Samantha a hug and then turns and hugs me. "I'm so glad to see you guys. Are you okay? This has been some crazy shit." I nod my head yes. "Look, we didn't want to worry you. Chris, Christina, Alina and AJ have been moved to a safe house. Christina has Alina's class work and has been teaching her at home. We didn't want to alarm you and have you come home but there was an issue. A woman posing as a substitute teacher yelled at Alina and said she was taking her to the principal's office. When she turned the wrong way in the hallway, Alina got spooked. Luckily, we had posted a detail at the school and we stopped her before they went out the side door. Well, I should say we assisted Alina in apprehending the woman. First Alina yelled that wasn't the direction to the principal's office. The woman started to put her hand over Alina's mouth. Morgan was posing as a janitor and was mopping floors. He ran down the hallway. Margaret was posing as a cafeteria worker and ran also. I have to hand it to Alina. She bit the shit out of the woman. By the time Morgan and Margaret got to them, Alina had bitten a hunk out of the woman's arm and was going in for another bite. They were about ten feet from the playground door but we took the woman down. Her name is Carrie Monk and she was a secretary at The Farm. After taking both her and Alina to the hospital, we took Ms. Monk back to our office. Alina was fine. Not a scratch on her. Monk needed nineteen stitches to close part of the hole. The rest will have to heal from the bottom up. It looked pretty nasty and she lost a lot of blood. I was worried about anything Alina might have caught from her but the blood work came back clean."

I know I shouldn't be laughing but I hear Samantha giggling also. This reminds me of the morning Tyler Braden tried to kill us and Alina lunged at him. She caught him off guard and I was able to wrestle the gun away from him and shoot him. We have told Alina ever since that what she did was brave but she had to be careful. Only attack back if she sees an opportunity but if anyone ever tries to kidnap her or hurt her again she is allowed to bite, kick and scratch her way free.

I hear the man who invited us speaking and turn to look at him. I know the voice sounded familiar and I find myself looking at the Speaker of the House. "My lady, gentlemen— if I may have you follow me. The other guests have already been seated and are waiting for you to arrive so that we might eat dinner. Please allow Brother Calvin Brant and Brother Leonard Timms take your pets ahead to

Blair House. Brother Timms is a veterinarian and you can trust him with their well-being. Food and water is waiting for them." He turns and walks through a wooden door. We follow him and find ourselves in a corridor lined with pictures of past Grand Masters and lodge memorabilia. I glance for a second at the portrait of George Washington dressed in full apron and jewel as the Grand Master. Ahead I hear the laughter and conversation of a group of people. The speaker opens the door and holds it for us to follow. "May I please introduce—Master Adam Clay and his wife, Sister Samantha Callahan Clay, Master Talmadge Bowdein, Master John Duncan, Brother Bernie Moll, Brother Tracy Davis, Brother Billy Gill, Brother Morgan Sykes, and Brother Chip Langley. Brother Macon, would you mind introducing our standing members present this evening?"

The Director pulls out a chair for Samantha, "Please, everyone have a seat and I will introduce everyone to you." I sit down and look across at the face of the current President of the United States. After everyone is seated, Director Macon begins the introduction of the lodge members present. "I think I should break protocol slightly and introduce down the table rather than by initiate. Of course you recognize Brother and President Mike Randall and Master and Vice President, Doug Lane, Rear Admiral Brother Peter Holmes, General Brother Howard Pike, General Master Roger Vandergraph, Congressman Brother Richard Houch, Brother Senator Derrick Poole, Master Congressman William King, Brother Congressman David Knight, Master Director Franklin Dubois from the Central Intelligence Agency and Grand Master Mason Peter Covington of the Grand Lodge of Washington, DC."

I look down the table at Frank Dubois. I did not expect to see anyone from the CIA in the room and it makes me nervous. Director Macon anticipates my concern. "Adam, do not worry about Brother Dubois. He has been helping us behind the scenes and working with Roddie Clark for a few years. He has wanted to bring John Wake down for some time and is glad this will give him the ability to jail him. He has been providing us with the communications from John Wake and Joseph Callan which identified the contract on your life. No one in this room means you any harm. We are here to protect you and to stop this coup in its tracks."

The President clears his throat and all turn to look at him. "If I might, may I say the blessing so that we may begin to eat. I don't mind talking shop, but the food is getting cold and it was graciously provided for us." Director Macon bows and sits on the other side of Samantha. The President bows his head and reaches out his hands. We all follow his lead and take the hand of the person on each side of us. "Our Heavenly Father and Grand Master of the Universe, we thank you for the safe journey to this place and for the food which has been placed before us. We ask that you watch over us as we face down the evil that has invaded our country and we ask that you give us strength and courage to complete this mission. Like our forefathers before us, we ask that you walk with us and guide us in the upcoming days. We ask that you protect this nation and the people who live here. We also ask that you comfort the families who have faced loss from this evil plague which swept over us and to deliver us to righteousness. To you, I pray. Amen."

We begin to pass heaping bowls of mash potatoes, gravy and green beans. There is sliced turkey and a bowl of stuffing. I am passed a bowl of fresh jellied orange cranberry and a basket of fresh hot rolls. The food smells delicious. We each have a glass of water and a glass of a blush wine. Everyone begins to eat.

Director Macon starts the conversation. "I guess we should bring the Clay's group up to speed. There were things we did not want to transmit to you. We were not sure if John Wake had your location or not and we did not want to have long transmissions if he was trying to pinpoint your exact location. As it is, we believe he was watching our chatter and figured out you were inbound to the city. This was one of the reasons we did not discuss times and our plans for your escort until you were within our perimeter. I hope you understand we kept you in the cold as long as possible for security."

I finish chewing and swallow, "I understand completely. Once Talmadge translated the scrolls, we were not sure what we had our hands on. I still am not sure of the entire story. We just know we have names, school and politicians that are woven together. We also know President Elect Hall is one of those names. I was hoping someone would tell us the rest of the story."

Director Macon gestures to CIA Director Dubois, "Frank, would you like to take this. It was you working with NSA that broke the plot open after Talmadge sent the information to me."

I look over at Frank Dubois. He looks older than I thought. Maybe the activities of the last week have aged him. He stops eating and takes a drink of wine. "What we do know, soon after the end of World War II a group of Muslim extremists visited Venezuela and tracked down certain Nazis who were involved in the eugenics program. From there, they went to Poland and offered some of the Lebensborn orphans a home. It was easy to bring them into America at the time as war refugees. Nathan Hall's parents were Lebensborn children."

"It took a bit of investigation into the churches and their schools to make sense of things. On the surface, they seem very Fundamentalist Christian. Anyone who walked into one of the churches on Sunday would have thought that everything was above board. That is until we dug a little deeper. You can learn a lot about comparative religions when you look at the basic tenants of Judaism, Christianity and Islam. They parallel each other in many ways—family, children, even God himself. When you get into the more Orthodox it can become even closer. You might change a name or location but the role of women is very similar. The needs for prayer and to follow the demands of God are very similar. It is easy if you remove the labels to mistake one for the other."

"This particular group sounded very Conservative Christian, except they believed in Sharia Law. In the school and church they never call it Sharia Law, they call it God's Law. The women in the group do not work outside the home. Their job is to take care of the house and to raise the children. This includes homeschooling and sending the children to the church run schools. It is not appropriate for a woman to go out alone or with her children. That is the job of a male. She must be escorted. They are told the world is too dangerous for them to be out among the rapists and murderers."

"They preach against homosexuality, pre-marital sex, teen dating, alcohol and dating outside the faith. It all sounds very above board on the surface. We had to ask ourselves why someone would develop a religion and organize breeding to a specific race and physical appearance. Why encourage specific sports to be more appealing? Why specify colleges and degree programs? Why breed a group of children to be politicians, nuclear scientists, lawyers and federal law authority? We kept asking ourselves what is there to win?"

"Isn't it more what is there to lose?" The entire table turns and looks at Samantha for that utterance. "No really, it isn't about winning something. It is about losing something. If this group controls the country, the role of women will revert back to the stone ages. Our jobs will be having lots of babies and raising them. We will lose our ability to drive, to shop when we want, to even go out in public without a man accompanying us! I have seen the role of women under Sharia Law. Men have the right to rape and live freely but a woman has to remain pure. If she is raped she is stoned to death. The rape is her fault because she has somehow caused it. A woman walking and showing anything but her eyes tempts a man sexually. Many houses have walls around the house so that the woman may walk out her front door. If there is no wall, she has to be completely covered except her eyes and finger tips to walk into her own yard. I had more rights and privileges in jail than a woman in these countries. I could at least feel the sun shining on my entire face!"

Frank Dubois raises his wine glass to her. "You are correct my dear." He takes a drink and sits the glass down. "If this was the only reason we might have been able to fight the group if it came into power, but that was not all. The group sees us as a country of infidels. We live in excess and abundance. Unlike many countries in the world, we have every convenience ever invented—from microwaves to electric fingernail files. With some exception, no one in America goes to bed hungry. We have made provisions for the homeless to get a decent meal and healthcare in many areas of the country, so even they live in the life of luxury compared to the poor in some countries around the world."

"We saw chatter on starving the fat and happy Americans. At first we didn't understand. Then we woke up to our freeway and rail systems being devastated by bombs. We are fighting to keep commerce moving. Our roadways and railways have been hit hard. Most grocery stores have a maximum of three days' supply of food. As we are sitting here today emergency shipments are being delivered by plane because we cannot get produce from point A to point B with the road destruction. Oranges in Florida are rotting in warehouses while steaks in Nebraska have been put into cold storage with drive times too long to transport to California. Bananas! There is an entire situation around bananas. Each and every banana in this country is imported. If you live in a port city you can buy bananas for ten cents a pound right now. If you live in land locked Kansas you are asking why there aren't bananas. More than eighty percent of the country cannot buy a banana now because they are shipped by truck on the interstate highway system. The other twenty percent is being suggested to make banana bread, banana pudding and lots of banana smoothies. If not they will soon fill a landfill with rotting bananas from the docks."

"The push is on currently by the Senators and Congressmen on that list for President Randall to address the nation on the food shortages. They want him to answer as to how he allowed terrorism to come into this country and destroy our roads, bridges and railroads. They want him to announce food and fuel rationing immediately."

Billy has been sitting there listening intently but he can't hold his thought in anymore. "So the prepper's were right? There was a terror attack to destroy the countries foundation and bring us to our knees. Do they expect us to beg them to fix the country and be grateful after they did?"

Frank Dubois is looking down at his plate. He is pushing his food around with his fork. When he looks up there are tears in his eyes. "Samantha—gentlemen, we sit here tonight with this plentiful food before us and dine in the lap of splendor and tomorrow may find us taking the last can of soup from the grocery store. Currently this group holds the fate of the country in their hands. We are gathered tonight to not only explain to you what has happened but to find a way to save the country. By this time next week, there will be noticeable gas and food shortages. We have a transportation system that can barely limp along. We have a group of politicians that have introduced bills, pushed them through, and voted to help wound the country more once their planned attack happened. They hold the majority vote in both houses and in a few weeks they will hold the White House. The freedoms of everyone in this country will be gone with no way to recover them without an uprising, one that has already been voted as illegal. Marshall Law exists in most of the country right now. Stepping outside the door of this building is currently illegal until seven o'clock tomorrow morning. Every person here is breaking the law of assembly, which passed yesterday and went into effect at midnight last night."

He pauses and looks back down at his plate a defeated man. I look at President Randall and he also looks pained and tortured. There is a look of sadness around the room. I think of my children and what life might be like if we allow this to continue, "I don't know about anyone else in this room, but I am from the Commonwealth of Virginia. Never in our past, nor our present have we taken life lying down. While Boston was throwing tea in the harbor, Virginians were writing the documents that would carry this country forward. I for one am not ready to roll over and hand this country to a group of terrorists!"

John laughs and I look down the table at him. "Well said my friend. I work with Adam every day. One of his favorite quotes is that history repeats itself. I find myself thinking of the Capitol in Williamsburg and the group of men who could not speak their minds in the House of Burgess or the House of Commons. So they took their meeting down the street to Raleigh Tavern. They had a choice to make. One was to allow tyranny to rule them. The other was to take the country and make it theirs. As I see it, we are fighting for the right to rule ourselves and to not lose our freedoms. I don't know about anyone else but I'm a cop. I think we need to go get the bad guys!"

Director Macon stands up, "Wait! We have to remain calm. While speeches against tyranny are great, we have a problem. This group of terrorists understands and utilizes social media to their advantage. They have painted a picture of themselves as the great saviors to society. Today around the country men and women lined up in employment lines. Some stood in line for hours and they expect to start working on Monday to rebuild this country. They see Nathan Hall as a savior. They see Marshall Law as a way to keep terrorists off the street. If we are going to take them down we are going to have to do it with the public's approval. If not they will condemn us and beg their saviors to rescue them from the mistakes we made."

Everyone seems to start talking at once. Some have ideas while others are shooting them down. I hear someone taking a knife and hitting the side of a glass. I look over and see Samantha gently tapping. People stop talking and look at her, "Thank you. I'm the psychiatrist here. My job is the human brain and their emotions. The collective vision of the country has put Nathan Hall on a pedestal. He is the voice of calm during the bombings. In two days, he has eliminated the entire unemployment situation. He is the face of God and family. The only way to take him and his organization down is to get people's attention. So what do we have on him? I need something that will rock the world. What do we know about him that is so dirty old ladies will faint? And if we don't have anything real, what can we manufacture that will stop people in their tracks and make them vomit."

Director Macon interjects, "He works with John Wake and they murdered Scott Llewellyn."

Samantha shakes her head, "No offense, but Scott was just a history professor. While his death is a loss to his family, knowing someone who had someone killed isn't enough to make him hated and lose the trust of America."

Frank Dubois lifts a finger in the air, "His first wife was eleven when they got married. He was twenty."

Samantha tilts her head to the side, "First wife? Does this mean there is a second wife?"

Frank Dubois nods his head. "There are three. The woman the people have seen is his third wife Natalie. They appear with their shared children. His first wife is Claire. She was eleven when they married and their first child was a son, Nathan. He's twenty-one next week. They have nine other children. His second wife was Kathleen. She was twelve when he married her and they have seven children. We just uncovered this information yesterday. Claire nearly died in child birth. Social Services got involved with a child who was still eleven giving birth. She refused to name the father and her parents said they would raise the child. The social welfare case was dropped by the state. We uncovered the church records of their marriage. Her date of birth was incorrect and stated she was nineteen."

"We began to put things together when Talmadge sent copies of the scrolls to us. This information is all still evolving. He had church weddings with all three wives but only a marriage certificate is on file with the state for his marriage to Natalie. Claire and Kathleen took part in religious ceremonies only."

I am confused. If no paperwork exists on these marriages how do we know they exist? I feel the need to ask even though I am not sure if I want to know the answer.

Frank Dubois looks around the table, "I think we need to drink something a little stiffer than wine. Grand Master Covington, does the lodge have something stronger. We will all need it after I finish speaking."

One of the men who have been standing guard outside the room leaves to bring back a bottle of scotch. Frank Dubois takes a deep breath before he begins. "Last night, after the church closed for the evening, we silenced their alarm system and broke in. Our original goal was to find information on the terror plot. We primarily found church records. My team was looking for information on Nathan Hall. They found the marriage records and had to dig deeper to find an explanation for some things."

"We found the eugenics records and a list of possible matches for breeding purposes. There were five names, so we investigated those five names. He is married to three of them. The fourth is eight years old. The fifth has been paired with someone else. Things got weird with the marriage certification within the church. When my team uncovered it they called immediately. There is a procedure. It's fairly graphic. The female is brought to the congregation after her first menstrual cycle. There a male member of the elders manually verifies her virginity. For three months her cycle is tracked for regularity. Once her body becomes regular, she is tracked for three months and on the first day of fertility during the fourth month the couple is brought together. Their first sexual encounter is in front of the male members of the congregation for verification. She is then held within the church so that she has no contact with anyone from outside who might inpregnant her. They wait to see if she has become pregnant. If she does not test positive for pregnancy, the procedure is repeated until she becomes pregnant. At that point, the union is blessed and she leaves the church and her parent's house to go home with her new husband."

Out of the corner of my eye I see Samantha take a big gulf of scotch. I notice others have drank most of the glass that was poured before them. The thought of a group holding ancient fertility practices is mind blowing. The torture and humiliation that these young girls must go through must be damaging. It is difficult to conceive that this practice is done to insure the child is of pure blood in their breeding practices. "Do we have copies of this documentation that we can leak to the press?"

Frank Dubois drains his glass in one gulp and looks down at the table before looking me in the eye. "Yes. There are pictures of the deflowering and signed documents by those who were witness. We have pictures of all of this."

None of this will hold up in court. It was from a break in. No one said a warrant was obtained. If there was any indication left behind of the break in, they have probably destroyed the evidence. Suddenly the food in my stomach feels alive. I drink some water to help calm it. "What is our game plan with the evidence?"

Before anyone else can speak I hear Samantha, "we have to release this to the press. They used the press against Adam. It's time to give them a dose of their own medicine. The court of public opinion will not stand for this."

President Randall is shaking his head, "It won't do any good. On January 20th, he will take the oath of office and he and his cabinet along with Congress will be able to pass laws and conduct business on behalf of the country. It will take months to impeach him. By then there will be so much damage it will be hard to reverse it all. Unfortunately, nothing has been put into place to stop an elected President from taking office. No one ever thought there would be a coup from within the government. It wasn't something our forefathers anticipated. We are in virgin territory. If for some reason Hall cannot take the oath of office, Vice President Michael Morris will take his place."

I look over at Derrick Poole, "So Senator Poole, as Speaker of the House, that would make you next in line. If we find a way to stop them, are you ready for this?"

He shrugs his shoulders, "I have never had any ambition to be President. I'm a gay man with a lot of skeletons in my closet. I never thought the country was ready for me. I mean sure, in San Francisco I am a local hero. I represent my community and had no problem coming out on the national front but we just had a Presidential election that voted for God and Country. Hall ran a campaign against homosexuality. What would the American people say when my husband and I moved into the White House?"

I look down the table at John. He has been extremely quiet. When he first told me that he was gay I wasn't sure how I would handle being his partner but he is one of the only men I would trust with my life and with the lives of my family. "I for one would support you. After the shock, the country will have for a polygamist, pedophile and sexual deviant I don't see a gay man as being a real issue. As long as you bring this country back from the brink that we are sitting at, I don't think your personal life will be that important. Sure there will be people who comment, but they comment out of fear of the unknown. It's easy to hate someone because you don't understand them. It's a lot harder to look into the eyes of a man who sexually abused a young girl in front of a group of witnesses in a deviant sex ritual."

"Samantha is right. We need to paint this guy as a pervert. We need people to imagine this young girl naked on a table being forcefully raped in a twisted Neo-Nazi breeding program. We need to pull the Muslim extremist card and how their children could wake up next week being either taken away to this breeding program or put into camps and sterilized like Hitler did in the concentration camps."

Samantha picks up from me, "We need women to fear being violated and losing their rights. In a few days, they will be hungry and there will be shortages. That is nothing. Imagine the outrage when they are mandated to have children, stay home with them and lose their abilities to walk outside without covering and being accompanied by a man."

From somewhere at the end of the table I hear a familiar voice, "we will never get that far." I turn with the others at the table and look at Bernie. "They are not going to let us get to the media with anything. They know by us coming to Washington that we know their plans or at least part of the plan. Right now it is a question of us or them. If we don't kill them; they are going to kill us. Given that choice, I don't think we have a choice. We have to kill them first."

General Vandergraph sounds amazed by his comment, "Do you have any idea how many people we would have to kill? That is insane."

Bernie responds, "Do you know how many they have killed and still plan to kill? Look around this room. We are all dead men walking."

Samantha chimes in, "And our families. They already tried to abduct my daughter."

Tracy puts his gun on the table. "I'm in. I agree with Bernie. They will not care about killing any or all of us. It's shoot or be shot. I don't mind taking some scalps. If it's terrorist hunting season, I will not cry one bit."

I put my gun down in front of me and look around the table. Samantha places her gun on the table followed by Talmadge, John and Malcom. Chip says, "What the hell, I'm in."

President Russell looks at us, "I really cannot be here for this conversation. I am going to stand up and go to the restroom. I will be back in five minutes. Let me know if it is clear for me to reenter the room."

I understand his reasoning. We are sitting around a table eating dinner and discussing the assassination of a President. This man or the people that he is connected to want to kill me. I'm not sure how many we need to kill but I do not see a way to get out of this room without planning to have blood on my hands. The door closes and I am sitting among a table of coconspirators. "I took an oath to defend, protect and uphold the Constitution of the United States of America. With that vow I offered to give my life for the betterment of the country and the citizens. I fight crime, but I never expected to fight my own government. How many do we have to kill and how are we going to kill them?"

Talmadge stands up and walks around the room. He stops at Director Macon, "Thomas, q ras al'afaa waljsm swf. Matha t'fal ma thaba'an thlathh?"

Director Macon nods his head. "al'qtl ba'asm Allah."

I recognized one word in the conversation, Allah. What does God have to do with anything and why suddenly are two people in the room holding a conversation in Arabic. I put my hand on my gun. "Would you mind explaining what's going on?"

Director Macon looks startled for a second. His eyes focus on my gun, which is now pointed at him. "I'm sorry. Talmadge told me we have to cut off the head of the snake and the body will follow. Then he asked, what do you do with a three headed snake? I told him kill in the name of God. Can you put the gun down? I can explain."

I lower my gun but keep my hand on it. Things do not feel right and I am afraid we have walked into a trap.

Thomas Macon waits for Talmadge to return to his seat. Once he is seated he begins, "The reason I sent Talmadge to you is because he has done years in the Middle East. He is a former CIA operative that came over to the FBI. Talmadge understands and thinks like the people we are dealing with. I think to answer the question we must kill the three at the top. Hall, Morris and Wake. They are the head of the snake. If we can, I think we should take out Callan as well. He is the neck that holds and supports the snake heads. He does their dirty work. Once they are dead, I think some of the other politicians will run figuring they are next."

Samantha is shaking her head, "We will be nothing but murderers. This will sign our death certificates. It is high treason. I know they are trying a coup of the country but the American people will never find that out. We need a plan that exposes them. That is the only way we walk away from this in one piece."

I see confusion cross her face and she tilts her head to the side. "Wait. Who is the head of the snake? There is someone calling the shots. Hall and Morris are the ass puppets of someone. If I understand this properly, they were born and bred in some Nazi/Muslim breeding farm to be the pretty boy faces that would get them the Presidency. The real heads are the ones with their fists rammed up Hall and Morris' ass. Who is that?"

Frank Dubois clears his throat and we all look toward him. "Saed al Hassan. We can't touch him. He was somewhere in the mountain region of Pakistan. He's nomadic and contacts John Wake via satellite phone twice a week. We have intercepted the communications and have determined Saed al Hassan is the current head of the organization. The communications are very short and we have been unable to lock in on his position. We also do not know what he looks like. After the election, he flew to the United States. The current phone calls are being tracked to Washington, DC and Northern Virginia. He is here. He is also the person who ordered the terror attacks last week. We didn't understand the chatter until after the explosions began."

"It seems there is a hierarchy in the organization. The top of the pyramid is Hall. He is the perfect male. Morris is the next level. Some of the Congressmen and Senators might be considered at this level as well. John Wake and Joseph Callan are on the third level. The people who died committing the suicide attacks are the ones at the bottom. It could have been something as simple as not being pretty or handsome. We think many of the drivers had no idea they were driving a bomb. They were told to drive to a specific place at a specific time. This put them closer to God. They died thinking they were doing a special favor to God. A few survived and we interviewed them. They had no idea that they were Muslim extremists. They had never heard of Saed al Hassan. They had no idea he was in charge of their clergy and elders. This is all about twisting the belief system of a group and the role of religion in a political agenda."

John interrupts him, "Does Nathan Hall know he is a part of a Muslim extremist group?"

Talmadge nods his head yes as Frank Dubois responds. "We have confirmation that Saed al Hassan has spoken with him and given him instructions. He is taking orders from the top. We have kept President Russell in the loop on this. They are aware that you have the cylinder and the scrolls have been deciphered. The race is on. They know that we know. The winner is the one that survives."

When Scott was murdered, I never thought it would come to this. Everyone in this room that has come together the help me clear my name has put their lives in jeopardy. Someone made an attempt to kidnap Alina. John and Samantha are with me and must help kill the incoming President and they risk being killed themselves. I wish now that I could walk away and just go to jail. "So where do we go from here? How do you get to and kill both the President and Vice President elect?"

I had forgotten Vice President Doug Lane is still sitting at the table. He has been silent the entire night. "A few weeks ago my family moved from the Vice Presidential home within the Naval Observatory grounds. We did so at the request of President Hall. He wanted to have a temporary residence in Washington, DC. He determined the Naval Observatory grounds were well protected and a perfect place for him and Vice President Morris to work on their transition. In his words, I was an incompetent boob anyway, no one would ever want to assassinate me. He also said, in my lame duck status, my being in Washington was just for show anyway. After he said this on the news, my wife and I decided to pack up and leave. She has gone back to New Hampshire to get our new home set up. I moved into a hotel. I will join her in our new home as soon as I leave office. I'm done with this town, or so I thought."

He sounds like a defeated man. I feel bad for him and his wife. Now he knows his job is being taken away as part of a coup. It has to be hard to stay in the limelight and being verbally assaulted by the incoming administration. Doug Lane has never been someone I looked up to or appreciated, but now I look at him with sympathy. He has just been a pawn in a power game. He has been a silent partner in this Presidency, now he has been kicked out of his home and is delegated to a hotel room.

Grand Master Covington suggests we review the tunnels. He picks up a remote control and with the push of a button a screen descends from the ceiling. He uses a red laser and points the dot to a position at the beginning of the tunnel system. "We are here. This is the northwest end of the system. The tunnels were put in during the early construction of the capital and added to over the years. The early designers dug the tunnels as a means to escape the capital if needed during an attack. Having the northwest escape through the Grand Temple was logical. This tunnel runs east to the Naval Observatory. The tunnel is just over a mile in length. You will need to be quiet through this section. Hall and his team will be directly over your head. You will be directly under the Naval Observatory when the tunnel opens up to the catacombs.

Originally, this was a secret arsenal. Then it became emergency storage in case the capital needed to be evacuated. Now it is part of the Homeland Security evacuation system."

He is following the tunnel with the laser pointer. I can see after the storage area the tunnel makes an abrupt turn southeast. "This tunnel dead ends at the Whitehouse in the bunker. You will run into a Secret Service agent there whom we have made arrangements with. He is one of our people. He will lead you though the bunker and to the door of the basement of Blair House. You will be safe there for the night. We need to find a way to get Hall and Morris alone and take care of them."

The door opens and President Russell returns and takes his seat. "Well, have decisions been made?" We all shake our heads no. I have no idea how we will get to Hall, Morris, al Hassan or Wake. I think Callan will come to us much too soon. "It is getting late and I have been informed by my detail that we need to get anyone who will be taken by vehicle to their destination. The National Guard is working with the police and they are blocking the roads. Everyone here will have to stay in the district tonight. Those of you taking the tunnels should head out. You have a three mile walk ahead of you. We would take you by vehicle, but it has been decided keeping you below ground will be safer."

John, Morgan and Chip join Tracy, Talmadge, Billy, Bernie, Samantha and I stand. Grand Master Covington leads us down a hallway. To my left I can see into the Colonial blue walls of the inner sanctum of the lodge. He stops in front of a door. It is a match to every other one in this hallway. He pulls keys from his pocket and looks over his shoulder, "Are you ready?" I nod and he unlocks the door and swings it open a few inches. He holds his hand out to me and we shake hands. "Good luck and God Speed. Stay as quiet as possible and follow my directions. Whatever you do, stay on the main tunnel. You could become lost for days down in the catacombs." We shake hands and I reach out and open the door.

I can feel the cold air flowing out as the dark mahogany door swings fully open. The air smells musty and damp. Wooden steps lead down into the dark. At the bottom, a single light bulb illuminates the stone landing. I look around and can see the marks in the stone showing where workmen with pick axes carved the tunnel from the granite rock bed beneath the city. The roof is about seven feet tall. I reach up and touch the damp rock over my head. Conduit runs down the middle of the ceiling to supply electricity to the light bulbs evenly spaced at about every ten feet. If nothing else, it is a weak attempt to light the area, but we can see enough to make our way down the tunnel.

The tunnel is relatively straight. Occasionally, water drops down from the air vents leading to street level above. Through the grates we can see that it has begun to snow again. Ahead is a junction where a tunnel crosses the one we are following. We slow down and allow Bernie and Talmadge to check the cross tunnel. They signal and we move forward.

A rat runs by us and Samantha stifles a scream. Sound travels in the tunnel and we try to move as quietly as possible. I try to count the light bulbs as I pass. I am using them to calculate a mile. I have to look for the main tunnel heading southeast. I was warned there are numerous side alcoves that can be mistaken for tunnels. At the mile mark, we will be in danger. This tunnel leads directly to the Naval Observatory. The doors leading up to it should be locked but we must pass this as quietly as possible.

I can tell this tunnel is old. I see a few small stalactites forming on the roof where water leaks through consistently. I am glad the floor is smooth with nothing sticking up to trip us. Occasionally a light bulb has burned out and visibility is almost impossible.

The sounds of our movements echo down the tunnel. I pause to listen. My heart provides a steady drum beat. I note that the stress and exertion is making it beat faster. The silence of the tunnel is pierced by the sound of water dropping from somewhere ahead. I can hear the claws of the rats as they run across the stone floor. Some chatter as they run. Maybe they are warning others, or encouraging friends to keep running. Their voices echo in the darkness.

After about half a mile the walls and ceiling change over to brick. I would love a chance to stop and examine them. I look as we pass. The brick appears to be colonial. These may have been hand shaped and fired in the kiln based near what is now the National Mall. The trees cut to clear the Whitehouse grounds were stacked in pits and burned to heat the earthwork kilns. The builders of the capital formed bricks from the brownish red Maryland clay they dug nearby and hauled in on ox carts. They coated the bricks in the sandy Virginia soil from the banks of the Potomac River. Then started the fires in the kiln in the fall. Throughout the winter months the heat from the kiln warmed the grounds of the Whitehouse as it was being constructed.

The number of side tunnels and alcoves increases as we approach the Naval Observatory. The number of rats increase as well. I wish they were not in our path but there is little I can do about them.

I hear a noise behind us and stop. I see a figure behind us dressed in black. He must have stepped out of the back of an alcove. "I've been waiting for you. Adam Clay, you have been a pain in my ass."

I hear another noise and look behind the man in black and see Joseph Callan. "I assume we are being faced by the illustrious Joseph Callan and John Wake, or is it Craig Willet? What name do you go by in your non-professional role?"

My mind is racing. I was not mentally on my game. I was drifting back in history to the building of the Whitehouse and somehow missed the Director of the CIA training facility and his henchman hiding in the shadows.

John Wake laughs, "So you have done your homework. Craig Willet died many years ago. He was a man with a family and people who would have lived at risk if he had lived. Something like the position you have put your family in. I must say, your daughter has quite a mouth on her. An associate of mine had to have over twenty stitches in her arm." He walks forward and approaches Samantha. "Absolutely beautiful." He runs his hand down her hair and she jerks her head away from him. He grabs her and spins her around with her back against his chest. I lung toward them and feel pain as Callan hits me in the back of the head. Samantha cries out and I roll onto my side to look up at her. Wake has his hand inside her sweater groping her. "How does it feel Adam? Do you like to see another man touching your whore?" He laughs again. "Yes, I did my homework also. So many men have felt up these tits. They are quite nice."

He reaches his hand in the front of her jeans. I hear a click and see Callan pointing his gun at my head. I look back at Wake and see his other hand moving inside her sweater. "Don't worry Adam. Everyone here will get to see me fuck your bitch. Joseph and I both decided we should get a test ride before we kill you. He thrusts his hand in her jeans. I feel like I am watching this in slow motion. He unzips his jeans and pulls his penis out, then shoves Samantha against a wall.

A gunshot rings out. The sound is incredibly loud and echoes down the tunnel system. I see Wake crumple to the ground. Callan turns to look in the direction of the shot and collapses to the ground. Talmadge is standing in the middle of the tunnel. He puts his gun back in its holster and walks over to me offering me a hand. John is running to Samantha. She is pulling down her sweater and adjusting her jeans. I can see tears streaming down her face. Talmadge looks at me and I see his lips moving but I can't understand what he is saying. I realize I am temporarily deaf from the noise. I finally understand what he is saying. "We need to move now!"

I nod and walk over to Samantha and give her a hug. She is still shaking but starts to walk with me as we head toward the bunker under the Naval Observatory. Behind us the bodies of John Wake and Joseph Callan bleed out. We need to find the southeast tunnel that leads to the Whitehouse.

I look down and glance at my phone. It is after midnight. We are somewhere in a tunnel under the streets of Washington, DC. We are walking away from two dead men. If caught and questioned we will try to claim self-defense. I wonder if the gunshots were heard on the streets above? We are in dangerous territory with nothing left to do but walk on through the tunnel and hope to find our destination. Instead we come face to face with another man with a gun.

Day Ten,
Washington, DC

He is blocking the entrance to the southeast tunnel with a semi-automatic gun. I hear him speaking above the hum still lingering in my ears. "I take it you have killed my men? I only wanted a few moments to speak to you. How violent Americans are. Now turn and go up the stairs on the right." He raises the gun as if to fire. Not wanting to have more gunfire to assault my ears I walk toward the stairs.

A door is open and I start up the steps. Samantha is behind me. I glance back and assume the entire group has elected to not resist and follow directions. The stairs lead to a door. I turn the handle and enter into a hallway. The walls are rough slats. It is lighted by naked light bulbs. I realize we are within the walls of the Vice Presidents house. I have heard rumors of secret tunnels in the walls. A set of stairs appear out of the darkness. The hallway ends at the stairs, so I have no option but to walk up them. I glance back again and see the entire party behind me including the gunman taking up the rear.

At the top of the stairs is a small landing and a door. I turn the knob and the door squeaks as it opens. The room is painted Prussian Blue with an off white trim. Dark Blue velvet covered chairs line the walls. This is some sort of a waiting room. I move into the room and put my arms around Samantha. "Are you okay?" She nobs and touches the back of my head where Callan hit me. Her hand comes away with blood on it. Adrenaline is still flowing and it doesn't hurt yet. I know in a while I will have a throbbing headache. I hope it holds off until after we get out of the situation.

Talmadge has come over and is checking my wound. "Damn Clay. You have one hard head. You just got pistol whipped and came away with a little scratch. One hell of a bump though. We need to keep an eye on you. You might have a concussion. I know this will sound crazy but try to take it easy for a while."

I finally get to see the man that forced us upstairs. He has a Middle Eastern accent and my theory is confirmed when he enters the room. He has black hair and olive skin. Dressed in black it is easy to see how he blended into the wall until we got close. I make a mental note of how callous he must be. He watched Callan and Wake being shot and killed and did nothing. I assume we are more expendable than they were. I also assume we have come face to face with Saed al Hassan, the man pulling the strings on the coup.

A door opens to my left and Nathan Hall walks out. "Saed, you should have told me you were bringing guests. I would have had refreshments sent up. Instead I have allowed the staff to go home for the night before the curfew." He looks at us. "I'm so sorry. After I get the information we need, there will be no one near enough to hear you. Although, Saed will have to get something with a little less fire power and I would hope a silencer. I don't want the guards on the grounds to come and investigate." He pulls the door open fully and steps aside. "Please, come into my office. Oh, and Saed— I heard about the misfortune in the tunnel. Please make sure you have all their guns. Wake got sloppy and it ended his life. I do not intend this to end mine."

Hassan walks through the group. "Put your guns on this table. All I have is this semi-automatic. I need something more appropriate to kill each of you. What better than one of your own weapons?"

He makes us each stop at the table and put our side arms down. I make a note that Samantha does not stop at the table. I know she had a gun in the waistband of her jeans. She gives me a knowing glance before stepping past. Hassan did not assume a woman can be armed. I hope she gets away with this. I don't want to have her roughed up because of the gun. My head feels a little foggy and I try to concentrate. I need to keep myself together.

I see Bernie looking at me and there is concern on his face. He moves over near Samantha and I. "Adam, are you okay? Hey Hall! If you want to get any information from Adam you need to get a chair for him. One of your goons cracked his skull with the handle of a gun."

Nathan Hall orders Hassan to get a chair for Adam. I find it interesting that Hall is making Hassan fetch and carry for him. He brings a chair over and Bernie helps me sit down. I whisper, "Samantha may still have her gun. Stay near us." He puts his hand on my shoulder and puts his arm around Samantha. Hall is asking about the cylinder. I try to focus on what he is saying.

Billy is standing across from Bernie and he nods slightly, "I have it." He pulls it from the inside pocket of his coat and walks over to the desk. He pulls the scrolls out and lays them on the desk with both the cylinder and the lid we sawed off. In my fog I am not sure what is happening. Out of the corner of my eye I see Bernie slip his hand up the back of Samantha's sweater. Both Hassan and Hall are looking at Billy. This gives Bernie time to get the gun out of Samantha's waistband.

Tracy's hand is inside his jacket pocket. I notice him make a slight nod to Bernie. Samantha walks closer to me and puts her hands on my shoulders. She whispers, "hang in there. I love you."

Hall notices her movement and focuses on her. "I need everyone to move together. I can't watch all of you scattered the way you are." He points at Talmadge, Tracy, Billy, Chip and Morgan. "Move over with the other four."

They hesitate for a moment. Hassan walks from the doorway toward their group. Billy yells "Now!" Tracy pulls his gun and shoots Saed al Hassan. Simultaneously, Bernie fires Samantha's gun at Nathan Hall. Saed falls back against a chair and slides to the floor. Hall has fallen face forward onto his desk. Blood is pouring out of a hole in his forehead.

The sound echoes through my head. I notice no one has moved. We are all looking at the two bodies in the room. I do not know if anyone outside the house heard the gun shots. "We need to get out of here. We just killed the President-Elect!"

Samantha is standing by the desk looking at the body of Nathan Hall. "Wait a minute. Let's think for a second. We have Nathan Hall bleeding all over the evidence. We have the Middle Eastern leader of a terror cell dead in the same room. In the bunker, we have the head of the CIA covert training and his primary assassin. We need to take these guys down right?"

Everyone is looking at her. My head is throbbing from the close gunfire and from the concussion. "Samantha, I can't think clearly. Talmadge is correct. I'm pretty sure I have a concussion. You might be on to something. Tell me what we should do."

Bernie speaks up, "I'm a little worried about evidence. We have witnesses at the Masonic temple putting us in the tunnels. We have probably left evidence in the tunnels and I know we have left finger prints and everything else in this room. What do we do about that?"

I realize Talmadge is on his cell phone. "I've got this." He nods his head. "Director, we have a little problem. I've got Wake and Callan dead in the tunnel and Hall and Hassan dead in the Vice President's residence. Clay has been pistol whipped and probably needs to see if his head is cracked like an egg. I need a clean-up crew and orders. Do you want us to continue to Blair house?" He is nodding again and begins to pace. "Yes sir. What about Clay? Understood sir."

He hangs up and looks at me. "We need to get the hell out of here. A clean-up crew is on their way here through the tunnel. We were never here. A doctor is going to meet us back at the Masonic Temple. He is a Mason. What happens there, stays there. As soon as the sun rises we are out of the city. Everyone goes home. We were never here."

Samantha is still next to the desk, "What about Morris? He will become President. We need to stop him and the rest of the crooks."

Talmadge shrugs, "Morris is at Blair house and we need to stay clear of that. I guess we leave it to the clean-up crew."

Samantha leans over the body and moves the mouse on the table. I see the glow of the screen light up her face. She reaches under the desk and wiggles the keyboard out between the body and the ledge under the desk. "Like hell I will! Wipe off my damn gun and put it in Hassan's hands. Gentlemen, we have ourselves a murder suicide between Hall and Hassan. Maybe Callan and Wake got in their way. I think Hall needs to confess for the crimes he committed and those he was planning on committing!"

She begins to type. Talmadge calls the director back and fills him in on Samantha's plan. "Okay, plans have changed. Adam sit tight, the doctor is coming to you. They have to walk through the tunnels. It might be better if you are checked out before we move. Samantha, let me help you with this letter."

Morgan, Billy, Talmadge, Tracy and Bernie walk over to the desk and stand around the body. John and Chip walk over to me. John looks concerned. "Buddy, you have blood down your back. You are still bleeding." He walks over to the desk and gets tissues from a box and puts pressure on the cut.

Talmadge walks to the door we came in from the tunnel and opens it. I see him disappear into the tunnel. It is probably a good idea to make sure anyone coming up the tunnel is one of ours and not one of theirs. I would hate to let the wrong person up here or shoot someone coming to help us.

Samantha is taking suggestions from the group on what to add into the suicide note. I agree that we do not want to put too many details. Suicide notes are short. They usually tell family they are sorry and goodbye. I agree we might need to add a little detail but we can't write too much. A long suicide note will be suspicious. She finishes and reads it out loud.

> *"As the inauguration grows closer I realize that I cannot go on with this charade. I was taught to be a man following Gods path, but my leaders have made me and my brethren stray. I therefore wish to turn over the evidence that outlines the program that I was born and bred to lead.*
>
> *My regrets are many. I am sorry that we murdered Scott Llewellyn. At the time I thought his death was justified. The archive explaining the lineage and breeding lines could not get into the public arena. I was wrong.*
>
> *I am sorry for the many lives we took with the bombings. I, like the men who gave their lives to Allah, did this for the better good. The American people must learn to suffer and feel the pain of the world.*

I am sorry to my wives, Claire, Kathleen and Natalie and to all of my children. My one regret is that I could not kill my brother, Michael Morris, so that he does not have to live with the prosecution for the many crimes we have committed.

Praise Allah and forgive me for what I have done!"

I hear Talmadge talking to someone down in the tunnel and he yells "We are coming up. Don't shoot at us!" There are footsteps on the stairs and in the walkway behind the walls. Talmadge walks out first followed by Director Macon. They are followed by nine other men.

Director Macon walks over to me with a man carrying a backpack. The man with the backpack puts it on the floor next to me. "Adam Clay, this is Doctor Richard Pollard. I heard you were pistol whipped and I want him to check out your head."

I reach out and shake his hand. He mumbles something and reaches into the back pack for a penlight. He mumbles again. "Good, your pupils are not dilated and you are following the light well. Do you have any dizziness or nausea?" I nod my head yes. "Any double vision or ringing in your ears?" I shake my head no. I'm not sure how to answer the ringing in my ears. Being at close range for a contained gunshot blast has nearly deafened me. It sounds more like static than ringing. He walks around my head and pulls my hair aside to look at the cut and with his fingers feels around the wound. I notice the area is beginning to throb. "I could give you two or three stitches to close this up. I'm not sure if you care. Unless you go completely bald the scar will never be seen. It will also be difficult to remove the stitches unless I shave that part of your head. I'm not sure if you want me to go to that extent." I tell him no.

He looks in my eyes again and in my ears. He turns to Director Macon. "He is fine to travel. He has a concussion but it appears to be minor. I think getting these people out of here and staging the crime scene can continue. I assume the woman is his wife?" Director Macon nods and Doctor Pollard walks over to her. "If he begins to vomit or loses consciousness get him to a hospital immediately. If you notice any change in gate, confusion or anything out of the ordinary get him checked immediately. I would have preferred to give him an x-ray and observe him overnight but I have been told with the current circumstances you need to be in southern Virginia a few hours ago. It is better for you to be out of Washington and away from the circumstances we have encountered. Get him out of here and make sure he is cleaned up before anyone sees him in public."

Samantha thanks him and turns to Director Macon. "Where are our vehicles and the dogs? We need to get our things and get out of town. What are your orders? Do we just go home like nothing happened? What about Billy and Bernie. Do they go with us or will you transport Billy home. I understand that we need to get out of town but there are some things we need taken care of before we can leave."

He agrees with her. "Adam, are you up for a hike? We have a subway train waiting for you just off the southeastern tunnel. Someone will guide your party there. The train will take you to Arlington. There you will find your vehicles and pets. Billy, a vehicle has been provided for you. Just call the number inside the glove compartment and let us know in the next week where to pick it up. Talmadge and Tracy, your bikes are in Arlington also. Talmadge, go out of town for a few days. The Arlington station will put you outside the curfew area. The station does not open for hours and you are on a special train. No one will see you. We will contact you later in the week. As far as you or anyone else knows you were not here today. You were not around this scene and you have nothing to do with this. Go home or go somewhere for a couple days. And Adam, as soon as the news breaks I will petition to drop the charges. Your life should be back to normal in a few days."

We thank him and stand up to leave. I feel a wave of nausea rush over me for a second. I grip the back of the chair to steady myself. I take a deep breath and nod to Samantha. One of the men who came out of the tunnel starts to walk through the door and we follow. I have a new insight for the passage between the walls. I try to distract myself from the throbbing wound and the slight dizziness. I begin to wonder what history has transpired here. How many mistresses and secret meetings silently walked through here? I can feel the chill from the tunnel as we approach it. I see other agents working on the two bodies and the tunnel. I assume they are staging the scene and cleaning up any evidence of our presence.

The cold dampness of the tunnel helps me focus. I adjust my eyes to the dim lighting and focus on putting one foot in front of the other.

The tunnel makes an abrupt turn. I can see bright lights ahead. The south eastern tunnel is tiled and bright. It widens after a few feet and there are golf carts sitting along the wall. The agent who is guiding us tells us to load into them. Once we are all on board the golf carts he takes off down the tunnel. He slows as we approach a set of blast doors and parks the golf cart. He looks behind and yells "these cut off two miles hiking the tunnels. I didn't think you would mind the short cut."

At the blast doors he puts his hand on the key pad and waits for recognition. I see a light flash on his face. He looks at me and smiles "seventeen point facial, eye and finger print recognition. It randomizes." When the door opens we are in an office hallway. To my left is the situation room under the White House, to my right a conference room and a small service canteen. Secret Service agents sit at desks in offices off the corridor. I see monitors in front of them as they monitor surveillance cameras throughout the White House grounds.

I realize we are in the basement of the White House. We turn the corner and I see President Randall sitting in a chair talking. He stands when he sees us. "I just wanted to shake each of your hands and thank you. I have been called about the suicide note. We will change very little. You have done a great service to your country. I only wish that I could publicly thank you and award you. Know that the gratitude of the country is with you, even though they will never know of your involvement." He shakes each of our hands and walks with us to the outer blast door. He stresses our need to get out of Washington as soon as possible. We leave him at the blast door.

I hear the door close behind us. Once again we are in a tunnel. I have no idea what direction we are walking. It isn't far before we come to a dead end. The agent pushes numbers on a key pad and the door swings open into another tunnel. He holds his hand up to stop us. I can see the tunnel in front of us. It is dimly lighted but I can see a vaulted roof. The walkway is narrow and drops off. I can see down into the floor of the tunnel and realize we are at a service door to the metro.

The agent lets us know the third rail is active. I know that metro stops at midnight and I am fairly sure the last trains have run for the night. I hear a rumble and feel the rush of wind as a train approaches. The single car stops at the White House tunnel and the door opens. I look at the driver and realize it is a suited Secret Service agent. We board and the doors ding as they close. In seconds we are riding out of Washington DC.

I notice the windows are darkened and as we blow through Metro stations the train does not slow down. I try to look out the window and see very few people. Most of them are sitting on benches appearing to be asleep. The train rocks and I can feel myself getting sleepy. I pull out my phone and the time is three forty two in the morning. We still have a three hour drive home.

It seems very little time has passed when I feel the train slowing down. It comes to a stop and the doors open. There is no announcement but we stand and get off the train. I look around on the platform. There is a single escalator working. It is going up into the main station, so we take it. The station is dark and empty. We walk down the ramp toward the lights of a parking lot. Outside the door I see the gates to Arlington National Cemetery and in the parking lot our vehicles sitting clumped together. As we approach I hear Max, Dee Dee and Sophie barking.

Billy walks to the vehicle with Dee Dee and Sophie. There isn't a key in the ignition. He opens the glove compartment and finds the key under the paper with the phone number to call. We are standing around. No one is quite sure how to say goodbye.

Samantha hugs herself in the cold wind. I had hoped the cold would help me focus, but my headache is getting worse. I know I need to get myself together. I don't want to ask her to make the drive. She has to be exhausted also.

Bernie is standing looking around for a moment. "Hey, my house is about fifty minutes from here. Everyone has at least a two hour drive. My house isn't big and I don't have beds for everyone but if you don't mind pulling a place up on the floor I have pillows and blankets. Does everyone want to come back to my place and when you wake up later this morning and we get some food before you go your separate ways?"

It is almost four in the morning. I am in no condition to drive home. I see John yawning. I am the first to agree to make the trip back to his house. If we are all together we can be each other's alibis. We get into the cars and drive north on I-95.

John is driving my Jeep. Samantha is asleep in the back. I find myself dozing off in the front. John tells me he is fine and I let myself relax and close my eyes. I wake up as we stop in Bernie's drive way.

When we get inside Bernie goes to a closet and gets blankets and pillows. Samantha and I take the guest room. Talmadge and Tracy each lay on a sofa. Billy lays down on a futon in Bernie's office. Chip and Morgan make themselves comfortable in recliners. John follows Samantha and me and sits in the recliner in our room. The last thing I see before I fall asleep is John making himself comfortable with his gun across his lap and his feet on the foot of the bed.

****

I wake up with a headache. Outside the sun is shining and I hear the sound of a television in the living room. I get out of bed and steady myself. I hear everyone else talking. They are sitting on chairs pulled from the dining room and on the sofas.

The news has broken from Washington, DC. A female reporter is at the microphone. Behind her I see the Vice Presidents house inside the Naval Observatory grounds. DC Police cars and ambulances fill the front of the house and are parked in the yard. The reporter is talking.

"Behind me as you can see Metro police are still investigating this incident. To recap what we do know. At six o'clock this morning a member of the house staff found the body of an unknown male in the hallway. She called security and they locked the residence down. President elect Nathan Hall was found dead slumped at the desk in his temporary office. It has been confirmed a suicide note was found at the scene. Further investigation of the scene found the bodies of CIA Operations Director John Wake and Special Operations Instructor Joseph Callan dead in bed. It is unconfirmed but it appears they were in bed together at the time of their death. Reports indicate a gun was found with them and might be a murder suicide."

"At six thirty this morning the Secret Service tried to wake Vice President Elect Michael Morris in Blair House. It is confirmed he has also died in some sort of suicide pack. We have not gotten a cause of death for the Vice President yet. President Randall and Vice President Lane were both at Camp David with their families at the time preparing for the holidays and were notified early this morning. The President is expected to speak about the tragic events within the next half hour."

"In other related news, police are on the scene of a residence in Georgetown. Pete Thompson is on the scene there. Pete, what can you tell us? Is this another crime scene?"

The screen switches to a middle aged man in a trench coat standing in front of a typical brick faced Georgetown townhouse. "Thank you, Veronica. For the last hour we have been watching police remove boxes from this Georgetown house. Earlier three women and nineteen children were loaded onto a bus and taken from the scene. In this group were Natalie Hall and her three children. We have an unconfirmed report that the other two women and sixteen children were President Elect Halls sister wives and their children."

"We have confirmation that the Georgetown home is rented by the oil magistrate, Saed al Hassan, from the French Oil Company, Kief Soleil, located in Iran. This house is unusual for the area. It is a triple house complex. It is listed as having nine bedrooms with a potential dormitory site in the basement. There is one large kitchen suitable for both catering and home use, a central great room and banquet room on the first floor. The second and third floors consist of the bedrooms, six bathrooms, an office and study."

The picture switches back to the studio and the anchor has his hand over his ear and is listening to something. "Okay, we now have confirmation of the identity of the second man found in the Vice Presidential house at the Naval Observatory. He was Saed al Hassan. Confidential sources are also informing us that CIA Special Operations Director John Wake was involved in a homosexual relationship with CIA Special Operations Instructor Joseph Callan. Among documentation found at the Naval Observatory were the marriage license for John Wake and Joseph Callan."

Samantha is laughing so hard tears are running down her cheeks. After the stress of the last few days seeing this plot fall apart is a relief. The spin put on the bodies is better than I could have ever imagined. I am anticipating the news to be leaked that they were part of a terror plot very soon. After all we have been through I never thought it would end in laughter.

The scene on the TV switches to the press room at Camp David. There is activity around the podium. We can hear the chatter and movement of chairs from reporters somewhere off camera.

President Randall and Vice President Lane are standing together behind a podium. President Randall looks tired. I wonder if he got any sleep last night. I assume after we saw him he left Washington for the Whitehouse retreat at Camp David. So much activity happened behind the scenes overnight to manufacture evidence and create the scenes needed for the cover up. We have gotten a few hours' sleep. He looks as if he has gotten even less.

I reach behind my head and touch the cut. I want to confirm last night was not a dream. My head is sore and I feel the scab on the back of my head. Last night was real but the country will never know. Instead, President Randall is about to provide a sanitized lie about the situation.

He smiles into the camera and raises his hand to quiet the reporters in the room. "I want to give a brief statement and then will answer your questions. Please keep in mind this is a story that is currently unfolding. I do not have all the answers and I'm sure more of the story will come out in the next several weeks. What we do know about the situation. President Elect Hall and Vice President Elect Morris were part of an Islamic terror group that was attempting to take over the country. As I speak, the FBI and local agencies are rounding up and arresting people who are part of this group. They hid under the cloak of a fundamentalist Christian group. They maintained their own churches and schools. Their families socialized in very close knit social groups. The goal has been to give birth to children and groom them into adults so that they are the perfect political candidate. What they didn't accomplish was manufactured so that they were exactly what this country was seeking to elect."

He shifts in front of the microphone and looks uncomfortable. "We have uncovered information about the group participating in polygamy and sexual acts with children as young as eleven years old. President Hall had a wife who at eleven gave birth to their first child. We have obtained the written records from the church with signed affidavits written by church elders on their witness to this young girl's virginity. The group of witnesses swore to the statutory rape of this young girl by Nathan Hall. They bore witness to the monthly rape of her until she became pregnant. At that time the marriage was consecrated and she was officially partnered with him as his wife."

Hearing this being broadcast makes me feel nauseated. While investigating the Co-op I dealt with pedophiles. In hindsight, I know some of the seats that became open in Congress after the Co-op was busted were taken by members of this group. In some ways my breaking this case opened the door to members of this group to become elected. It gave them the opportunity to take over more seats and gain a bigger majority. By shutting down one group of pedophiles I helped open the door for the next group of deviants.

President Randall is still speaking and I try to focus on him once more. I make a note that my headache has not changed since last night and concentrating is difficult. I should not drive home today and I need to ask John or Samantha to drive. "The goal of this group was to strip the freedoms of woman and elevate the role of religion in social and political decisions. We were destined to become a country under religious law."

Vice President Lane reaches up and puts his hand on President Halls shoulder. They glance at each other. President Hall looks back into the camera. "The next part of the plot pains me to discuss. While the sexual abuse of minors and deviant sexual practices of the group are abhorrent, the link to the death and maiming of thousands of people is beyond comprehension. The group orchestrated the bombings, not just in America, but around the world in order to bring about the collapse of commerce, causing food shortages, starvation and suffering. There was a desire to bring the people to their knees and teach them the lessons of humility so that they could appreciate what they were allowed to have and to possess. It was engineered to create reliance and dependability on the group as a means of control. We were to accept and adapt to the laws given down by Muhammed, or die defying them."

He pauses for a moment and takes a drink of water. I don't know if this is for effect or if like me he needs to take a drink and force the bile back down in his throat. "America came close to the brink, but through the diligent work of law enforcement we were able to halt this attempt to overtake our government and enslave us all. We are still the home of freedom. I will now take question."

A reporter asks what will happen Inauguration Day. President Randall shakes his head. "We aren't sure. It seems our forefathers did not anticipate something like this happening. For today our government continues as normal. On Monday a special Congressional committee will be formed to determine the continuation of the government and the next step. There are options. The first is a run-off election with an extension of my Presidency for a few months. Another is for the Speaker of the House to be sworn in as President on January twentieth. This is not a decision that I can make, it may take some time for Congress to make an intelligent decision based off their interpretation of the Constitution."

My head is throbbing and I stand up to find the prescription that was handed to me last night. The pain is making my stomach turn. John walks out of the kitchen and hands me a cup of coffee. "How is your head? The doctor didn't think your concussion is that bad but you aren't making fast moves. This is between you and me. What are we dealing with?"

I don't think it's too bad but I know John is worried that I might have a brain bleed. "I have a headache and some nausea. No blurry or double vision. I'm tired but I think that is due to lack of sleep. I have had worse concussions in my career and will hand over the keys to drive home because I'm hoping to get some sleep."

When we walk back into the room Tracy, Talmadge and Billy are preparing to drive home. Talmadge lets me know that I am no longer wanted in Virginia and a story is being released to the press linking a fictitious name to the murder. This is being done to protect both the CIA from further embarrassment and move Scott's murder out of the headlines. John jokes that I can go back to work tomorrow. I think I am going to take a vacation first. I throw my keys to him and laugh. Maybe a couple days nursing a mild concussion isn't a bad idea.

What a strange week we have had. I have gone from discussing the early settlers to Virginia and the impact they had creating this country to the fragility of our country and freedoms. We came close to the end of this dream of liberty and freedom. In November we voted on a dream of making our country better only to find now this was a lie. While voting to preserve our freedoms we were unknowingly voting to give them away. It was so easy for us to believe what we were told and to be led to slaughter. Even after a horrific terror attack we still wanted to believe we could follow a vibrant leader and make things better.

I wonder where the country goes from here? The terror attacks crippled commerce. Our transportation system is limping along. I'm not sure if the employment situation will continue and we use it to rebuild, or have these people woken up this morning to realize the job they have today is because of the terrorist we elected. How do we heal?

How do we learn to trust again? If the voters can be convinced to vote politicians into office that blew up our roads and bridges while killing family, friends and neighbors who can we believe? For me it is more fundamental. The government I worked for murdered my friend to keep their activities secret. I was set up to take the fall for them. They went after my daughter and I doubt they would have stopped there. I was in their way and meaningless. Even the FBI that I have been loyal to and after Elizabeth died gave my entire life to, threw up their hands and stepped away from me until I proved there was more to this than the CIA planted evidence.

I can never thank any of the team who has helped me these last couple days as they should be thanked. It is hard separating and going our own ways. Tracy and Talmadge leave with plans for us all to get together for a spring fishing trip. Billy and Bernie make plans to meet for lunch next week. We may not have trusted each other but we have become friends. I invite everyone to our house any time.

Samantha and I are the last ones out the door. Bernie gives Samantha a hug and shakes my hand. Samantha is sniffling and wiping tears. He is smiling from ear to ear and brushes a tear off Samantha's cheek. "Don't cry. You aren't getting rid of me. I'm thinking about taking you up on the offer to come down for a visit. I have more vacation time to burn before the end of the year. Besides, I need to celebrate." She looks at him with a puzzled look on her face. He laughs, "this is more excitement than I have had in a long time. I have never been allowed to shoot my gun on the job. Last night I was part of the assassination of the President elect of the United States. I don't have to go through an internal investigation. I don't have to answer questions. Hell, the Secret Service, FBI and CIA have covered up the entire thing. Since 9/11 I have wanted to take down a terrorist. Last night I got my chance. Any time you have a case you need help with you have my number. Just call me."

We laugh as we walk to the Jeep. John is sitting behind the wheel. Samantha gets in the back as I lean the seat back and close my eyes. Now that this is over I feel exhausted. It is time for me to get some sleep.

I wake up as we weave through Washington, DC and ask if we can stop at Scott's grave. I want to say goodbye. I doze off again and wake as John stops at a florist shop in Fredericksburg. Samantha gets out of the Jeep. She walks out of the flower shop minutes later with an arrangement of pine and holly. It smells like Christmas when she puts it on the seat behind me. The smell reminds me that this will be the first Christmas AJ will begin to understand. Of course his big sister, Alina, will teach him the ropes of Santa. We need to get home and decorate the house for Christmas. Life goes on and the holidays are coming. My life and the people in the country have to find a way to get back to normal.

John makes the turn into the cemetery and winds his way around the hillside. I see a car parked near a tree and a woman sitting on a bench near a fresh grave. She has the hood up on her coat and I am not sure from a distance if the figure is Karen or someone else. As we come to a stop I am glad to see Karen and not Kathryn. I know I will eventually have to meet Kathryn but I am not ready for that encounter.

Karen walks up to me with tears in her eyes. "Samantha called me. She said you and I need to talk. I haven't been out of the house since the funeral. I haven't wanted to face the public. I don't know if I ever will." I wrap my arms around her and we cry together.

I feel an arm around my waist and see Samantha next to me. She whispers, "We are alone in a graveyard. Karen, there are some things Adam has to tell you that cannot leave this place, but it will explain what happened." She looks at me with tears in her eyes, "Adam, she needs to hear it from you. Karen deserves to know the truth behind why Scott died."

I nod my head and lead Karen back to the bench. We sit down and she puts her head on my shoulder. Samantha walks back to John at the Jeep. They are standing together watching the road and watching over us. "Karen, it is hard to know where to even start. I guess I should start at the beginning. After we left you we drove to Baltimore. I know I didn't kill Scott but if I didn't find out, no one would ever know...."

I tell her everything. Once I start to speak I feel as if I cannot stop. The story behind the last few days has been stranger than fiction and ended with me watching the newly elected President of the United States die. It was the only thing that could be done to stop a terrorist head from becoming the leader of the free world.

When I finish she pulls out her phone and shows me a picture of Scott's son. For better or worse Scotts heir lives on. He has moved into Scott's family home along with Kathryn. Karen walks a fine line between acceptance and alienation from her former in-laws. The child is part of the man she loved, but he is also the blatant reminder of his secret life. It will take her time. I know it took me time to accept the secret life Elizabeth led. Like me, she has a future, she needs to find a new path to follow.

We part and return to our cars to drive away. I gratefully hang up the title of fugitive from the law for family man. I think I need a vacation. I'm not sure how to handle the thoughts swirling in my head. Scott's death has brought up many things I have never dealt with after Elizabeth died. I have just kept running away from all that happened. I have been afraid to stop or to think. I still close my eyes and feel the loss and hopelessness I felt when Elizabeth's body was found. Now, I keep replaying my last conversation with Scott. If I would have left him talk I may have listened and saved his life. Instead, he was murdered and I was accused of his murder. My accuser was the very government that employed me. I don't know who to trust anymore. I know I have my friends and family, but outside that circle I feel betrayed.

I will return to the roll of FBI agent in a couple week but for now I just want to be father, husband and friend. I have two children, a dog, two rabbits and a house to go home to. It's time for me to put my life back on solid ground and stop running. I look at Samantha and smile. I am a lucky man and my future began the day I met her. It's time to stop running.

ABOUT THE AUTHOR

Sharon Dobson lives in her home in Maryland. The scenes in Maryland, Virginia and Pennsylvania are places she knows well. Middle Plantation is her third book in the Adam Clay series.

Made in the USA
Middletown, DE
03 June 2017